**Praise for the *New York Times* bestselling
Ghost Hunter Mystery Series**

"A quickly paced and cleverly constructed mystery . . . Laurie's character work is, as always, first-rate. M.J.'s one of my very favorite cozy heroines; endearingly goofy, insanely brave, and loyal to a fault, she injects both humor and heart into a story."　　　　—The Season

"A series that combines suspenseful tension with humor, romance, and mystery."　　—Kings River Life Magazine

"Filled with laugh-out-loud moments and nail-biting, hair-raising tension, this fast-paced, action-packed ghost story will keep readers hooked from beginning to end."
　　　　　　　　　　　　　　　　—Fresh Fiction

"Paranormal mystery fans, look no further."
　　　　　　　　　　　　　　　　—SciFiChick.com

"Fabulously entertaining. . . . [Laurie] has a genuine talent for creating unique spirits with compelling origin stories and then using those creations to scare . . . her characte...　　　　　　　　　　　　　　　　...pect

"Parano...　　　　　　　　　　　　　　　...ose
of fun an...　　　　　　　　　　　　　　　...nce

The Ghost Hunter Mystery Series

The Psychic Eye Mystery Series

NO GHOULS
ALLOWED

A GHOST HUNTER MYSTERY

Victoria Laurie

AN OBSIDIAN MYSTERY

OBSIDIAN
Published by the Penguin Group
Penguin Group (USA) LLC, 375 Hudson Street,
New York, New York 10014

USA | Canada | UK | Ireland | Australia | New Zealand | India | South Africa | China
penguin.com
A Penguin Random House Company

First published by Obsidian, an imprint of New American Library,
a division of Penguin Group (USA) LLC

First Printing, January 2015

ISBN 978-0-451-47008-9   5544 0720 01/15

Printed in the United States of America
10 9 8 7 6 5 4 3 2 1

For Ruth Margret Laurie

Love you, Gram

Acknowledgments

Deepest thanks go out to my editor, Sandra Harding, for all of her hard work, patience, perceptive advice, patience, wise observations, patience, lovely praise, and especially her patience. I totally pinkie-swear that someday, SOMEday I will actually turn in something on time. Pinkie. Swear. (But maybe don't hold me to that.) ☺

More thanks go to my fantabulous agent, Jim McCarthy, who ROCKS and whom I adores. The longer I work with Jim, the more convinced I am that he's just the greatest thing since chocolate sprinkles on a triple scoop of peanut butter–chocolate ice cream in a waffle cone. And, if you knew how much I love sprinkles on a triple scoop of peanut butter–chocolate ice cream in a waffle cone, you'd tooootally get how much I adores him.

I also want to take a moment to mention how much I count on and totally appreciate my copy editor, Michele Alpern. I've never, *ever* had a better copy editor, who so totally gets my style and gently corrects all the little (sometimes big . . . doozy!) imperfections in my manuscripts. Thank you, Michele, for always being so awesome, for always suggesting just the right alternative, and for catching all of those echoes. I always sweat

it until I hear you're available to copyedit my latest book, and sometimes I know you work extra hard just to fit me in. I hope you know how very much I appreciate you. ☺

More thanks go to my awesome, awesome team at New American Library, namely Danielle Dill, Claire Zion, and Sharon Gamboa. You guys are so great. Truly.

Last, allow me to take a moment to thank those very special friends and loved ones who support me in so many ways and are the best cheerleaders on the planet! Sandy Upham, my sister, who gets me in ways that no one else in the world ever will. For that understanding alone I'd give you the moon if you wished for it . . . and if I could throw a lasso that far. ☺ Brian Gorzynski, whom I love more than I can ever possibly say. You're one of the very best people I've ever known, and I will love you with all of my heart to the very end of my days. Katie Coppedge, Leanne Tierney, and Karen Ditmars, aka Team Lo . . . how would I ever survive without you amazing ladies in my life? I love each of you so, so much. Thank you for always having my back. Know that I will always have yours in return. And, of course the rest of my peeps, Steve McGrory, Mike and Matt Morrill, Nicole Gray, Jennifer Melkonian, Catherine Ong Kane, Drue Rowean, Nora, Bob, and Mike Brosseau, Sally Woods, John Kwaitkowski, Matt McDougal, Dean James, Anne Kimbol, McKenna Jordan, Hilary Laurie, Shannon Anderson, Thomas Robinson, Juliet Blackwell, Sophie Littlefield, Nicole Peeler, Gigi Pandian, Maryelizabeth Hart, Terry Gilman, Martha Bushko, and Suzanne Parsons.

Chapter 1

"*This* is where you grew up?" my boyfriend, Heath, asked me as our van came to a stop.

I stared up at the large plantation home of my childhood and tried to see it through Heath's eyes. The stately six-bedroom, five-bath home sat atop a large hill that I used to roll down when I was little. I had found such joy in rolling down that hill. And the grand, ancient sixty-foot oak tree that dominated the far right side of the yard, where I'd had a swing that I used to ride for hours. And the long wraparound porch where I'd spent lazy summer days cuddled up with a good book and glass after glass of pink lemonade.

Of course, all of that was before my mother died. Before all the joy went right out of my life and right out of that house.

Looking up at the dark redbrick manor with black shutters and a gleaming white porch, I could see that not

much had changed about the house in thirty years. It still looked as grand, charming, and pristine as ever, but inside I could feel the ghosts that haunted the old Southern home. Literally.

"Are we there yet?" Gil yawned from the backseat. Gilley is my BFF. He's been my best friend for over twenty years, so he knows my history well.

"We're here," Heath said, arching his back and stretching. It'd been a long drive from Boston to the southern Georgia city of Valdosta. "I didn't know this place was gonna be so . . . big."

Gil sat up and leaned forward. "M.J. didn't tell you?" he asked, like I wasn't in the van. "Her daddy's a *very* wealthy man."

I scowled. Gil made it sound like that was something to be proud of. But since my mother's death, Daddy had always put his work before me, so I hardly thought it a positive thing. Plus, he'd never once offered to help me out in all those years Gil and I had struggled to make ends meet in Boston.

"Yeah, he'd have to be to afford this place," Heath said. My gaze shifted to him. He looked intimidated, and I thought I knew why. Heath came from far humbler—but perhaps more honorable—circumstances.

"Hey," I said, reaching for his hand. "It's his money, not mine."

Heath tore his eyes away from the house. "Yeah, but, Em, I mean . . . *look* at this place."

"It's just a house," I said, leaning in to give him a quick peck before getting out of the van.

As we walked from the van toward the house, the

front porch door opened and out stepped Daddy. My breath caught in surprise at the sight of him. I barely recognized the man standing there.

My father had always been a tall and imposing figure. Well over six feet, he'd been a big barrel of a man who'd gone gray, then silver prematurely, and whose countenance had always appeared to be tired and overworked. The man on the porch, whom I hadn't seen in several years, was still tall and imposing, but he'd trimmed down by at least forty pounds—pounds he'd always carried around his middle and which he really had needed to lose. His hair was also darker, but it suited him and made him look ten years younger, and his face, always set in a deep frown, was actually lifted into an expression I hadn't seen him wear since I was ten. The man *actually* looked happy.

"You okay?" Heath whispered, and I realized he'd taken up my hand.

"Yeah," I said, shaking my head a little. "He just looks . . ."

"Amazing," Gil said on the other side of me. "Lord, M.J., is that *really* Montgomery Holliday?"

"Hey there, Mary Jane," my father called from the porch with a wave. "I was expectin' you a little later. Y'all must've made good time."

"Hey, Daddy," I replied as we started up the walk toward the stairs. "We did make good time."

My father nodded and adopted something halfway between a grimace and a smile, but I couldn't really fault him for it. If you don't ever smile even once in twenty years, I expect you'd be out of practice.

The porch door opened again and out stepped a lovely-looking woman perhaps in her late fifties or early sixties. She had a regal quality about her with short-cropped and perfectly coiffed blond hair, bright blue eyes, and a trim figure. Her smile was brilliant and contagious and she clapped her hands at the sight of us. "Ooo!" she exclaimed. "Monty, is *this* your daughter?"

I had climbed the steps and now stood in front of Daddy and the woman who must be his new fiancée, Christine Bigelow. "This is her, dear," Daddy said, stepping forward to open up his arms to me.

For a moment I just stood there confused. Daddy hadn't hugged me since the day my mother died. In fact, that was perhaps the last time he'd ever touched me tenderly, so this open display of affection was throwing me a little and I didn't know how to react.

Next to me I heard Gil clear his throat, then push me with his hand a little, and I sort of took two awkward steps forward and Daddy hugged me with three neat pats to the back before letting go. He continued to wear that strange half smile, half grimace.

And then I was wrapped up in another hug from Christine. She squeezed me tight and added another "Ooo!" Then she stepped back and held me at arm's length. "Mary Jane, I have heard *so* many wonderful things about you! Your father simply raves about how smart and amazing his little girl is!"

"You have?" I said. "He does?" I wasn't trying to be a brat—I was actually really surprised that Daddy would say anything even remotely kind on my behalf.

He'd spent decades letting everyone else know what a disappointment I was to him.

"Well, of course!" she said, and then her bright eyes turned to the two men at my side. "Now, don't tell me. Let me guess," she said to them. Pointing to Heath, she said, "You must be Heath Whitefeather, Mary Jane's boyfriend, and you," she said next, pointing to Gil, "must be Gilley Gillespie, Mary Jane's best friend—am I right?"

"What gave it away?" Gil said, and I wanted to roll my eyes. Gilley was actually wearing mascara and blush today, along with blue nail polish. He loved flaunting his flamboyant side in my conservative Southern Baptist father's face.

"Your mama described her handsome son to a T," Christine told him slyly. The tactic worked; Gil blushed and I knew she'd just claimed another ally.

"It's very nice to meet you, ma'am," Heath said, extending his hand to her.

Christine laughed lightly and shook her head, stepping forward to hug Heath. "Oh, none of that formal stuff for family!" she said.

I hate to admit it, but the lovely warmth and charm of the woman had an effect on me. I liked her. A lot. And I couldn't understand what she'd first seen in my father, but looking at the dramatic change in him, I had to be grateful, because it was a world of difference.

Once she'd had her fill of hugs, Christine took up my arm and Gilley's and said, "Now! Let's all step inside and have ourselves a proper lunch, shall we?"

We began to follow her and Daddy inside when a

pickup truck came barreling up the drive at an alarming rate of speed, honking its horn to get our attention. Daddy's posture and countenance changed in a second and he stepped forward to the edge of the porch, ready to handle whatever came next.

Heath moved over to stand next to Daddy, and I could tell that my father approved of the move and perhaps even of Heath in that moment. The truck came to a stop and out jumped a man in jeans, a plaid shirt, a stained cowboy hat, and work boots. "Mrs. Bigelow!" he called urgently.

"Clay," my father said, his voice full of the authority that used to send me scurrying.

Clay removed his hat and nodded to my father. He looked out of breath. "Mr. Holliday, sorry to trouble you, but we've had another situation at the work site."

Daddy moved down two steps toward Clay, and Heath followed him. Next to me Christine stood rigid, biting her lip as if she knew the news was bad.

"It's another accident," Clay said.

"What happened?" Daddy demanded.

"The scaffolding in the ballroom gave way, sir. Two of my men were sent to the hospital."

"Oh, no!" Christine exclaimed. "Clay, are they badly injured?"

Clay clenched and unclenched his hat. "Not real bad, ma'am, but bad enough. Boone's got a busted ankle, and Darryl might have a broken arm."

Christine's posture relaxed a fraction. "Oh, that's dreadful," she said. "But I'm so grateful it wasn't worse! Monty, after lunch we should go straight to the

hospital to see the men. And of course I'll cover their medical expenses."

"Now just hold on here," my father interjected. "Clay, that scaffolding is your responsibility. If it wasn't properly put together, Christine ain't gonna be responsible for no medical expenses."

It was Clay's turn to stiffen. "Mr. Holliday, sir, that scaffolding *was* put together correctly. Why, I checked it myself this morning. Just like I checked all the other equipment and rigging that's somehow managed to come apart, or blow up, or fail on us and cause nothing but accidents at this jobsite. It ain't us, sir."

"Well, then who's responsible?" Daddy snapped.

Clay fiddled with his hat and looked at the ground. "It's like I told you last time, Mrs. Bigelow," he said, avoiding my father's sharp gaze. "We think your place is cursed, and, ma'am, I truly am sorry, but I'm pulling my crew."

"You're what?" Daddy roared loud enough for Clay to jump.

But the foreman wasn't backing down. Donning his hat, he looked directly at Christine and said, "I'm real sorry, ma'am. But that estate has something bad creeping through those hallways. I've tried to tell you that I don't think it's a good idea to keep messing with it, and maybe you'd best to cut your losses too, before you or someone you love gets hurt same as my men. Anyway, we're leaving. I just wanted to come tell you in person, is all."

With that, he turned and headed back to his truck, even though Daddy called after him to come back and talk about it.

As Clay's pickup drove away, I turned to look at Christine. She looked stricken.

I knew from the gossip mill that Daddy's new fiancée—a wealthy widow originally from Florida—was also fairly new to our small city. She'd told folks here that she had come on a retreat to Valdosta with her then-ailing husband a few years back and had fallen in love with the place. After Mr. Bigelow's death, she'd sold her home in Naples, which was also rumored to have been a sizably valuable property on the water, and she'd set her sights on the estate of what had once been a prominent family here, the Porters of Valdosta.

The Porters had made their money in tobacco, but as smoking declined beginning in the late 1970s, so had the family's wealth. Through mismanagement and family greed, much of the once vast fortune had been squandered, and many of the two dozen or so Porter family members had fled Valdosta in shame.

Only one group of Porters had stayed in the area after 1985 to keep up appearances and inhabit the once proud estate, but I'd heard that the mansion had fallen into disrepair of late, ever since the only two remaining Porter family members—a brother and sister—had moved out in the early 2000s. Still, no one had ever expected the remaining Porters to put their family's estate up for sale—the house came with over three dozen acres of gorgeous woodlands, and I think everyone in town thought that either the brother or the sister would eventually start a family and move back in, but the years went by and that never came to pass. And then there were rumors of the heavy tax burden

that the Porter estate carried, and ultimately, that, and the fact that neither sibling seemed interested in moving back home, could have been the motivation for the sale.

Whatever it was, the house and its surrounding land had been put on the market, and Christine had promptly jumped on it. I'd been told that's how she'd met Daddy, in fact. She'd hired him to handle the transaction, and he'd asked her out to coffee after she'd signed the closing documents. Gilley's mom had said that they'd been inseparable ever since.

Still, Mrs. Gillespie also said that the Porter house needed to be gutted and completely renovated, which made me wonder if Christine had known what she was really in for when she'd purchased the place. And now there seemed to be a troublesome ghost in residence as well.

"That's the third contractor to quit on us in as many months, Monty," Christine said, her voice holding a slight note of panic.

Daddy turned and came back up the steps, reaching out for her hand, which was still looped with mine. "Now, now, Christy, don't you worry. We'll find another, better contractor. As I recall, you had half a dozen contractors bid on Porter Manor. After lunch I'll look at the list and pick the contractor with the most experience. Someone who won't be using any rickety scaffolding, unskilled labor, or poorly kept tools."

I could see that Christine's eyes were beginning to water, and she blinked rapidly to fight the tears. "But what if Clay's right?" she whispered. "Monty, what if

there really *is* something in that old place causing all those accidents?"

Daddy adopted a patient look, but I could see he didn't believe a word of it. That didn't surprise me—even though I'd shown him enough evidence through the years to convince most anybody, Daddy never admitted that he believed in ghosts. "Bah," he said. "Christy, Clay's just covering his tracks, is all! He's trying to avoid gettin' sued by his workers, honey. I'll bet money he or his crew didn't rig that scaffolding right, and it's his fault it fell down."

"We could check it out," Heath said. "M.J. and I could go over there and tell you for sure if there's a spook haunting the place."

My gaze cut to him and I shook my head subtly. But he was focused on Christine, who was obviously distressed. I knew he wanted to help, but he didn't know my father.

And just as I suspected, I saw Daddy's eyes narrow, and his lips compress into a disapproving scowl.

But Christine had already stepped forward and reached for Heath's hands. "Oh, would you?" she asked. "I'd be most grateful, Heath." Turning to me, she added, "Most grateful to both of you!"

I stood there dumbstruck, not really believing what'd just happened. One minute we were headed in for a nice get-to-know-you lunch, and the next Heath was committing us to a ghostbust on our vacation. Which of course was just my luck.

"It'd be our pleasure," Heath assured her, nodding his head and smiling encouragingly at me.

"Of . . . of course," I stammered. Christine clapped her hands happily, then hugged first Heath, then me and showered us with thank-yous.

Daddy cleared his throat, his irritation quelled but barely below the surface. And then Christine turned to him and said, "Oh, Monty, your daughter and her beau are angels! I'll sleep well tonight knowing a pair of experts can put all this craziness to rest!"

"I'll go too," Gil offered, and Heath and I both widened our eyes. Gil seemed to realize what he'd just committed himself to, because he followed that quickly with, "You know. I'll monitor things from the van. Like usual."

Christine put her hand on his cheek and smiled sweetly. Gil, like Daddy, seemed to melt under her charms. "Thank you, Gilley. That would be most kind of you." Gilley blushed and Heath and I hid smiles.

Then Daddy did something most unexpected. He chuckled and gave Heath a good-natured pat on the back. "Well, now that's settled, maybe we can all go in and enjoy our lunch. Heath, you sit next to me. I hear you like to drop the occasional fly come salmon season. It's been a long time since I had someone to talk fly-fishing with. . . ."

As we filed into the house after Daddy, Gilley sidled up next to me, wearing a mocking grin. He was enjoying this a little too much. "Shut it," I warned.

Gil adopted an injured expression. "I didn't say a word!"

My eyes narrowed. "Oh, but you will."

"Well," Gil replied. "That's a given, sugar."

We entered my childhood home and I was stunned to find that so much had changed since I'd last been to see Daddy. For the past twenty years Daddy had left the home exactly as it'd been on the day my mother died. It'd been like living in the moment of her passing for most of my childhood, and I'd probably resented Daddy for making us stay in such a sad place. But now as we all stepped into the foyer, I was struck by the fresh coat of light beige on walls that had previously been a dull yellow.

Gilley widened his eyes a bit at me and nodded his head, like he had also noticed the change and approved. Daddy led the way toward the back of the house, saying, "We've set up on the back porch for brunch. There's a nice cross breeze and you'll have a chance to admire the gardens. Christine's done wonders back there."

As everyone trailed behind Daddy, I held back for a moment and turned to look toward the entrance of the parlor, and there too the walls and the trim had also received fresh coats of paint, in a slightly deeper shade of beige. A new set of deep brown leather sofas and cream-colored accent chairs had also replaced the dingy blue couches that'd once occupied the room. Additionally, built-in bookcases had been installed, turning the parlor into something more like a library, but I saw that Daddy's extensive book collection had been organized and assembled in such a clean, crisp way as to beckon fellow book lovers to run their fingers along the volumes.

My head swiveled then to the left and I took in the

new dining room with a gorgeous oak table and beautifully upholstered burgundy chairs. Like just about everything else, the curtains were new, replacing the dusty peacock blue window coverings from before. The look was lovely and elegant and exactly reflected the full potential of the space. I sighed and turned my attention back to the parlor, taking a few steps forward to investigate it. Out of the corner of my eye I saw that Christine had come up next to me. "Your father finally let me tackle this old house and bring it into the twenty-first century," she said with a hint of pride in her voice. "I've let my decorators loose in every room including yours, which I hope you like, Mary Jane. I didn't want to change too much in there, but it desperately needed some fresh paint and updated furnishings."

I turned to face her, feeling that warmth for her at our initial greeting expand even more in the center of my chest. "Your taste is lovely. I've wanted Daddy to fix up this old house for decades."

Christine wrapped an arm around my middle. "It took him a long time to get over Madelyn," she said, almost as if she knew how truly hard it'd been for both of us. "And he sure made me use all of my charms to break through that big bleak wall of his. But when I first met him, I thought there was something so sad about Monty, and I couldn't let him carry on like that without trying to find the good heart I knew was inside. As I got to know him, it was like someone just coming out of a deep sleep, you know? Like gently shaking someone awake from a place so dark and withdrawn that even the smallest acts of kindness

worked on him like sunshine peeking through the blinds."

I looked up at Christine and I couldn't help the water that filled my eyes. She was radiant and beautiful and I knew exactly what she meant by the sun finally waking Daddy from that long slumber. In that moment I felt my mother's presence so intensely that I wanted to weep, because I knew . . . I just *knew* she'd been the one to place Christine Bigelow on my daddy's path.

Thanks, Mama, I called out to her in my mind, and I felt her presence come even closer for a moment, as if she were giving me a hug before withdrawing again.

"You all right, Mary Jane?" Christine asked me, obviously noticing how emotional I was getting.

I swallowed hard and blinked a few times, but I still had to wipe at my cheeks a little. "Yes," I said, with an embarrassed laugh. "I don't know what's come over me."

"Aww," Christine said, squeezing my middle a little. "Coming home is always such an emotional thing. But we're so glad you came for our wedding. It wouldn't have been the same without you, honey."

I inhaled deeply and nodded, still a little embarrassed. Trying to change the subject, I said, "So, where will you live after you're married?" I couldn't imagine Daddy in any house other than the one I'd grown up in, but then I also couldn't imagine Christine spending all that money on renovations to Porter Manor if she didn't intend to live there.

Christine seemed to know I was treading on a potentially touchy subject because she looped her arm

through mine as she led the way out of the parlor and said, "Well, now, that's something that Monty and I have talked a great deal about, and I think we've decided to live here until renovations are complete at the Porter house, and then he'll go ahead and put this place up for sale."

I nodded, and tried to tamp down the tinge of bitterness that rose inside me as I heard that my childhood home would soon be sold. "I guess it's time Daddy moved on," I said with a sigh.

Christine squeezed my arm. She seemed to understand. "If it helps, renovations won't be complete for at least two years, Mary Jane. We'll be here awhile yet."

I smiled. That did help. "So, what's the plan for the wedding?"

"Well, it'll be a very small affair. Your father and I are both veterans of the big wedding, so this time around we'd like just a few very close friends and family to gather here next Saturday. Monty's friend Judge Michaels will be doing the honors, and we'll have a lovely catered dinner afterward. With any luck the whole thing will be over by eleven o'clock!"

I eyed her with surprise. "Really? That's it? Just a small ceremony and a catered dinner with only a few friends and family?"

Christine laughed lightly. "Yes, that's all! Why? Did you really think your father and I would have a big, grand affair?"

I shrugged. "Well, maybe not really big, but, I mean, between the two of you, you've got to know a whole lot of important people."

She laughed again. "Well, the only important people we absolutely needed to be here were you, Heath, and Gilley, and of course my son and his family. Speaking of which, Tom will be here Saturday morning, and I just know you'll adore his wife, Kelsey. She went to school in Boston, you know. . . ."

Christine continued to chat happily at me while we made our way out to the garden for brunch. As she spoke, all the reservations I'd had about attending the wedding melted away. For the first time in forever, it felt good to be home again.

A few hours later I was hugging Christine and Daddy good-bye. "You sure you won't stay with us?" Christine asked me again.

"Oh, no—thank you—but we've already settled in at Mrs. Gillespie's. We'll be back in the morning, though, and we'll let you know what we've discovered at the Porter house."

Christine bit her lip. "I'm nervous about you going there alone, Mary Jane."

Heath put a hand on my shoulder. "She won't be alone, ma'am. I'll be with her and we've done plenty of these investigations. We know what we're doing."

Except that we didn't have any of our equipment or safety gear. I'd had one too many mimosas at lunch, and I'd promised Christine that I'd check out Porter Manor that very afternoon. Now that the buzz was wearing off, I was beginning to wonder if I'd done something stupid in committing to investigate without the proper equipment.

Judging from the size of Gilley's current frown, I'd probably done something stupid.

"Well, then," Christine said with a sad smile as she gave us a little wave. "Y'all be safe over there and come back first thing in the morning. I'll have Ruby send over some of their croissants and Danishes."

Daddy seemed a bit aloof as we said our good-byes for the night. I knew he and Christine were disappointed that Heath and I had decided to stay with Gilley's mom instead of at the house with them, but I also knew that Daddy would've thrown a fit over Heath and me wanting to stay together in the same bedroom. He'd been pretending to overlook the fact that Heath and I were living in sin up in Boston, and as that was an argument just waiting to happen, I'd cut it off at the pass by asking Gil's mom if we could stay with her. She'd been more than happy to host us.

As we got ready to take our leave, Christine squeezed my hands one last time and let me go, but before I could get into the van with the boys, Daddy stepped forward and gave me a buss on the cheek. My breath caught and I stood there rather stunned for a moment. I could remember exactly the last time Daddy had given my cheek a kiss. It'd been the night before Mama had been diagnosed with stage-four breast cancer. From that moment on, he'd never bussed my cheek again.

While I stood there, a twinkle came into Daddy's eyes, and he smiled like he knew he'd caught me off guard. "Y'all have a good rest of your day, Mary Jane," he said, laying a hand on my arm to squeeze it gently. "Drive safe and we'll see y'all tomorrow morning."

I waved to Daddy and Christine as I got into the van, and then we were all waving at them as Gil took us back down the long drive toward the road. For several moments no one in the van spoke until Gil said, "Who *was* that man masquerading as your daddy, M.J.?"

I laughed. His question was so earnest that it fit exactly the train of my thoughts. "*That* was Daddy," I said, and felt my voice quaver. "At least, the Daddy I remember from before Mama died."

"I like him," Heath said.

I sighed happily. "He likes you too, honey."

"Oh, hell," Gil scoffed. "He *loves* you, Heath. I mean, M.J., did you see the way Monty was asking Heath about the fly-fishing in New Mexico?"

"I did," I said, my brow furrowing. Daddy had always been hard on my boyfriends, and by hard I mean awful, terrible, and despicable. "I can't get over the change in him."

"Was he really that bad before he met Christine?" Heath asked.

"Yes," Gil and I said together.

"Huh. Well, he seemed nice to me. And, Em, I didn't want to bring this up at brunch, but your mom was *all* over me from the minute we stepped outside for brunch. She talked me up the whole time we were eating."

"What'd she say?" Gil asked eagerly.

I felt my stomach muscles clench. I often felt Mama close to me in spirit, but she rarely communicated directly with me the way she did with other mediums like Heath, which is a common practice for the spirit

world. I think it's because the way we hear spirits is
often so subtle that it can feel as if it's imagined, and
when we hear from our own loved ones, there's that
seed of doubt that plants itself in our brains and begs
the question, is this really my loved one, or me just
making it up?

The fact that she communicated to me so clearly
through Heath made Mama's words real and undeni-
able, but I will admit that I both loved and hated hearing him relay her messages. I loved it because I missed
her so much, but I hated it because it always reminded
me that she was physically absent from my life, and no
matter how often I "heard" from her, I'd still never feel
her arms wrap around me or hear the lilt of her sweet
voice in this lifetime again. Unless of course she came
to visit me in one of my dreams, but even that fell short
of having her here with me in this world.

"She said that she loves Christine," Heath said.
"And she loves the way your dad has come out of his
shell, Em." Looking meaningfully at me, Heath added,
"She also said that she's happy you and your dad are
talking to each other again. She's super proud of how
you're handling all this."

My eyes misted and I blinked furiously. Nothing
touched me more than hearing that Mama was proud
of me. "Thanks, sweetie," I whispered, and had to look
away until I could compose myself.

The van fell into companionable silence as Gilley
drove us through Valdosta's beautiful streets. I had a
sudden pang of homesickness for the place that, only a
dozen years before, I couldn't wait to get away from,

and found myself leaning my head toward the window to catch the lovely breeze and the sweet smell of fresh peaches, which was so much a part of my history. Summer was just gearing up and the smell more than the sights of my home city was taking me back to a time when I was young and carefree. Before Mama died and the gray cloud of sadness settled into our lives.

"Hey!" Gil exclaimed, jerking me from my thoughts. "There's Christine's place—Porter Manor! They cut down all the trees along that ridge, M.J."

I turned to look out Gilley's window, and sure enough, the massive house could now be clearly seen at the top of a ridge that'd once been thick with trees. The Porters had been a very private family, and they'd done nothing in the hundred and fifty years of owning the manor to make it more visible to the people of the town. "Huh," I said, a little sad to see all the trees gone, but also impressed by the size of the place, which I'd never realized was as big as it now appeared.

"Whoa," Heath said. "It's at least as big as any castles we've investigated overseas."

"It's the largest single home in Valdosta," Gil said smartly. "Mama sent me the listing when it went on the market. It had all the historic details, and the square footage posted at ten thousand square feet."

Heath whistled his appreciation. "That's huge. Have either of you ever been inside?"

Gil pulled over just below the ridge and we all gazed up at the manor. "No," Gil said. "But I've always wanted to take a peek."

I cocked an eyebrow at him. "You have?"

He nodded. "Haven't you?"

I squinted up and nodded. "Yeah. I suppose I have."

"Well, we told Christine that we'd investigate it to-day, so we'd better get to it," Heath reminded us.

Gil put the van into drive and pulled away from the curb. I could see his curiosity was getting the better of him.

Gilley had gotten a little braver about interacting with spooks in recent months and I thought that his boy-friend, Michel, was responsible for the change. Michel wasn't fazed by much and that seemed to calm Gil down considerably on all fronts. Of course, I fully expected him to wait in the van until Heath and I completed the investigation and gave the all clear, but still, his enthusi-asm for a ghostbust was something to be noted.

After winding our way up the hill, we finally arrived at the bottom of the drive leading to Porter Manor. The entrance of the manor was a dirt drive flanked by two huge crumbling brick pylons. The drive was at least a quarter mile long and lined with ancient oak trees drip-ping with Spanish moss. At the end of the road was the manor, a regal-looking three-story Greek Revival plan-tation home, with white paint and black shutters, which was now a bit haggard with age and neglect. Only a large section of the middle was visible through the trees. Even so, what could be seen was impressive. As Gil hes-itated at the bottom of the drive, I felt goose pimples rise up along my arms and I glanced back at Heath only to see his brow furrowed.

"Cool, isn't it?" Gilley said, his enthusiasm never waning.

"It is," Heath agreed, his gaze darting to me, and when I held out my arm to show him the goose pimples, he smiled and nodded. The place was ringing with spectral energy all right. "Let's have a look, then," Heath said.

Gil took his foot off the brake and we made our way slowly down the drive, kicking up a good cloud of dust as we went. The closer we got, the more intrigued I became. The house was even bigger up close than it had appeared from down below at the bottom of the hill. It loomed like a behemoth at the end of the drive, growing in size as we approached until, when we parked near the front door, it seemed to block out the sun and cast us in shadow.

An involuntary shudder snaked its way down my spine and I couldn't help but smile. I've spent many years now creeping through haunted spaces, and what I used to fear, I've now come to appreciate in a way that only repeated experiences with the spirits of the dead can foster: namely, a wealth of admiration for historical landmarks that soak up the memory of the living so intensely that some spooks find it hard to leave. I love the mystery of digging through the ether to figure out the history of a haunted space; the identity of the ghosts haunting the hallways and why they haven't moved on are the mysteries that continue to captivate me.

"Do we have anything in here for protection?" Heath asked from the backseat, and I saw him looking over his shoulder into the back of the van.

"I doubt it," Gil said. "M.J. made me get rid of everything not nailed down in here before we set out from Boston."

He said that like it was my fault we didn't have any of the magnetic spikes or the gear we normally used to ward off the more aggressive spooks. "The van was filthy, Gil, and you know it. Besides, I only told you to clean it out, not get rid of everything useful in it."

"How was I supposed to know we were gonna do a ghostbust down here?"

I put a hand on his arm. "You didn't. So this isn't your fault or mine."

"Do you want to wait?" Heath asked, turning back to me.

I eyed the house. "Nah. At most it's probably some crotchety old relative of the Porters who just needs a good talking-to. We'll be fine."

Gil offered me a level look. "You know who else always says stuff like that?"

"Who?"

"Velma, right before she, Shaggy, Scooby, and the rest of the gang go running for their lives."

I chuckled. Since our show, *Ghoul Getters*, had started to air on cable, Gil had become obsessed with the comments section of the show's Web site, and a few of the "fans" who had compared us to *Scooby-Doo*. I'll admit that it'd stung a little at first, reading their less than kind jabs, especially when I kept getting compared to Velma, but now I could actually see the humor in it. Gil was also starting to come around, to a lesser degree of course, but that was likely because most everyone compared him to either Shaggy or Scooby.

The three of us stepped from the van in unison, and in silence, each of our chins tilted upward toward the

second and third stories. High overhead was a circular balcony and my attention seemed drawn by it in particular. As I squinted to the black ironwork railing, a flicker of movement made me suck in a breath.

"What?" I heard Heath ask.

I pointed toward the railing and said, "I thought I saw something up there."

Heath said, "Huh. I saw something in that window." And he pointed toward a large picture window to his right.

In the next second I felt a great force hit me from the side and I was airborne, flying sideways into Heath, who let out a grunt of pain as we both tumbled to the ground in a heap. Somewhere behind me I heard a loud crash, and a spray of rocks bit painfully into my back and shoulders. "What the . . . ?!" I cried, just as I realized Gilley was also lying next to me, his arm still wrapped around my middle.

Bewildered, I watched him shake his head and try to untangle himself from me. "You okay?" he asked.

I brushed a little of the debris out of my hair and lifted my left arm to allow him some room. "What happened?"

Gil brushed at his own head, and small chunks of black debris clinked to the ground. Instead of answering me, he pointed behind him. "That planter," he said, a little out of breath. "The second you turned your head, it came off the balcony and headed straight for you."

My eyes widened. The remnants of a large black planter lay smashed and broken exactly where I'd been

standing. If that thing had hit me, there's no way I would've survived.

"Whoa," Heath said, but I was too shocked to speak. "Em, you okay?" he asked after a moment.

I nodded dully, still amazed that I'd come that close to death and hadn't even known it. And then I focused on Gilley, who was looking a bit pale and shaken himself. Throwing my arms around him, I hugged him fiercely. "Thank you, sweetie!"

Gil let out a small chuckle. "It was nothing," he said humbly.

I released Gil, and Heath helped me to my feet. We all moved tentatively over to the planter to inspect it, our gazes moving from the planter up to the third-story balcony, where it must've come from.

"I'd say that somebody in there isn't so happy we've stopped by," Heath whispered. "Maybe we should go and come back another time? Like when we're covered in magnets."

"You know," I said, still staring up at the balcony, "I think that's a great idea."

The three of us turned back to the van and got in. Gil's hands were shaking a little as he reached down to turn the key, but all of a sudden there was another gigantic crash and the front windshield imploded.

I screamed and so did Gil. In the next moment the three of us were back out of the van, and Gilley and I were shaking the broken glass off us. "Guys!" Heath said, pointing our attention back toward the van. "Look!"

I was so stunned that all I could do was stand there with my mouth agape. On the top of the hood was an-

other huge planter, which had cratered itself on the hood and imploded the windshield.

"Another six inches and it would've killed us!" Gil exclaimed.

"There's no way we can drive out of here now," Heath said. He was right. The van was at best inoperable and at worst totaled.

"So what the hell do we do?" Gil squeaked, his gaze moving from the van to the house and back again.

I turned toward the front door of Porter Manor, anger fueling my thoughts. "We find the son of a bitch throwing planters at us!"

"We can't go in there!" Gil screeched, and suddenly there was another loud crash and I ducked low, covering my head with my arms. Slowly I craned my head to look back at the van, which had been struck on the right front quarter panel by a third planter.

Heath came up next to me and grabbed my arm, pulling me toward the front door. "At some point whoever's up there has to run out of pots."

Hurrying to the door, we were passed by Gil, who streaked up to the porch and trembled pathetically next to the door. "What the hell is going on?" he practically shouted when we joined him.

"Don't know," I said. "You might wanna stay right here, though, honey. At least until we know what else could come flying off the balcony."

I then put my hand on the door and Gil said, "What if it's locked?"

I hadn't thought of that, and tried the knob only to discover it was locked. "Dammit," I muttered. "I

should've gotten a key from Christine before we left." No sooner had I finished that sentence than the front door suddenly clicked and swung open with a loud creak.

"Whoa!" Heath whispered again.

We stood there for several beats, frozen to the spot while we contemplated the fact that the door had just unlocked itself and opened wide. "I think maybe I should make a run for the road," Gilley said, his eyes wide with fright.

I grabbed his arm to stop him; something told me not to let him out of my sight. "Hang on," I said, that foreboding getting stronger. A moment later a paint can came flying from somewhere above, hit the drive, and paint splattered everywhere. A second after that, several bricks smashed to the ground, kicking up debris that found its way to the porch and hit our legs.

Both Gilley and I shrieked while Heath grabbed me around the waist and hauled my butt through the door. As I was still holding on to Gilley, he had no choice but to stumble along with me. The second we were through the door, however, it slammed behind us and we were plunged into the dim interior.

"What the hell?!" Gil cried, his voice now quavering with fear.

I let go of him and pulled away from Heath to go back to the front door and give it a tug. I wanted to know what'd happened outside, but the door was now locked again, and no matter what I did to the lock, it wouldn't open.

"It's stuck!" I growled, yanking on the handle.

Heath moved up next to me and I let him try, but he couldn't get it to open either.

I put a hand on his shoulder. "Leave it. We'll find another way out."

"I don't like this place, M.J.!" Gil said, sidling up next to me close enough to share my shirt.

I took his hand again and squeezed it. "It'll be okay, Gil. We just need to find another exit and we'll be on our way."

"How're we gonna get out of here, though?" Gil pressed. "We can't drive the van in that condition."

I lifted my cell phone. I'd been clutching it the whole time we'd been at the house. "I'll call Daddy," I said. But as I pressed the HOME button, the screen remained dark. I pressed it again, with no luck. I muttered under my breath and tried to think of what to do.

"Please don't tell me your phone's dead," Gil whispered when I covered my eyes with my hand.

"Try yours," I told him.

Gil reached into his back pocket, but his hand came up empty. Then he began to pat himself. "Where's my phone?"

"You don't have it?" I asked.

Gil shook his head even as he continued to pat himself down.

"Here," Heath said, handing me his cell. I pressed the HOME button, but his phone wouldn't come on either. Meanwhile, Gil had dashed to a nearby window to peer through the pane. "It's out there!" he wailed. "I must've dropped my phone when I pushed you fools out of the way."

"We'll get it back," I reassured him, moving up next to him to look through the pane to see where he'd dropped his cell.

"Come on," Heath said, taking charge. "Let's find an exit and get the hell out of here."

I took his hand and grabbed up Gil's hand too. Silently I berated myself for being so foolish as to arrive here so unprepared and unprotected. "We should've geared up before coming here," I muttered angrily.

"Well, we're in the thick of it now," Heath said, his head swiveling back and forth as he considered which way to go. "There's nothing left to do but find a way out as quickly as we—"

At that moment there was a loud *slam* from somewhere above us.

"What was that?!" Gil squeaked.

Heath tilted his head toward the stairs at the end of the entrance hall. "A door slammed shut somewhere upstairs. The spirit energy in here is pretty active."

"The ghoulies in this house don't waste time, do they?" I asked.

As if in reply there came another *slam!*

Next to me, Gil jumped and squeezed my hand hard. "Where's the exit?" he whispered.

Heath moved forward a few paces with us in tow. "Kitchens always have exits," he said wisely. "And they're usually at the back of the house. Come on, maybe we'll get lucky and it'll be down this hallway."

But luck wasn't with us. The hallway we were in passed several large, empty rooms before it came to a dead end with no obvious sign of the kitchen or an exit.

Heath frowned when we came to a stop and muttered an expletive. "I would've bet the house there'd be a door leading out down here."

"Let's open a few of these doors and see if one of the rooms has an exit," I suggested, pointing to the few remaining rooms between us and the end of the corridor.

Heath nodded, but as we headed to the nearest closed door, we heard another nearby door open, then slam. Next to me Gilley jumped. "That wasn't on the second floor!"

"The spook is on the move," Heath whispered, and he glanced at me as if to gauge my reaction.

I pointed to my bare arms, which were lined with goose pimples. "I don't like it," I mouthed, careful not to let Gilley know I felt we could be in even worse danger. He was scared and trembling enough as it was.

Heath still had ahold of my hand and he stepped a little closer to me before whispering, "Stick tight by my side and keep your antennae up."

He didn't have to tell me twice. We walked quickly but quietly to the next doorway, which was the last one on the right, and peered in. To my relief I spied what looked like an exit in the far right corner of the room. "There!" I said, pointing to it so the boys would see. "That window looks big enough for us to get through. Let's just open it and hop out."

"Oh, thank the baby Jesus!" Gil cried, letting go of my hand and dashing into the room. Heath and I were about to follow when the door slammed shut in our

faces. It happened so abruptly that I cried out and stumbled back.

Heath held his composure and reached for the door handle, but the second he laid his hand on it, he pulled it back and hissed through his teeth. "Dammit!" he swore, shaking his hand back and forth as if he'd burned it.

"What happened?" I tried to reach for his hand to see.

But he was already focused back on the door. "It's nothing," he said, using his shirt to cover his hand this time as he reached for the handle again.

From inside the room we heard Gilley yell, "Guys? What's going on?"

"Gil!" I called as Heath struggled with the door handle. It appeared to be locked tight. "Can you let us in?"

There was a slight pause, and I had a feeling Gilley was weighing whether to come back to the door and unlock it for us, or dart out through the window to save his own skin.

"Gil?" I called, trying to ignore the fact that the air all around us had taken on a fetid sort of odor.

To my relief I heard footsteps approach the door, while Heath tried in vain to get the handle to turn. And then there was a click, a creak, and another *slam*. Heath and I both jumped. "That was right behind us," Heath whispered, pointing to the door opposite us.

No sooner had those words left his lips than there came another *slam!* and then another, and another, and another, until it seemed that all the doors in the entire

house were opening and slamming closed one after another with enough force to shake the walls and rattle
the floorboards. Startled and more than a little scared,
I pressed myself against Heath, who wrapped me in his
arms while we waited out the percussion of sound. But
it seemed to go on, and on, and on, echoing all over the
house, and so violent in its nature that I wondered if it
ever would stop.

And then . . . abruptly . . . it did.

A silence fell upon us that was startling, given the
cacophony of noise from just a moment before, and I
noticed that both Heath and I were breathing heavily.
My heart was pounding away against my rib cage and
I felt clammy and dizzy. The air was oppressive and
thick with something dark . . . something evil.

Heath squeezed me in his arms and whispered, "We
gotta get out of here, Em. Right now!"

I nodded against his chest and pulled back slightly,
reaching for his hand. He hissed a little when I took it,
and I turned it over to look at his palm. That's when I
saw raised red blisters on the inside of his hand, and I
winced too. But we didn't have time to discuss what'd
happened to his palm. We needed to get out of that
house, so I stepped back to the room where Gilley was
and gave a light tap. "Gil?" I called softly.

There was no reply.

Putting my ear to the door, I called out to him again,
and this time I heard a small sob. "M.J.?" he said at last. I
had a feeling he was pressed right up against the door.

"You okay, honey?"

"N-n-n-nooooo."

I looked at Heath and he moved closer to the door. "Gil, we're gonna need you to unlock the door, but use your shirt to cover your hand before you touch anything metal, okay?"

I listened close and heard sniffling, then saw the handle jiggle slightly. "You need a key to unlock it," Gilley said. "There's no dead bolt or lock on this side. Just the keyhole."

I shifted my focus to Heath. "Can we kick it in?"

With a frown, he stepped back to consider the beautiful antique door with the brass handle. "I could, but Christine might not be too happy about it."

Upstairs there came a *slam!* That was followed by another, then another, then what felt like ten more. Reflexively I squeezed Heath's arm. This place was starting to get to me. "Kick it in!" I yelled above the noise as I forced myself to let go of him so he could do the deed.

Heath called to Gilley as he stepped back, "Gil! Get away from the door!" Then he turned slightly to the side and raised his knee high. Just as he gave a serious thrust with his leg, the door flew open. Heath's foot failed to connect and this caught him off-balance as the thrust of his kick tilted him awkwardly. I reached out to grab onto him, missed, and out of the corner of my eye I saw Gilley standing in the room, gaping in confusion as Heath tumbled forward, barely able to catch himself from falling to the floor.

I got ahold of his shoulder to help steady him, and just as I did that, the door came swinging right at us with terrific force, slamming Heath in the face. There was a god-awful *whack* and my sweetheart let out a

horrible grunt of pain as he was propelled right into me. We both flew backward, and I hit the wall with a hard knock to the back of my head. For several seconds I saw stars and my vision closed in around the edges.

To make matters worse, the full weight of Heath's body was pressed against me, making it impossible to breathe. Feebly I pushed at him, but he was slow to move off me. "Can't . . . breathe . . . ," I wheezed, but then I realized that Heath wasn't likely to hear me above the noise.

It was as if the entire house had come alive and was protesting our presence by opening and slamming shut every single door in the entire mansion. The walls, floors, and ceiling vibrated with bone-jarring intensity, and it was almost too much for me. My vision darkened even more while I struggled to get a full breath.

And then, at last, Heath moved off me, but the uproar around us kept on and on. And then I felt myself pulled away from the wall, which was shuddering so much that it was painful to lean against. Immediately, Heath enfolded me into his arms and I managed to cling to him until my head cleared a little. But still the slamming carried on and on, and I thought it would never stop.

"We have to get out of here!" Heath shouted.

I nodded weakly. I felt disoriented and my head throbbed both from the noise and the smack on the head. Belatedly I realized that Heath's forehead was bleeding. I took a deep breath and forced myself to focus on his face. There was a huge bump on his forehead with a jagged cut through the center. I couldn't imagine

how much that likely hurt, but he seemed somewhat oblivious to the pain while he looked this way and that, searching for a way out.

The door to the room on the other side of the hallway where Gilley was currently imprisoned was opening wide and slamming shut in perfect rhythm with all the others in the house, and I caught glimpses of Gil huddled near the floor, his fingers in his ears as he squeezed his eyes closed, trying in vain to block out the chaos.

And then a shadow passed in front of the door inside the room and my breath caught. The shadow was large, in the shape of a man. It was enough to raise every hair on the back of my neck. "Gil!" I shouted, but there was no way he could hear me above the noise. The door continued to open and slam closed, offering me only small glimpses into the room. The shadow appeared in the doorway, then on the other side of the room, then by the window, then right next to Gilley, and finally, it obscured my view of Gilley altogether.

I shouted his name at the top of my lungs, trying to get his attention, even though I didn't know what I expected him to do. At that moment Heath seemed to become aware of what was going on too, because he released me, whipped around, dipped his shoulder, and charged straight at the door.

He caught it just as it was about to slam shut, and the force with which he hit it sent it flying open to pound hard against the wall. Heath then bore all his weight on the door, keeping it open while yelling for Gilley.

But Gil was still hidden behind that large black shadow. I didn't waste another moment. I flew through the open doorway, heading with bared teeth right for the shadow. As I approached, it seemed to crouch a little, as if it was anticipating my physical connection with it. *"Gilley!"* I screamed, trying not to blink while I reached my hands forward, hoping I could simply push my way through the menacing spook and grab hold of my best friend. However, at the point of impact I felt the most intense blow to my midsection, which knocked the wind right out of me. In the next instant, I was sent flying backward for the third time since arriving at the manor.

I hit the ground in a heap, landing on my right shoulder and hip. My hip took the brunt of the force and I would have groaned if I'd had enough air to make a sound. I rolled onto my back in a daze, and reached my left arm up feebly, hoping that Heath was coming to my rescue. I tried to suck in some air, but my diaphragm seemed paralyzed. I felt that reflexive panic that comes with the wind being knocked out of you and you have to consider, however briefly, that this inability to breathe could be a permanent condition, but then a little air leaked down my windpipe and I closed my eyes to concentrate. I know from experience that if you push too hard to get your diaphragm to react, you can further hamper your ability to begin breathing again.

I tried to calm myself, but with the noise of the slamming doors, Heath's shouts, and Gilley's screams, there was just too much chaos, not to mention the fact that

I'd just been hurled across the room by an incredibly powerful—and likely very angry—spook.

Shutting all that out the best that I could, I focused on taking another tiny breath. I managed that one okay. And then I took another, a little deeper this time. Trouble was, my lungs were starting to protest mightily. They needed more air. Right. Now.

Around me the noise and chaos kicked up and I knew I absolutely *had* to get my breathing to start again, and I also wondered why Heath hadn't yet come to my rescue. It was then that I opened my eyes, but what I saw stopped my breathing all over again.

Chapter 2

With effort I managed to get myself into a sitting position, and take in a few more breaths. I blinked and rubbed my eyes to be sure I was seeing what I thought I was seeing, but the scene in front of me remained.

"What the hell?" I whispered as I looked warily around. "Heath?"

There was no reply.

"Gilley?"

Again, no one answered.

My brow broke out into a cold sweat and I drew my knees in close, continuing to look all around, stunned by what I saw. "I must've passed out," I told myself. And yet I felt certain I would've remembered that sinking feeling that happens right before you pass out, like the whole world is receding from you until you let go into darkness.

There'd been none of that. Just an effort to take a

breath, followed by full consciousness in an entirely different place.

It appeared that I was in a hallway that was dimly lit by the glow of the moon. How it'd gone from late afternoon to middle of the night was only one part of the puzzle. The hallway I recognized by its configuration and the wallpaper. A strip of it next to me was aglow with moonlight, and there were the telltale bluebirds, hurrying to build a nest, one with a bit of string and another with a small twig in their respective beaks. The pattern had fascinated me as a child and it was one I'd spent a lot of time studying during the lonely days of my mother's long illness when I'd been sent to spend time with my maternal grandparents.

I reached out to touch the wallpaper, and it felt real enough. Shakily I got to my feet and leaned against the wall. "Heath?" I tried again. "Gilley?"

This time my call was answered by a noise from behind a closed door at the end of the hallway. I felt another cold chill go through me and I shuddered. The sound had been human—I was sure of it—but it hadn't belonged to any voice I recognized.

As my heart hammered in my chest, I crept forward, feeling like a cliché right out of a B horror movie. I got to the door and hesitated. This had been my mother's bedroom when she'd been little. I used to sleep in it when I spent the night, but I hadn't been in it, or the house really, since my grandparents had passed away nearly a dozen years ago.

I rested my palm on the door handle, unable to control the shivering of my limbs. I felt cold and scared

and very much like I had when I was nine and knew
that my mother was never going to get better.

For a second I entertained the idea of turning around
and dashing down the stairs and out of the house, but
then that noise came again from the bedroom, and this
time it was more distinct. It sounded like a child in dis-
tress.

Taking a deep breath, I gripped the handle firmly
and turned it. As I entered the room, I saw the most
terrible sight.

Hovering three feet in the air above the bed was a
skinny little girl with long dark hair, a pale complexion,
and the most terrified expression on her face. She was
dangling above the bed like a rag doll, held up by an
unseen force, but she seemed to be clutching at her
throat, as if an invisible hand held her by the neck.

I took a step forward to help her, but then her eyes
shifted to me and I came up short, stunned to my core.
The little girl was unmistakable.

She was me. Eight-year-old me.

I stood there for several heartbeats too shocked to
move. And then the much younger version of myself
stopped clutching at the invisible force holding her and
she actually reached her small hand out to me.

I reacted out of instinct. I ran to her with outstretched
arms, and as I got to her, whatever was holding her by
the throat suddenly let go. She fell into my arms and I
wasted no time turning tail and running out of the
room. Cradling her protectively, I rushed down the
stairs and right out the front door.

I didn't stop running until we reached the huge elm

tree at the edge of the drive. Once I'd come to a stop, I simply stood there, holding her trembling form and trying to figure out what the heck was going on.

Everything felt real enough to be an OBE—out-of-body experience—but why I was having one I couldn't be sure. And of all the OBEs I'd had in my life, and I'd had quite a few, I'd never had one with a version of myself in it. I could only wonder at the meaning of it.

The little girl in my arms trembled and shook and I hugged her tighter. "It's okay," I told her as she cried quietly into my shoulder. "You're safe now."

"I'm never safe," I thought I heard her whisper.

I continued to hold her until she settled down and all the while I kept wondering what the purpose of this OBE was. "What's your name?" she asked suddenly.

I wondered what her reaction would be once I told her. "I'm M.J."

"M.J.?" she repeated.

"Mary Jane," I said, pulling my head back so that I could look down at her. It was such an eerie thing to see my own young face staring curiously back up at me.

"That's a nice name," she said.

I nodded. "The same as yours, right?"

Her brow furrowed. "No. I'm DeeDee."

I shook my head a little. "I'm sorry. You're who?"

"DeeDee."

For another moment I remained confused, but as I stared down at her, I noticed a few things that helped me put the puzzle together. It was in the little girl's nose and the set of her eyes. Her nose was a little thinner than mine had been at her age, and her eyes were a bit

more almond-shaped. "DeeDee?" I whispered. "As in DeeDee, short for Madelyn?" My mother's nickname from childhood had been DeeDee. The story was that when she'd been a toddler, she couldn't pronounce her own name, so she'd introduced herself as DeeDee. For the most part the nickname had stuck, although Daddy never used it, preferring her given name of Madelyn.

The little girl in front of me nodded and added a shy smile. "Thank you for saving me," she said.

For several long seconds all I could do was stare down at this slight, sweet child. The fact that I was holding my own mother was a bit too surreal for me to really take in. While I stared at her, she took a lock of my hair and studied it. "I like your hair," she said.

I stroked the back of her head. "It's dark like yours."

DeeDee smiled again and let the lock fall. "Mary Jane?" she asked.

"Yes, sweetie?"

She lost her smile and her eyes drifted up to her bedroom window. "Don't make me go back there."

My own gaze traveled up to her bedroom. "What the heck was that, DeeDee?"

"The Sandman," she whispered, and she shuddered in my arms.

I hugged her tightly, troubled by both what she'd said and what I'd seen in her bedroom. "Tell me about him," I coaxed, hoping she felt safe enough to trust me.

DeeDee gripped me around the neck and I rocked her back and forth. I didn't know if she'd be able to tell me about her experience, but I hoped she found the courage. "He comes at night to put sand in my eyes."

"Sand in your eyes?" I asked. What I'd seen in that bedroom had had nothing to do with the childhood fable.

DeeDee nodded against my shoulder. "He never does, though." She paused then and I patiently waited her out. At last she continued. "I tried to tell Mama about him, but she says I'm only dreamin'. She says the Sandman won't hurt me. 'Cept he does. He hurts me every time."

I hugged DeeDee tighter to me again, and I couldn't help wondering if I'd actually entered an alternate reality, or if I was somehow revisiting some element of my mother's past.

What troubled me was a memory I'd had when I was close to DeeDee's age, and I'd woken up in the middle of the night to find my mother sitting in the rocking chair next to my bed. I'd asked her what was wrong, and she'd leaned over to kiss and reassure me, whispering, "Nothing's wrong, child. I'm just here to keep you safe."

I'd never asked her what she meant and I remembered only the smell of her perfume as I drifted back to sleep, but there'd been other nights when I'd awakened to find her watching over me protectively. And then she'd soon become too sick to continue the practice.

Still, I also remembered around the age of seven when I'd started sensing the spirits of our deceased loved ones, how concerned Mama had been. She'd ask me all the time if any of the spirits I sensed had ever tried to hurt me. None had until I was much older and started doing ghostbusts with Gilley.

I wondered if any of what I was currently experienc-

ing was part of that vague memory of my mother hovering close by me while I slept. Could this be just a very vivid dream instead of an OBE? If it was simply a dream, then it would explain encountering my mother as a child, but what I couldn't get over was how *real* everything felt. The little girl pressed tightly against me was as real as real could be. Her skin was warm, her hair soft, and I could even smell the lingering scent of soap on her skin.

Tilting my chin up, I could see the stars in the night sky and feel the breeze stirring the leaves of the elm tree above us. No dream I'd ever had had felt this vivid and clear.

So what the heck was going on?

And, for that matter, what had my mother experienced as a child?

"How long has the Sandman been hurting you, Dee-Dee?" I asked softly.

Her small shoulders shrugged. "I don't know. A while. Ever since Everett told him to come find me."

My brow furrowed. "Who's Everett?" I asked.

"Glenn's cousin." She started to say more, but at that moment a light came on in the house. DeeDee gasped.

"DeeDee!" we heard from inside, and my own breath caught. It was the voice of my maternal grandmother, clear as day.

"I have to go!" DeeDee said urgently, already wriggling to get down.

"*DeeDee!*" my grandmother called again. "Child, stop hiding and come out right now!"

I frowned as I set the little girl down on the ground.

My mother's mother had been a stern, religious woman. I'd always preferred my father's mother to her, especially after Mama had passed away. "DeeDee!" I whispered, catching her hand before she could hurry away. "I know you have to go inside, but I want to tell you to get some magnets. Lots of magnets and put them under your bed and in the four corners of your room."

DeeDee appeared torn between nodding impatiently so she could get back to the house before she got in any more trouble and wanting to ask me why I was telling her to get some magnets.

"As long as those magnets are in your room, the Sandman won't bother you," I told her. "His power will drain around the magnets—they'll stop him in his tracks—so ask Grandmama—I mean . . . your mama to get you some."

DeeDee nodded and offered me a tiny smile. "Thanks, Mary Jane." Then she was off, racing up the hill toward home.

I watched her slip through the front door just as more lights in the house came on. I waited until I heard my grandmother exclaim, "There you are! Oh, you bad child! Why would you hide like that when you knew I was looking for you? And what on earth has you out of bed at this time of night?"

I frowned again as my grandmother's harsh words echoed out the open windows. I had half a mind to march up to that door and to lecture her, but at that moment I heard the sound of breaking glass coming from right behind me. I whirled around, but immedi-

ately lost my balance and began to fall to the ground. What was even odder was that as soon as I began to fall, I became totally disoriented, and for what felt like several long seconds, I had no idea which way was up. Flinging my arms out to try to catch myself, I felt something sharp cut into my arm and I hissed through my teeth. "Em! Can you hear me?"

I blinked, but my vision was blurry and the world still felt like it was spinning. I thought I was about to throw up when I heard Heath say, "Steady, babe. I've got you."

And then Heath lifted me into his arms and I knew we were on the move. Try as I might, though, I couldn't get either my vision to focus or the world to stop spinning. I clutched at Heath's shirt and hoped that he'd set me down soon, because I was very close to tossing my cookies.

And then I was aware that Heath was extending me away from him, and another set of hands had me under the arms. "Got her?" Heath asked.

"Let her go!" Gil said. "I've got her!"

"Gil!" I cried out a little desperately, so happy he was okay and the spook hadn't harmed him.

"I'm here," he said with a grunt, taking firm hold of my torso and pulling me out of Heath's grip.

"What's happening?" I asked, covering my eyes with my hand, hoping that would stop the spins.

"We're getting the hell out of here," he told me, his voice strained as he took my full weight. "Sweet Jesus, girl. You gotta lay off the cupcakes."

I smirked in spite of my discomfort. If anyone needed

to lay off the baked goods, it was Gilley. I was the same weight I'd been since high school.

"Heath!" Gil called. "Get out of there!"

I moved my hand and blinked furiously. At last the world came into focus, and just like that, the spins stopped too. I looked over Gilley's shoulder as he carried me away from the house, and I realized the boys had broken a window and passed me through it to get me out. I looked anxiously for Heath and then he appeared in the window and began shinnying out of it. I didn't relax until his feet were on the ground and running toward us.

Meanwhile, Gil had finally had enough of carrying me, because he was easing me to the ground as carefully as he could. "I'm okay," I told him, trying to squirm out of his grip to make it easier on him.

"Hey!" he barked. "Settle down, sugar. You've been out for like five whole minutes, so just let me put you down, okay?"

I held my hands up in surrender and Gil set me on the ground with another grunt. Then he held on to my shoulders and peered into my eyes. "Where the hell did you go?"

"How is she?" Heath asked, coming up behind Gil.

"She's awake and seems alert," Gil said.

"I'm fine," I repeated. "At least now I'm fine."

Heath reached out and took hold of my hand. "You look pale."

I nodded. I could imagine I did look pale, given how shaky I still felt, but then Heath was the one with the giant bump on his head, which was still bleeding. He

wiped absently at it, but his focus was still all on me. "I'm fine," I assured him. "I think I just need a minute to get my bearings, but I'm okay."

Heath and Gilley both looked at each other, then back at the house; then both of them turned to look back at me. "What happened to you?" Gil asked me.

"I have no idea," I said honestly. "One minute I'm trying to stop that spook from attacking you, and the next I'm having an OBE."

Heath's eyes widened. "You had an out-of-body?"

I nodded. "Yeah. And it was so weird." I then gave them a brief overview of the encounter with my mother as a child.

"That's crazy!" Gilley said.

Heath's brow was creased with worry. "So you didn't see this spook that was attacking your mom as a little girl?"

"No. I mean, I saw DeeDee suspended in midair by an unseen force. She was being held by the throat."

Gilley bit his lip and slid his gaze toward the house. "What?" I asked him, and then I realized I had no idea what'd happened to Gil and Heath while I'd been having my OBE. "What went on in there?"

Instead of answering me, Heath lifted up my arm and made a face. "That's a mean-looking cut, Em," he said.

I turned my arm and saw that I had a good-sized slice to the back of my arm, probably from a piece of broken glass. Of course, the second I set eyes on it, the damn thing began to throb. Clamping his hand over the cut, Heath said, "Gil?"

"Yeah?"

"Do we still have that first-aid kit in the van?"

Gil's head turned toward the van. "Yep. It's in the back."

Heath eyed the house warily and I noted that all the slamming doors had stopped and the house seemed to be relatively quiet now that we were outside. "Do you think you can get to the kit while I stay here with Em?"

Gil stood and bounced from foot to foot, eyeing the house, then the van. "Yeah. I think so."

"Good man. And see if you can retrieve your phone too," Heath said. "We'll need someone to come get us, and that cut on M.J.'s arm might need stitches. And watch out for anything coming off that third-floor balcony."

Without another word, Gil got to his feet and raced toward the back of the van. The second he was out of earshot, I focused on Heath. "Tell me what happened in there."

Heath sighed. "What's the last thing you remember?"

I blinked. "Well, I remember trying to get to Gilley before that spook did, and immediately after that I was having an OBE."

Heath's expression was grim, and the lump above his eye was large and still swelling. I wasn't the only one who needed medical attention.

"You went diving for Gil," Heath said, turning to look back toward the house. "I tried to stop you, but that damn door was fighting me. I thought if I let it go, we'd get shut in."

"So what happened?" I asked.

The corners of Heath's mouth quirked. "I let go, and we got shut in."

I eyed the broken window. "But you guys figured out how to break the window and get us out, right?"

"Not exactly."

I sighed and rubbed my temples. I was still feeling a tiny bit queasy and I could also tell I'd have a raging headache before this was all over. "Honey, please just tell me what the hell happened in there, would you?"

Heath nodded. "Sorry, Em. I'm caught between full disclosure and the possibility of upsetting you."

I stopped rubbing my temples and stared hard at my boyfriend. "Spill it."

Heath cleared his throat and said, "The second you made contact with that spook, you just went out."

"Out?" I repeated. "Like unconscious?"

Heath shook his head. "No. Not exactly. Your eyes were open and you were breathing, but there . . ." Heath paused as if he couldn't find the words.

"There what? What happened to me?"

He sighed and looked over his shoulder toward Gil, who was rooting around in the van still. Then he turned back to me and said, "It's like when we looked at you, there was no soul. You were totally gone. For a second we even thought you'd died. It scared the shit out of me, but then I saw you take a breath and I felt your pulse, but you . . . well, you were gone, Em. Like . . . *gone.*"

"Wow," I said. I didn't know what else to say.

Heath shook his head and cleared his throat. "I gotta tell ya, I've never seen anything like what happened to you and I've never been that scared in my life."

I gazed at my incredibly brave sweetheart. Coming from him, that was saying a *lot*. "How long was I like that?"

Heath's expression turned grim. "Long enough. And then, all of the sudden, you just jumped to your feet and started thrashing around. That's when you broke the window. I barely had a chance to grab you before you cut yourself to pieces, and that's about the time that you started to come around, back to us."

"Mission accomplished," we heard Gilley say. Heath squeezed my hand tight and we both looked to see Gil coming up to us, wiggling his phone.

"Did you call someone to come get us?" Heath asked.

"I called Mama, and a tow truck."

My eyes narrowed at Gil. He wore a very slight smile and I had a bad feeling. "*Which* tow company?"

Gil pursed his lips to keep from smiling even more. "I called Robby."

"Oh, Gil!" I snapped. "Why?!"

"What'd I miss?" Heath asked.

Gil folded his arms and looked crossly at me. "If you must know, I called two other tow companies, but when I told them where the van was parked and what'd happened, they both refused to come out here to this nightmare on Elm Street. So, as a last resort I called Robby because we need a tow and I was hoping your history with Robby would override any fears he

might have of helping us out." Focusing on Heath, Gil added, "Robby Reynolds was M.J.'s ex-boyfriend."

I glared at Gil. "He was *not* my boyfriend." I hated that Gil was stirring up trouble for Heath and me. My sweet man had had to put up with another ex of mine recently, and it'd caused more than a bit of tension between us. Turning to Heath, I explained, "Robby asked me to prom my senior year of high school. Stupidly, I said yes. It was a total crap fest."

"That's not how Robby tells it," Gil said, and I offered him a murderous look. At least Gil had the decency to appear chagrined and he got busy opening the first-aid kit and squatting down next to me. "Anyway, he's reliable and he has a body shop that should be able to fix the van. He promised to be here in ten minutes to give us a tow and Mama says she's on her way as soon as Miss Dalia finishes her hair, so probably in an hour." When Heath frowned disapprovingly at him, Gil added, "Hey, I couldn't tell her we'd been attacked by some spook 'cause it would've freaked her out. Mama's old, Heath. I'm not gonna give her a heart attack my first day back in town."

Turning to me, Heath said, "Em, we can call your dad or a cab to get you to the hospital for that cut."

I twisted my arm a little to take another look at the slice from the glass just as Gil sprayed it with antiseptic, which had me hissing through my teeth. "Sorry," he muttered. He then dug into the kit again and brought up one of those instant ice packs. Breaking the gel inside, he handed it to Heath and said, "Put that on your forehead, honey. I'll clean you up after I help M.J."

While the two of them were busy with the ice pack, I eyed the cut on my arm closely. "It's actually not that bad," I said. "The bleeding has nearly stopped and I think we can put a few butterfly bandages on it and avoid the emergency room."

Gil pulled my arm out straight so that he could apply the first bandage. "Mama can stitch that up for you if it comes to that, M.J."

I blinked. Of course she could. Gil's mom was a retired registered nurse. "What'll we say happened?" I asked him. Gil hadn't been lying about his mother's reaction; she was as scared of spooks as Gilley was.

He shuddered. "As little as possible. In fact, the less said the better. I told her we'd meet her at the bottom of the drive—that way she won't get too close. And, speaking of being too close, how about after I help Heath, we head toward the road? We can wait for the tow truck there."

I held in a groan. The only thing worse than dealing with a dangerous, havoc-wreaking spook was seeing my senior prom date after all these years.

Robby had used every trick in the book to try to get me to sleep with him the night of prom: groping me on the dance floor, trying to coax me into the janitor's closet, and repeatedly offering me a swig from the silver flask he'd stolen from his grandfather. He'd only quit his antics when I'd used a particularly tricky dance move that'd involved my knee in his crotch. The night had ended abruptly with him doubled over and me stomping off. It'd been a terrible memory to end my high school career with, and to make matters worse,

the following week I'd learned that Robby had told everyone that I'd gone all the way with him.

I think I was still a little furious about that because most people believed I'd lost my virginity to Robby Reynolds, who'd been a good-looking guy but a total himbo, even back then. I'd only agreed to go to the prom with him because the guy I'd really liked, Mike Newcomber, had chosen to take "Double-D" Debbie Campbell to prom even though he and I had gone to the movies and made out a couple of times.

I could only hope that when Robby showed up to tow the van, he'd be sporting a paunch belly and a receding hairline.

"Come on," Heath coaxed after Gilley had done his best to tend to his forehead. Taking my hand, he added, "Let's get as far away from the house as we can."

Heath had pulled me to my feet, but I couldn't help looking back over my shoulder. The mansion was giving off a seriously sinister vibe, which I hadn't detected when we'd first pulled up to it. Turning to Heath, who was also glancing nervously over his shoulder, I said, "Can you feel that?"

"Yeah. It's pretty thick, right?"

"What's thick?" Gil asked.

I shuddered and moved a little faster. "The energy coming off the manor. It's thick with something big, bad, and evil."

Gilley rolled his eyes. "Well, *duh*."

"It wasn't like that when we first entered the home," Heath told him.

I nodded. "Odd that we wouldn't sense it immediately, right?"

"It is. Energy as thick as that should be oozing from every crack and crevice. We should've picked up on it like a bad smell."

"What if it was like Godzilla?" Gil said.

Heath and I both turned to him. "Come again?" I said.

He shrugged. "What if it was like Godzilla, you know, asleep, and then we came around—or rather, you two fools with your abilities to talk to dead people—and that thing detected that in you and it woke up?"

"You're seriously comparing that spook to Godzilla?"

"He may have a point," Heath told me. I cocked an eyebrow at him. "Seriously, Em, things were a little bumpy in there until all the doors started slamming. Something shifted. Didn't you feel it?"

I thought back, but I honestly couldn't say that I'd felt any sort of shift. "I didn't," I told him. "But then, I might've been more focused on getting to Gilley before that spook did. After that, I ended up on a whole other plane."

A rumble alerted us to an approaching vehicle. I tensed when I realized it was Robby.

Gil nudged me with his elbow. "Are you wondering if he's still as gorgeous as he was in high school?"

"Uh, no," I said crisply as I reached for Heath's hand and hoped that he and I didn't look too beat up. Little did Gilley know that I was actually hoping Robby appeared fat and bald.

Chapter 3

The person who stepped out of the tow truck was somewhere in the middle of what I'd hoped to see. "Hey, y'all!" Robby said, after opening the door to his truck and leaning out to wave at us across the cab.

He looked much as he had in high school, except his hairline was receding (yes!) and he was a little thicker around the middle (yay!), but there was also that same underlying handsome smile and twinkle in his eye, which had always made him so appealing to the girls in my high school (dammit!).

We waved and said hello and then Robby squinted at me. "Well, hell! Is that Mary Jane Holliday?"

I offered another lackluster wave. "Hey, Robby. How ya been?"

Instead of replying, Robby jumped down from the cab and came racing around, heading straight for me with outstretched arms as if he fully intended to sweep

me up in a giant bear hug. I braced for impact, but right before Robby reached me, Heath stepped to my front, squared his shoulders, and thrusted out his hand. "Heath Whitefeather," he said, introducing himself while making it *really* clear whom I was currently attached to.

Normally, I would've rolled my eyes at such manly theatrics, but the truth was, I was relieved Heath was acting as a buffer between me and that big embrace. I'd been through enough for one afternoon, and I wasn't in the mood to be squished too.

Plus, I still harbored a bit of a grudge against Robby.

For his part, my old prom date stopped short and at first seemed puzzled by the fact that Heath had stepped in front of me, and then he seemed to get it. Shrugging slightly, he grasped Heath's hand and squeezed hard enough for Heath to grimace. And then Heath's already pronounced biceps bulged, and I knew he was squeezing back for all he was worth.

I sighed and pointed to Robby's truck. "Is your parking brake on?"

Immediately Robby let go of Heath and whirled around, taking three steps toward his truck. "Wha . . . ?"

I smiled and put my hand on Heath's back. The ruse had worked, and judging by the white handprint on Heath's already injured palm, not a moment too soon. "Oh, sorry," I said. "Thought it was rolling forward."

Even though the truck clearly wasn't moving, Robby headed there anyway and we heard him set the parking brake. Then he came back to us. "This is my fourth trip out here," he said, with a smile that didn't quite reach his eyes. Looking nervously down the road toward

the manor, which loomed large and formidable in the distance, he added, "Ever since they started working on this place, I been gettin' at least a call a week."

"You have?" Gilley asked, expressing the surprise I think we all felt.

"Yep. And every time it's something really weird. First call was for Sean Cadet's crew. M.J., you remember Sean?"

"Vaguely," I said. The Cadets had had six boys come up through our schools, but none of them had been in my grade. Sean, the oldest of the six, had been a senior when I was a freshman. "I remember his brothers Steve and Cal better."

Robby nodded. "Steve works construction for him now, and Cal went off to Florida to open up a fish shop. Anyway, Sean called me one afternoon and said he'd just gotten the job to fix up this old place. He was real excited, you know? He's always been talkin' about how much he wanted to see inside of that house, but the Porters, well, they was a weird bunch. Never invitin' nobody over who wasn't filthy, stinkin' rich, like they couldn't stomach the rest of us common folk or somethin'. And all along they was burnin' through their money until there wasn't much left for themselves."

I mentally sighed. Robby was taking a long time to get to the point, so I thought I'd help him. "You say something happened to Sean when he came to work here?"

Robby blinked like he'd just remembered what he'd been trying to tell us. "Oh, yeah. So, anyhow, Sean calls me and says that he needs me to tow three of his trucks.

I say, '*Three* of your trucks, Sean? What'cha all been doin' out there?' and he was like, 'Weren't us! There's somethin' spooky goin' on with this here house!' and I was like, 'How's that?' and he was like, 'Boy, you'd best come here and see for yourself!' So I came and shooo-eee! Three out of four of Sean's trucks had bricks all over their hoods and smashed clean through their wind-shields!"

I glanced sideways at Gilley, who'd made a small squeaky noise. He was staring bug-eyed and pale at Robby. "That's what happened to our van! Well, except that it wasn't bricks, but some pots from the balcony."

Robby nodded again, like he just knew we'd had trouble like that. "Good thing y'all didn't get hurt. Sean lost three members of his crew before he finally called it quits."

I gulped. "They . . . *died*?"

"Oh, sorry, no. I mean, three of his boys, including his brother, walked off the job. Said all sorts of crazy stuff was happening inside and they wanted no part of it. But as I hear it, there's been a bunch of accidents out here that folks is sayin' weren't no accidents. Every-thing from scaffolding falling, to workers sayin' they was pushed down the stairs, to power tools losin' all their power and the extra batteries being out of power too. Yep," Robby said with a sigh. "You ask me, I'd say this place is cursed."

We all fell silent as we each turned to look back to-ward the house, and I couldn't suppress the shudder that vibrated down my spine. "Our van is parked in front of the house," Gil said after a moment, jingling

the keys in Robby's direction. I knew he wanted Robby to go take care of it so that Gil could hurry to the road and be as far away from the house as he could get until Mrs. Gillespie could pick us up.

Robby grimaced when he took the keys. "Gonna make me head over there by myself, huh?" he said, trying to make light of it.

"I'll go with you," Heath told him, and the look of relief on Robby's face was unmistakable.

"Good," Robby said. "I'll need someone to be my lookout so my truck don't get damaged."

Heath and Robby set off in the tow truck while Gil and I stood guiltily under the shade of a tree.

"They should be all right," Gil said, but not like he really believed it. He then got on the phone with our insurance company to report what'd happened so that they could start processing the claim. At one point he covered the phone mic and said, "I probably shouldn't say that a spook threw planters at the van, huh?"

I shook my head. "Keep the details to a minimum if you can, Gil."

"We had the van parked in front of an old historic home that's having work done to it," Gil explained to the insurance rep. "I think the third-story balcony may have become compromised during the construction, causing the planters to slip down from the ledge and onto the hood of the van." I gave him a thumbs-up for that one.

After Gil was finished filing the claim, we both waited tensely for nearly ten additional minutes until

Robby's tow truck appeared with our wrecked van behind it.

Robby came to a stop next to us, and Heath got down from the cab while I offered up my credit card to pay for the tow. "You sure I can't give y'all a lift?" Robby said as he swiped my card through his portable card reader.

I eyed the front of his cab. There'd be no way Heath, Gilley, and I could all squish in there with Robby without the aid of a Twister mat. "Thanks, Robby," I said. "But Mrs. Gillespie should be here to pick us up anytime now." At least I hoped that was true.

"Okay, then," Robby said, handing me the receipt before offering me a two-finger salute. "I'll tow your van to Grady's on Bemiss."

We watched Robby pull away and I knew I wasn't the only one who wished we could've all fit inside his cab.

"Come on," Heath said. "Let's get to the road."

As it happened, we only had to wait a little while for Mrs. Gillespie to show up. She came plodding along in her trusty white Buick and waved at us as she approached.

Mrs. Gillespie had been driving the same car since Gil and I were in high school, even though I suspected she was wealthy enough to afford a fleet of cars. She believed in using things until they wore out, not just until something prettier came along. I admired that about her. I admired a lot of things about her.

She'd been a surrogate mother to me since my own mother's death, and because Daddy had all but checked

out of my life after Mama died, Mrs. G. had pretty much raised me.

She was almost a decade older than my mother had been when she'd had Gilley. Her husband—Gil's father—had abandoned the family when Gilley was quite young—around five, I think. The rumor was that Gilley had insisted on parading about in a tutu and his mother's feather boa (which Gil still held a fondness for) and it soon became clear that the Gillespies' only child would grow up preferring the company of men to women. This had caused a rather violent reaction on the part of Mr. Gillespie, but I never knew the specific details as Gil claimed not to remember too much about it and Mrs. G. sure wasn't talking.

All I knew was that she'd come home to find her husband violently abusing her son (trying to smack the gay out of him, is what I'd specifically heard) and she'd shown Mr. G. the door that instant. The divorce had been nasty, and I knew that because my daddy had handled it and once I'd snooped through his old files and read a few pages of the transcripts. I'd never met Mr. G., but within the context of those transcripts, I thought that he'd come off as a first-class douche bag.

Anyway, Mr. G. had relinquished all parental rights to Gilley without ever being asked, and he'd written Gilley right out of the family will. The Gillespies had been worth a fair amount of money at one time, and it still upset me that Gil would be denied his family's inheritance simply because his father was a pigheaded bigot of a man.

Still, his mom had done pretty well for herself in

spite of being on her own all these years. With Daddy's help, Mrs. G. managed to win a good settlement from her ex-husband and she'd used that money to purchase several homes that she'd then fixed up mostly on her own and turned into rentals. She liked to rent to single mothers, and was considered a very fair and good landlord.

Her real estate ventures had blossomed over the years and now she owned nearly thirty properties, which she managed almost single-handedly—well, at least the business side. She had several contract workers who kept the properties up to code and solved any maintenance issues. Meanwhile, Mr. Gillespie had moved right out of Valdosta and had never come back. At last word, he was said to be living north of Atlanta.

As Mrs. G.'s car came closer, I felt myself exhale at the sight of her and I smiled as I recognized the calming effect Gilley's mom always had on me. Mrs. G. looked very much like her son; she's rather short in stature, a little plump around the middle, and loose curls adorned her head. Her face was kind even if her nose was perhaps a bit prominent, but there's always a twinkle in her eye that's disarmingly charming. "Yoo-hoo!" she called to us as she pulled to a stop. "My, my! Y'all look like three lost frogs waitin' on a lily pad!"

Heath and I chuckled, while Gilley simply got into the Buick's backseat. He was obviously anxious to be away from Porter Manor. Heath opened the door to the front passenger seat for me, and I thought it was cute he was on his best behavior in front of both my dad and Mrs. Gillespie.

As I got in, she smiled brilliantly at him to show him she approved. "You sure you weren't raised in the South?" she asked of him. "Such good manners for a Western boy."

Heath gave her one of his lady-killer smiles, and bless her heart, Mrs. G. blushed. But then she squinted at him again and said, "Heath, is that a bandage on your forehead?"

Heath put a hand to his head. "Yes, Mrs. G. I bumped my head on a low-hanging branch. Gilley fixed it up for me, though."

"Well, I should probably have a look at that when we get to the house. It looks like you have a good knot forming under there."

After Heath got in, we set off and I settled into the familiar leather seat with another contented sigh. There was something so comforting about the Buick's slightly bouncy ride and worn but squeaky-clean interior. "So tell me again what happened to your van?" Mrs. G. asked.

"It's nothing, Mama," Gil said.

"Well, it must be something, Gilley, or y'all wouldn't need me to pick you up." Mrs. G. was not to be so easily dismissed.

"One of the planters dislodged from a third-story balcony and hit the van," I explained.

"Oh, my," Mrs. G. said, her hand going to cover her heart. "None of you were hurt, were you?" I noticed that she was looking in her rearview mirror at Heath again as if she suspected he might've lied to her about the way he got the bump on the head.

"No, ma'am," Heath said, sticking to his story. "We were all out of the van when it happened."

"Well, thank goodness! You know that Porter house is the talk of the town these days. I can't believe Christine hasn't abandoned the place yet. People are saying it's cursed."

"Yeah, we heard that too," I admitted.

Mrs. G. suddenly cut her eyes to me. "Y'all didn't enter that place, did you?"

"No, Mama," Gil said quickly. "We stayed outside."

Mrs. G.'s eyes never left mine, which made riding in the car with her a bit precarious. Mrs. G. was someone I'd never been able to lie to, and she knew it. "Uh, Mrs. G.?" I said, extending my hand to steady the wheel as we began to drift a bit to the right. "The road?"

She sighed and focused back on her driving. After a bit she said, "Mary Jane?"

"Yes, ma'am?"

"Did you go inside that house?"

I tensed and felt Gilley's and Heath's gazes on the back of my head. "I did," I told her, trying to leave the boys out of the confession. "But only for a minute. Christine asked if I could check out the house because a few of her construction crews had been complaining about strange goings-on."

Mrs. G.'s brow rose with interest. "And what did you find?"

I squirmed, picking my words carefully. "Nothing definitive. I'll probably do a little more background research before I go back for another look."

"We're going back?" Gilley squeaked, and when his

mother raised her skeptical eyes to the rearview mirror, Gilley blushed and flashed her a toothy, innocent smile.

"I think we might have to, Gil," I said, turning slightly in my seat to look at him. "Christine sank a lot of money into buying that old place, and I can't very well let her keep sending crews there who might get hurt. I think we'll need to figure out what's causing the activity and do our best to clear it."

Gilley frowned and settled down into the seat for a good pout. Heath's expression was unreadable, and I suspected that he felt a little conflicted about committing ourselves to another encounter at Porter Manor. I knew he knew I was right, but still, it'd be dangerous work; of that we could both be sure.

"We'll have to gear up," he said at last. "We'll need some spikes and some vests."

My sweetheart was referring to the magnetic spikes we used to close up the portals the more evil spooks utilized to float between the lower planes and our plane of existence. Not all ghosts are bad, of course. In fact most spooks are quite harmless albeit somewhat annoying at times. Those spirits were often easy to deal with through conversation and persistence and a reminder that their bodies had stopped living, and it was time for their spirits to go on home.

The ones we had to be cautious of were the evil spooks who had no interest in crossing to the other side, or what most people thought of as heaven. These more malevolent souls enjoyed causing mayhem, and some even lusted for hurting the living. These spirits were especially dangerous because most of them had

figured out how to create a portal—a hole between two planes of existence—that they could travel through, and they'd spend much of their time on a lower plane, where most dark energies lurk. Here, they could gain power and know-how, and plot against the living.

Often the only way to stop these spooks was to shut down their portals and lock them into the lower realms, and to do this we used magnetic spikes, which, when driven directly into the center of a spook's portal, would cause total havoc with the electromagnetic energy that held the portal open, and it would disintegrate and collapse, leaving the spook safely locked on the other side.

Heath, Gilley, and I had encountered more than our fair share of these rather rare entities, and all of them had been incredibly difficult to deal with, but somehow we'd managed to shut them all down. Each really creepy spook taught us something about dealing with the next, and I had to admit that we'd become very good at tackling even the scariest of entities.

And even though we'd only encountered a bunch of slamming doors and a big creepy shadow, something told me that whatever was haunting Porter Manor would require all of that expertise and, of course, some ghostbusting equipment.

For added protection we usually wore our bubble vests, which were ordinary down vests with much of the down in the front removed and replaced with magnets. "We'll need to get some bubble vests," I said, thinking out loud.

"Where the hell are we going to find a bubble vest

during the summer?" Gilley complained. "It's June, M.J. It's not like they're at the local department store."

"I might have the perfect solution," Mrs. G. said with a sneaky grin.

I eyed her curiously, but she didn't give up any more details.

"We'll need more than just the vests," Heath said from the back. "Maybe we should have someone in Boston send us some of our equipment."

"Yeah!" Gil said. "M.J., call Teeko and see if she can send us our stuff."

Teeko was my best girlfriend, Karen. She'd gotten the nickname Teeko from Gilley, who'd elongated it slightly from TKO, total knockout, which appropriately described my bestie.

"I'll call her as soon as we get back," I said.

"Have her send the Smasher!" Gil insisted, tapping my shoulder.

"The Smasher?" his mother repeated. "My goodness, Gilley, what's that?"

"It's an invention Michel came up with," Gilley told her, realizing that if he explained what the Super Spooker Smasher really was (an improvised tennis racket strung with magnetized wires), she'd catch on that we were dealing with something pretty intense—aka dangerous.

"What kind of invention?" Mrs. G. pressed.

"One that compresses the electromagnetic frequency of any ghost we come across," Gil replied easily. I had to hand it to him; the explanation was both accurate and a bit misleading.

"Why would you need to do that?" she asked next.

"If they're in a heightened state, Mama, it calms them down."

I almost laughed. By "heightened state," Gilley really meant "about to kill us," and "calms them down" was code for "squishes them like a bug."

"Ah," said his mother with a nod, and I swore everyone else in the car breathed a sigh of relief.

Mrs. G. chatted with us amicably for the rest of the ride and at last we arrived at her home, a lovely sprawling ranch with a stone facade, black-stained trim, and the most gorgeous garden both in front and back. Mrs. G. loved to get her hands dirty, and nothing gave her greater pleasure than playing in her massive gardens. That love showed, because everywhere I looked, flowers were bursting with blooming joy.

The scent of gardenia, a favorite of mine, hung heavily in the air, as dozens of monarch butterflies flittered drunkenly on the fumes while feasting on the coral blooms of butterfly weed, purple coneflower, and blue salvia.

For a moment I stood at the entrance of the walk leading up to Mrs. G.'s and simply allowed myself to drink in the scene with all its beauty and heavenly scent. In that moment I felt the softest touch on the edge of my energy and I knew my mother was close. She had loved to garden too, and it was one of the things that had made me feel especially close to Mrs. Gillespie in the early days after I'd lost her, a time when I was so broken and muted with sadness. Back then, Mrs. G. would pick me and Gilley up from school and bring us

here to help her weed or water or feed the gardens, and held within such a gorgeous nurturing setting, I'd felt a semblance of security and peace that no other place at that time could have possibly afforded me.

I'd also felt my mother's presence almost constantly here. She seemed to know how much I missed her and needed her close, because her spirit floated on the edge of my energy for many months after she passed. I always felt it the most clearly right in these gardens.

"Em," Heath whispered, sidling up next to me on my left. "Your mom is like, right behind you. I think she's trying to hug you."

I laughed and also felt my eyes mist. It was incredible to me that I should be so lucky to have found someone like Heath, who understood more than anyone else ever could what it was like being a medium, and also who freely gave his impressions to me when I most needed a confirmation. "I can feel her," I told him. "She used to be a regular here."

He grinned, but then his smile faltered. "Your mom has an urgent message for you."

The second before Heath had spoken, I felt a shift in the ether around us, as if Mama had gone from being playful to super serious in the span of an instant. "What is it?" I asked, turning to face him.

Heath's eyes shifted to the right, as if he were listening to someone next to him. "She says that something's going to happen soon that will change how you feel about her, but she wants you to remember the love you feel for her right now, because she's giving it back to you tenfold. She's afraid you'll turn away from her—"

"What?" I interrupted. "That's crazy. I'd never do that. She has to know that."

Heath frowned, and I felt he was trying to communicate that to my mother, but for some reason she was still pushing back. "She says the truth will come out, and it could change everything."

I shook my head. "I don't know what she means."

Heath focused on me again. "Neither do I. But she keeps insisting that this truth has the potential to change the way you feel about her."

I let out a small laugh. The idea was so absurd. "Nothing could ever make me change the way I feel about Mama." Heath shrugged. He had no answers. I tried a different tack. "Does she say anything about what truth I'm supposed to be looking for? Is it about Daddy?"

Heath's gaze shifted to the right again. "No. It's about . . ."

"What?"

"The sound man?" Heath had spoken slowly, as if he was trying to translate what he was hearing inside his head.

My breath caught on his words and I felt all the hairs at the back of my neck stand up on end. "You mean, the Sandman?"

He blinked. "Yeah! The Sandman. I think that's what she's trying to say. Do you know what she means?"

"No. But in the OBE I had at the Porter house, my mother as a little girl had mentioned that the spook terrorizing her was called the Sandman."

"Whoa," Heath said. "She won't give me any other

details. She just keeps telling me that we need to be very careful of him. And also that she loves you very much."

I felt my mother's energy from behind again, and this time she enveloped me in a bubble of love, which was her version of a hug. I drank in that feeling for the long moment it lasted, and then it vanished.

"She's gone," Heath said.

We were left to simply look at each other, both of us wondering what the heck Mama was talking about.

"Are you two still out here?" Mrs. G. said, peeking at us from the front door. "Come on, y'all! I've made up some lemonade and a few snacks for us to eat on the back porch. If you two want any, you'd best hurry. Gilley's already through his first helping."

Heath and I grinned and nudged each other before heading inside.

Before joining everyone out on the back porch, I claimed to need a visit to the powder room and instead I called Boston. "How's Georgia?" Teeko asked by way of hello.

"Beautiful. Sunny and eighty degrees today."

"And?"

I grinned. We both knew her question hadn't been about the weather. "And it's nice. Daddy seems really happy with Christine, who is a genuinely lovely person."

"Oh, good!" Teeks said. She would never admit it to me, but I knew she wanted very much for me to get close to Daddy. She'd been very close to her father until he'd died of lung cancer quite suddenly the previous fall while we were off in Europe shooting *Ghoul Getters*.

Teeks and I caught up with each other for a bit before I casually said, "Hey, before I forget, I need a favor. Can you please go to my place and dig out our bubble vests from the front hall closet?"

There was a pause, then, "Your bubble vests? You mean the ones you wear on ghostbusts?"

"Those are the ones," I said, trying to keep my voice nice and light. "Also, in that same closet you'll find a duffel bag with our *Ghoul Getters* logo on it. I need that and everything that's in it."

"Is that it?" Teeks answered, and I knew that although she was playing it cool, she was dying to ask me why I wanted her to ship my ghostbusting equipment down South.

To her question I replied, "Almost. On the top shelf you'll see about a dozen spikes. If you could put those into the duffel, along with the weird-looking tennis racket with the metal strings, I'd really appreciate it."

There was another pause. This one nearly ten seconds long. "Sounds like you've got one hell of a spook on your hands, M.J."

"That we do."

"How bad is it?"

I shuddered again. I'd been doing a lot of that lately. "Not as bad as that thing that destroyed your patio furniture in New Mexico, but probably every bit as wicked as Hatchet Jack." I was referring to two of the spooks that Teeko was personally familiar with.

"Yikes. You sure you don't need a magnet grenade launcher or anything?" she said with a chuckle.

I laughed too. That was funny to imagine. "Naw.

What we have in that closet should be good enough. I need it to get here as soon as possible though, Teeks. I mean, I know it's a lot to ask this late in the day, but can you find a way to overnight it to us?"

"Well, if I head there right now, that should be doable," she said. "John and I are leaving at nine tonight for New Zealand."

I slapped my forehead. "Ohmigod! I totally forgot about your big trip! Do you have time to do this?"

"For you, girl, I'll make time," she said.

I wished I could reach through the phone to hug her, because I knew my favor would most certainly be a hassle, but Teeks had always come through for me. It's just how she rolled. "Remind me to take you to the spa as soon as you get back," I told her. "My treat."

"I'll look forward to it. But I should probably go now if I'm going to make FedEx with your stuff by five."

"Wait! Let me give you my credit card number—"

"Pay me back when you get home," she said easily. I wanted to hug her again because I had a feeling it was going to be a few hundred bucks to ship all that heavy equipment overnight to us. Still, I knew there'd be no way to argue with her, so I accepted her offer, made her promise to keep the receipt, then gave her Mrs. G.'s address here in Valdosta.

As I sat down to some lovely treats that Gilley's mom had prepared for us, I winked at Heath and gave him a thumbs-up to let him know I'd made the call and our stuff was on the way. However, about a half hour later I got a call on my cell from Teeks. "Hey, girl!" I

answered cheerfully. "That was fast. Did everything get sent off okay?"

"No, M.J., there's a problem. I can't get the key to work."

I gulped as the realization hit me that Teeko had the old key to the lock on my condo. Heath and I had changed it—twice—to stop Gilley from just walking in on us, and I'd never given Teeks the new key. I explained all that to her and begged her forgiveness for wasting her time. "It's fine," she said easily. "Don't worry about it, but, M.J., I've got to go meet John for dinner before we head to the airport. Can you call Mama Dell?"

"Sure," I told her, not wanting her to worry, even though Mama D. and her husband were currently making their way down to North Carolina to visit with family, and I only knew that because I'd had to board Doc, my beloved parrot, at the local aviary when he would've much preferred Mama Dell's company while we were away. "Now, you have a fantastic time on your vacation with John!"

The second I hung up, I said, "We're screwed."

After I'd explained what'd happened, Gil said, "What're we supposed to do without any of our equipment or protection?"

"Maybe we can hit a hardware store and pick up some spikes?" Heath said. "And somewhere around here we should be able to find some magnets."

Mrs. G. set down her drink and said, "Oh, you three! I told you I had a solution for you. Now, come inside so I can show you the surprise."

We followed dutifully after Mrs. G. and she led us straight to the guest room, where Heath and I were staying. Opening the closet, she pointed to the top shelf and said, "Heath, would you please pull that big box down for me?"

He did and she directed him to set it on the bed. Then we gathered close as she lifted off the lid and parted some tissue paper, and there she revealed a bright green, yellow, and vivid orange plaid fishing vest. "Ta-da!" she said, pulling it out and holding it up for us to see.

All three of us took a step back. "Um . . . wow," I said.

"Whoa," Heath said.

"Oh . . . my . . . God!" Gil said, and I braced for whatever insult was about to come next. But he surprised me when he grabbed the vest out of his mother's hands and exclaimed, "It's *gorgeous*!"

"Oh, you really like it?'

Gilley immediately put the vest on. It sagged a little on him and he reached into the pockets to pull out several thin magnets. "Mama!" he said. "This is awesome!"

Heath and I stood side by side with wide eyes and I secretly hoped that in that big box there was only one fishing vest.

It wasn't our lucky day. Mrs. G. reached back inside the box and pulled out another two brightly colored vests. "I was going to give these to y'all right before you started filming the next season of your show. Gilley said that some of your locations were too hot to

walk around in those down vests, so I thought a fishing vest might be a good alternative."

Heath and I pushed giant smiles onto our faces and tried our best to look grateful and thrilled. Truth be told, the fishing vest *was* a fantastic alternative to the sometimes sweltering heat of the down vests, and it had ready-made built-in pockets to store plenty of magnets. The only problem was the ungodly awful plaid.

"Can you believe these were on sale down at the sporting goods store? I mean, who could pass up such a gorgeous pattern?"

"Mama, they're perfect!" Gil sang, and he paraded around in his vest while he secretly flashed me a mocking smile because he knew Heath and I were struggling to appear delighted by Mrs. G.'s gift.

I was so tempted to tell him his butt looked fat in that vest, but managed to hold my tongue and instead said, "Thank you so much, Mrs. G. These are great."

"Yes," Heath said, slipping his on with slightly wooden movements. "Oh, and they fit too."

Mrs. G. clapped her hands. "Well, I had to guess on the sizes, but I knew you were a little taller than my Gilley."

I held in a chuckle. Heath was nearly a half a foot taller than Gil. "Well, it was so thoughtful of you," I told her. "And they will definitely come in handy when we go back to the Porter house."

"But what about weapons?" Gil asked. "And meters and monitors. I mean, there's no way we can do a full-fledged ghostbust without the rest of our equipment."

I sighed. "For now, we'll have to plan a trip to the hardware store for magnets and spikes, and make do with that."

Gil nodded in agreement, and I wondered if he wasn't a bit too enthused by the fact that if he had no equipment with which to monitor Heath and me from the car, he'd be kept well away from Porter Manor.

The rest of that evening we were busy wrapping things up from that afternoon. Gilley made a call to the shop where our van had been dropped off to give them the insurance claim number and coordinate with the insurance adjuster when our van would be looked at. In the meantime he also rented us a four-door SUV. I was happy that he'd rented us something roomy because Gilley could be stingy when it came to saving a few bucks. A few years back when he and I had vacationed together in the Florida Keys, he'd rented us a car so small and so slow that I thought it must've been purchased by the rental company from a few clowns at the circus.

While Gilley was dealing with our transportation, I bit the bullet and called Christine. My call went straight to voice mail, so I blurted out a short message for her to call me and left it at that. I knew I could've called Daddy and asked him to pass the phone to Christine, but I just didn't have the energy to hear him ask me why and then grill me for details once I told him about visiting Porter Manor. Where Daddy was concerned, I was still a bit of a chickenshit.

At ten we all turned in for bed, and I hadn't heard back from Christine, but decided not to worry about it. I was almost too tired to think.

The next morning I woke up to the smell of fresh coffee and cinnamon buns. Heath was still asleep and I didn't want to wake him, so I slipped out of the bed and, after donning a sweatshirt, hustled down to the kitchen for some gooey goodness. At the kitchen door I inhaled deeply. "My God, Mrs. G., that smells like heaven!"

"Oh!" she replied. "M.J., you startled me half to death!"

"Sorry," I said quickly, moving forward to give her a giant hug. I'd missed Mrs. G. more than I'd realized.

She hugged me back, then shooed me into a chair before pouring me some coffee and handing me a plate for the buns already on the table. "Best eat quick before Gilley wakes up," she said with a grin.

I reached for a bun, took a bite, and closed my eyes to savor the wave of buttery, fluffy, sweet goodness that played like a beautiful symphony across my taste buds. "These buns should be outlawed," I told Mrs. G. "It's gotta be a crime to make anything this good."

Mrs. G. laughed delightedly. "Oh, Mary Jane," she said, reaching over to squeeze my arm. "If you think that's good, just wait until you try my peach cobbler tonight!"

I smiled, but there was a part of me that inwardly groaned. Heath and I were currently training for a marathon in the fall and we'd both sworn to eat nothing but healthy meals during our training. Then again, I'd been eating super healthy for a few weeks now, so I figured a few days off the regimen wouldn't hurt much. Especially if I kept up the training. And then I realized that I should've gotten out of bed and gone for a run,

especially since I was having an eight-hundred-calorie breakfast. It'd take me nine miles to burn that all off.

"Penny for your thoughts?" Mrs. G. said, and I realized I'd lapsed into silence while I worked through the algorithm of miles/cinnamon buns.

"Your new kitchen is gorgeous," I told her, admiring the open floor plan she'd chosen when she redid her kitchen—a recent and much needed update, as the old one, dominated by the avocado cabinets, appliances, and even the countertop, had dated back to the early seventies.

By contrast the new kitchen was something straight out of *Elle Decor*, with gleaming white windowed cabinets, a gorgeous smoky gray granite countertop, a large central island, Wolf appliances, and the addition of a huge bay window, which had expanded the breakfast nook and gave tons of morning light to the room. Mrs. G. beamed with pride. "It was expensive but worth it," she said. "My next project is to get rid of all the old carpet in the house and replace it with something more modern. Did you know they make tile that actually looks like wood flooring?"

Before I could answer, we heard a voice say from the hallway, "Mama? Are those cinnamon buns I smell?"

Mrs. G. winked at me. "No, Gilley. Just a new air freshener. Go back to bed, honey love."

A second later Gil's head appeared in the doorway. "You know I can always tell a real bun from a fake one, right?"

I hid a smile. Only I knew that Gil wasn't referring just to baked goods.

Mrs. G. offered her son a skeptical frown. Huh. Maybe I wasn't the only one who knew Gilley's penchant for the double entendre. "What's on your agenda for today?" Mrs. G. asked, setting a hot mug of joe down for Gilley, who was already four fingers deep into the rolls.

Gilley looked at me as if I were the master of schedules. I wished there were nothing more to do than hang out with Mrs. G. in her beautiful home and let myself relax. But as with most of our vacations of late, there was no way that was happening with some menacing ghost to deal with. "Well," I said, "I'll have to get ahold of Christine and tell her about the accident, and warn her not to send any more workers over there until we have a chance to fully investigate the source of the spook activity."

"You know, Mary Jane, I've been thinking," Mrs. G. said. "Maybe the source of the activity has something to do with that young boy who went missing from the Porter house all those years ago."

Gil and I both turned curiously to her. "What boy?" Gil asked.

Mrs. G. tapped her lip thoughtfully. "Maybe y'all are too young to remember. I was just about to enter my senior year, and at the end of that summer I'd landed my first real job as a typist for the sheriff, which I was so happy about because it meant that I got a chance to get out of workin' at my mama's boutique with all those gossipy ladies goin' on about how they couldn't find good help, or their husbands spendin' too much time on the golf course, or how the butcher was chargin' too much for his pork roast—"

"Ma!" Gil interrupted as Mrs. G. began to get wildly off tangent. "What boy?"

She chuckled. "Sorry," she said. "I spend so much time alone these days, it's hard to remember how to tell a story! Anyhoo, it was on my second or third day at the sheriff's department when a call came in about a missing boy—a cousin of the Porters', as I recall, had come for a visit and turned up missing. No one knew what'd happened to him and people searched for him that whole summer, but it was like he'd just vanished into thin air.

"His parents lived in another state, Alabama, maybe. North Carolina? I can't remember. Maybe Tennessee?"

"So, they never found him?" Gil said to move things along.

Mrs. G. shook her head. "No. It was so sad and so scary. People didn't know if he'd been kidnapped or if he'd just wandered off into the woods somewhere and gotten lost. The prevailing theory was that he'd died of exposure and his remains were simply never found."

"How old was he?" I asked, feeling a sense of familiarity. Had I heard this story before?

"Oh, I think he was fourteen or fifteen at the time. A good-looking young man too, from the photo that got printed in the paper."

"Do you remember his name?" Gil asked.

"I do," she said. "Everett Sellers. Such a good name, don't you think? I remember looking at his photo and thinking he could have easily been a movie star with those good looks and that name. He was particularly

close to Glenn Porter, who was just a few years older than your mama, if I recall, Mary Jane."

My breath caught.

"What?" Gil said.

"Nothing," I said, not wanting to go into detail in front of Gil's mom, but my heart beat a bit faster as I remembered DeeDee telling me that the Sandman had been brought forward by someone named Everett who was Glenn's cousin. I hadn't had any idea whom she meant, but now there was an apparent connection, and what an odd connection it was. It might even explain why I was pulled into that OBE with my mother as a child. Maybe it was to give context to something having to do with Everett Sellers, or, taking it one step further, maybe there was a connection to this Sandman and Everett's disappearance. It was something I knew I'd need to check out, sooner rather than later.

Chapter 4

"M.J.?" Gil said as his hand landed on my arm.

I jumped. "Huh?"

"You were deep in thought there, sugar. Where'd you go?"

"Nowhere. Just thinking that maybe we should check out the story of Everett Sellers." No sooner did those words leave my lips than I had the most overwhelming foreboding come over me. I'm not the best when it comes to predictions—my psychic sense is much more firmly rooted in communicating with the dead—but sometimes I'll get the most intense image in my mind's eye, and what came to me was the picture of the swirling strobe lights of first responders playing against the front entrance of Porter Manor. It was so clear, so vivid, and came with such intensity that I abruptly shot out of my chair and began racing down the hallway. "M.J.!" I heard Gil call after me, but I

didn't slow down or even pause in my flight to the guest room. I heard the pad of Gilley's bare feet behind me and was glad for it. I'd need him too.

Flinging open the door to the bedroom, I yelled, "Heath!"

"What?! What?!" he said, jerking upright before jumping out of bed and looking around as if he expected to fend off an attack. I'd obviously woken him from a dead sleep.

"What's happening?" Gilley asked me. "M.J., what's going on?"

"Get dressed," I said to both of them as I reached for my suitcase. "We're about to have a situation."

As if on cue my phone rang. It was Christine. She was sobbing. "Mary Jane!" she wailed, and then she couldn't seem to form any coherent sentences.

So I did the talking. "Christine," I said as calmly as I could while making a hand motion for the boys to hurry up and get dressed. "We're on our way. You stay put and I'll call Daddy. He'll come to you, and I'll head over to the manor and figure out what's going on."

"N-n-noooo!" she cried. "D-d-don't go over there! Everyone who goes there gets hurt or . . . or . . ."

"Shhhhh, honey," I coaxed, sitting on the bed to pull on my jeans. "Just try to tell me who's hurt. Can you do that?" My hand shook as I pulled up the zipper to my jeans.

"The . . . the . . . construction man! He's dead! I only hired that crew last night and this morning one of them is *dead*!"

Dammit, I thought. If only I'd had a chance to speak

with Christine and warn her about not letting any work crews go over to the Porter house until we'd busted the violent ghost there. I could only imagine that a new, unsuspecting work crew had shown up this morning and perhaps was hit by a planter or another heavy object thrown from the third-floor balcony. "Where's Daddy?" I asked her.

"He . . . he . . ." Christine was starting to breathe too fast, and she didn't seem to be able to form words.

"Shhhh," I tried again as I spun in a circle, looking for a shirt, and located one on the top of my suitcase. "Don't worry about it, Christine. I'll find him. You stay put until you hear from us, okay?"

"D-d-d-d-don't go over there, Mary Jane!"

I paused with my shirt half on and said, "We won't go inside. We'll just figure out what's happening and call you. We'll be okay. I promise. You just stay put. I'll be in touch as soon as I know something."

I then hung up because I knew my insistence to head over there was only going to stress her out more. The second I pocketed my phone, Heath said, "Tell me."

"That was Christine. Before I had a chance to talk to her, she hired another crew to go work on the house this morning."

"Shit," Heath swore, his forehead creased with worry.

"It gets worse."

"How much worse?"

"I think someone might be dead."

Gil stared at me as if he couldn't believe what words had just come out of my mouth. "Come again?" he said. "Someone *died*?"

"Maybe. Christine was pretty hysterical, and I can't be sure of any details. That's why we need to go."

I turned to head out of the room but was stopped in the doorway by Mrs. G. She was toting our vests and she handed me mine, then Gilley his, and finally offered the largest vest to Heath. "I don't know what's going on, but I'll want a full report the second you get back, and don't even think about taking these off for the rest of the day."

I kissed Mrs. G. on the cheek and put my vest on in haste. We had to get going. "Thank you so much! You're a lifesaver!"

With that, we were finally out the door.

Gilley drove us over to Porter Manor and the moment we turned down the long drive, he gave a whistle. "Lots of first responders," he said.

I could feel myself tense when I saw the scene that had been almost exactly captured by my mind's eye just fifteen minutes earlier. Then I counted three sheriff's patrol cars, a fire truck, and a paramedic truck all on scene with their lights flashing. As we passed the patrol cars, I was a little surprised there was no deputy standing in the road, ready to turn us away. "Everybody must be inside," Heath said from the backseat.

"Look, M.J.!" Gil exclaimed suddenly. "Your daddy's car."

Sure enough, parked right in front of the steps was Daddy's dark blue Lincoln. A jolt of alarm added itself to the anxiety brewing in my stomach. "Why is he here?"

Gil parked and we all hopped out, but while Heath

and I headed toward the front door, Gil hung back by the rental car. "I'll stay here, if y'all don't mind," he said, the Southern creeping into his speech again.

"I'll text you from inside," I told him. Assuming my phone would work this time, of course.

Heath and I hurried up the steps and through the front door, where I very nearly ran right into Daddy. "Mary Jane," he said, quickly taking hold of my shoulders and gracing me with a disapproving frown. "Why are you here?"

I thought I could ask him the same thing. I craned my neck, trying to peek around him, but Daddy's a big man, and I get my petite stature from my mother. "Christine called us," I said, trying to shrug out of his grasp, but Daddy is also quite strong for a man his age. "Daddy, please, let me go. I'm here to help."

His disapproving frown intensified. "There's nothing to be done, honey. You'd best get back in your car and go on now before you get in somebody's way."

"Montgomery," said a familiar voice behind Daddy. I leaned out to see Sheriff Kogan, who'd been the Valdosta sheriff for as long as I could remember. "We're ready to bring out the stretcher. Mind stepping aside?"

I felt my breath catch even though Christine had warned me that a man had died.

"Come on, Em," Heath whispered, and I felt his gentle hand on my back. "Let's go back outside so we'll be out of the way."

Daddy's eyes flashed with a brief note of approval for Heath before returning to me. "Wait for me in the drive," he said, his tone brooking no argument.

With a heavy sigh I turned and headed back outside with Heath to wait next to our rental car, which was parked well out of range of projectiles. Gilley came out from the SUV to join us, but he kept glancing warily up toward the third-floor balcony. It was now empty of flowerpots, but after our earlier experience, I could understand how cautious he was being.

After a bit there seemed to be some movement visible in the front hallway and soon enough two paramedics appeared with a stretcher between them. They carefully eased it down the steps and it wasn't until the stretcher was even with us that I could see who was on it.

A man with salt-and-pepper hair and a thick mustache was totally strapped down, complete with head and neck brace. His hands were struggling against the straps and his fingers were extended and slightly curled, resembling claws. He was also growling and spitting while trying to twist his head this way and that. Abruptly, he stopped growling and emitted a laugh that could only be described as a cackle. It was a terribly creepy sound, and as it faded, he returned to growling. I felt Gilley latch onto my arm with both hands and step close enough to hug me.

"What the hell is that?" he whispered.

But I knew that he already had that answer. "Something's got ahold of him," I said to Heath, who wore a grave look on his face.

We watched as the paramedics maneuvered the stretcher toward the ambulance, and all the while the medic at the helm attempted to talk softly to the man

and reassure him, but it was as if his words were falling on deaf ears.

No one else spoke although a slew of other first responders was now coming out of the house. I focused on them for a moment and I saw how strained their expressions were. There was something about the way they were holding themselves so tensely, as if they were quite disturbed by what they'd witnessed inside.

Daddy came out at that moment with the sheriff and a few men wearing hard hats who were pale and visibly shaking. They scrambled down the steps and over to three pickup trucks parked among the patrol cars and fire truck, and hustled inside.

"What do you think happened?" Gil asked, his grip on my arm becoming painful enough that I pried some of his fingers loose.

"Somebody died," Heath answered, his gaze far away as he stared in the direction of the house.

"You're trying to make contact?" I asked him.

He nodded. Then he frowned. "There is some *really* bad juju in there."

"We already knew that," I told him.

"Yeah, but, Em, I think it's actually gotten worse from yesterday."

"Maybe we should go?" Gil said, a hopeful note in his voice.

I pulled my arm out of his grip and walked with determination toward Daddy. He saw me coming and excused himself from Kogan. "You can't go in there," Daddy said, obviously mistaking my purposeful walk toward him at the top of the stairs.

"What happened?" I asked when I reached him.

Daddy shook his head and wiped a sheen of sweat from his brow. "Nothing you should be concerned with, Mary Jane. It's a terrible sight in there, and nothin' I want my baby girl to see. Now please, let me handle this, and you and Gilley and Heath go on back to Minerva's house."

A knot of anger formed in the center of my chest. Daddy was forever treating me like a child, as if he was oblivious to the fact that I'd seen far more terrible things just in the past few years than he could even imagine. "Daddy," I said sternly, refusing to budge or go away. "That man who was just taken away, what happened to him?"

Daddy sighed. "We don't really know, Mary Jane. He seems to be havin' some kind of psychotic break."

I held his gaze stubbornly even as he laid a hand on my shoulder to gently remind me he wanted me to leave. "That was no psychotic break," I said, knowing a possession when I saw one. "I'm assuming he was part of the construction crew that Christine hired?"

"Yes," Daddy said, but I thought his patience was beginning to wear thin. "He was part of Mike Scoffland's crew."

"Did anyone else see what might have triggered the . . . uh . . . psychotic break?"

"No. Well, no, I expect, except Mr. Scoffland."

"Can I talk to him?"

"No," Daddy said firmly, applying more pressure to my shoulder and trying to turn me away from the house.

I shrugged out of his grasp and crossed my arms to show him I wasn't going anywhere. "Daddy, I might be able to help that man, but I need to know specifically what happened inside that house, and if Mr. Scoffland can tell me what he witnessed, I might be able to help his crew member."

"You can't help him, Mary Jane, and you can't talk to Mike. Now please, go on home, all right?"

I shook my head and refused to turn away. "Daddy, you need to listen to me. There's something evil inside that house. Something spiritually evil. We had a bad encounter out here yesterday, and I tried to call Christine to warn her, but I never got ahold of her, and she hired another crew without knowing how dangerous it is."

Daddy's eyes widened at my admission. "What kind of bad encounter?" he demanded.

"It's not important," I told him, because it wasn't right now. "I need to talk to Scoffland—"

My argument with Daddy was cut off by the sound of his cell phone chirping. He pulled it out of his pocket, glanced at the display, and promptly answered it. After a moment his eyes got big and he gasped, "She's what?!"

I held my breath again, focused on Daddy's shocked expression, willing him to blurt out a detail that might tell me what other bad thing had just happened.

"Which hospital are y'all at?" Daddy said, and my anxiety increased. I had a bad feeling the call was about Christine. "Right, I'm on my way, June. You stay with her until I get there, all right?"

Daddy hung up the phone and eyed me, then his

car, as if he couldn't decide whether to bolt to his vehicle or explain to me what'd happened.

"Christine?" I asked him.

"Yes," he said, already turning away from me. I walked with him while he fished in his pocket for his keys. "She's had some sort of panic attack. Mrs. Lindstrom found her on the lawn, struggling to breathe. Thank God June was out for her daily walk around the block."

As Daddy opened his car door, I gave his arm a squeeze. "She'll be okay," I assured him.

For a brief moment he paused and there was something in his eyes, something I hadn't seen since a few days before Mama had died. There was a sweet tenderness in the look he offered me, and he patted my hand gently and said, "Go back to Minerva's, Mary Jane. I'll call you in a bit."

I nodded, even though I had no intention of heading anywhere until I found out what'd happened inside the mansion. Once Daddy's car was comfortably rolling down the drive, I turned on my heel and set my sights for Sheriff Kogan.

He was over with one of the firefighters, patting him on the back as the man turned toward the truck, presumably to be on his way.

Before I could reach the sheriff, however, I was stopped in midtrack by the most horrible bloodcurdling scream coming from deep within the house. Everyone turned to look through the open door, but I was the first to fly into action. Tearing up the steps and

into the front hall, I headed for the back of the house, following much the same path that Heath, Gilley, and I had used the day before.

Behind me I heard Heath call out, but I was motivated by the fact that that scream had sounded so desperate, as well as the fact that most of my torso was covered in magnets, and I was at least somewhat protected from the unseen evil in the house.

Reaching the end of the corridor, I stopped abruptly in front of the only open door.

There was a large swath of blood across the threshold.

The scream sounded again, only this time it came from practically right in front of me. Pulling my gaze off the floor, I realized it was coming from a deputy who was pointing to the opposite wall and screaming bloody murder. From my angle I couldn't see what he was pointing to, so I stepped over the line of blood to look, and . . .

"Oh, God!" I gasped. "Oh, my God!"

The deputy screamed again. Clearly he was having his own nervous breakdown. Diverting my attention away from the wretched sight on the far wall, I moved quickly to him and grabbed his arms, shaking him. "Hey!" I yelled. "Deputy! Focus on me!"

The second I grabbed him, he seemed to settle down just a bit. Well, actually, he still looked terrified, but at least he'd stopped screaming.

"Holy shit!" I heard Heath swear behind me. I knew he'd seen the awful scene too.

"What in hell is going on here?!" Sheriff Kogan

roared from the hallway, and the sound of additional pounding feet could also be heard getting closer.

"Deputy," I said firmly, still holding tight to his arms. "Can you hear me?"

He nodded, but was trembling so violently that his teeth were clicking together. The bronze name tag above his left-hand pocket read BRESLOW. "Deputy Breslow!" I said loudly. "You need to come out of this room." I tried pulling him toward the door, but just then the sheriff and another deputy arrived and they crowded our exit.

"Beau!" Kogan yelled. "What the hell is the matter with you?"

Feebly, Deputy Breslow lifted his hand and pointed toward the opposite wall, where the bloody corpse of a man who'd been crucified hung limply. "It moved, Sheriff! It moved!"

I blinked. So the corpse wasn't new information to the lawmen? And then I remembered what Daddy had said about not wanting me to go into the house to see a terrible scene. Was this what he was talking about?

"Beau," Kogan growled, his face a red, sweaty, furious mess. "Scoffland's dead. The medics checked him, I checked him, and Levi here checked him. He's got no pulse. He's dead, son."

Beau shook his head vigorously. "Sheriff, I swear! I was standing over here taking my photos and I heard a noise behind me, and when I turned . . ." Beau paused to gulp loudly and close his eyes against the memory

of whatever he'd seen. "He was staring at me. And he was smiling. All evil-like. And then, Sheriff, I swear to God, he laughed at me!"

We all looked from Beau to the corpse of Mike Scoffland, which was sagging listlessly, his head bent forward, almost completely obscuring his face.

At that moment a chill filled the room. It was a familiar kind of chill and I tensed. Heath edged close to me and caught my eye with a meaningful look. He'd felt it too.

Sheriff Kogan appeared a bit rattled by Beau's story. I had a feeling he'd known the young deputy long enough to know he wasn't the type to make up wild stories, because I'd heard enough eyewitness accounts from people who'd claimed to see something terrifying to be able to pick out the truth tellers. I was absolutely certain that Beau wasn't making up the story, nor did he seem to be exaggerating.

"Maybe you should check him one last time, Sheriff?" I suggested, nodding toward the dead man.

Kogan narrowed his eyes at me, but instead of telling me to butt out, he sighed heavily and moved stiffly toward the corpse. I tensed when he reached up to feel for a pulse on the dead man's neck, and we all waited with bated breath.

"Beau," the sheriff said.

"Yes, sir?"

"He's dead. Hell, he's even cold and rigor has set in, son! There's no way this corpse could've smiled or laughed at you."

Beau sagged a bit against me and in a flash Heath

was there to help support him, and the other deputy also stepped forward to hold him up. "Easy there, Beau," said the other lawman.

Heath nodded at him and motioned with his chin to the doorway. "Why don't we take him outside for some air?"

The other deputy nodded and they began to shuffle with Beau over to the exit, but then the frightened man seemed to think of something. "Wait!" he said, planting his feet. "I think I took a picture!" With trembling fingers the deputy lifted the camera he was still clutching and fumbled with the viewfinder. He then pushed the whole camera at me. "Look! Look!"

I took the camera and moved over toward Heath, holding it so he and I could look at the screen. Meanwhile I heard Kogan's bootheels beginning to cross the floor toward us. I ignored him and focused on the image, and it was so terrifying that I almost dropped the camera.

The photo was at a bit of an odd angle, but I could clearly see the body of the dead man, tacked to the wall, still limp and lifeless; however, obscuring his head was the smoky black face of a demon with fangs and red eyes. It was wearing the most wicked smile and my blood ran cold at the sight of it.

"Jesus!" I muttered, my eyes flickering to Heath, who looked just as alarmed and rattled as I felt.

The other deputy leaned way over and said, "I can't see it at that angle. Tilt it toward me."

I began to when Kogan snapped, "Let me see that!"

I handed him the camera and watched his face

closely. If I'd been frightened by that image, then Ko-gan, who'd probably never seen anything like it, was gonna be downright terrified.

He surprised me by saying, "Looks like a dead man to me."

Kogan showed it to the other deputy and he agreed. "Beau, there ain't nothin' here."

"Wait. What?" I asked, reaching for the camera, which Kogan handed to me. I looked again and myste-riously the image of the demon was gone. "How is that possible?" I said, angling the viewfinder toward Heath.

Beau leaned in too. "Where'd it go?!" he exclaimed, grabbing the camera out of my hands and fiddling with the image tabs. "What'd you do?" he then demanded, glaring hard at me.

"Nothing!"

"You had to!" Beau looked desperately to the sheriff. "Sir, I swear! It was there, just like I said!"

"Beau," Kogan said softly, as if he were speaking to a frightened child. "Why don't you head on home and let Levi and me finish up here? Get some sleep, son, and we'll talk about this in the morning."

Beau was still trembling. I couldn't blame him. I was a little shaky too. What I felt Beau needed more than any-thing right now, though, was someone to believe him, so I moved over to the other deputy, whose name tag read COOK, and eased Beau's arm away from him. With a squeeze of support to his biceps I said, "Hey, Deputy, come with me and Heath. We can talk about it outside."

At first Beau looked like he wanted to protest and stay to argue with the sheriff about what he'd seen, but

as he looked around the room, he seemed to understand that no one but us was going to believe him. With a small nod he allowed me to lead him away.

We passed the threshold on our way into the hallway when the sheriff said, "Come on, Levi, let's get this poor son of a bitch off the wall and loaded into a bag."

I grimaced. Murder was such grisly work; I'd never know how anyone could become desensitized to it.

Heath was still supporting Beau's other side, and once we were out in the hallway, the deputy seemed to settle down a little as we got closer to the front door. I knew that he'd be safe between us, what with all the magnets zipped into our fishing vests.

We stepped onto the front porch and I saw Gilley wave and get out of the SUV. He looked anxious himself, and I thought he was probably wondering what was going on inside. I waved back and was about to lead the deputy over toward Gil when a loud crash from inside the house echoed out to us.

Everyone froze.

And then there came a sort of sickening scream. Heath, Beau, and I all turned as one and went running back into the house only to hear more crashing and more screaming, but this time there were words mixed in. *"Levi! Levi! Stop! Dammit, STOP!"*

Heath was in the lead this time, but I was hot on his heels, and although we raced down the hallway, it felt like we couldn't move fast enough. I knew that the screams were coming from Kogan, and I couldn't imagine what he was begging his deputy to stop doing. Ten more quick strides brought Heath to the door and I saw

him pause in the doorway, his trajectory brought nearly to a halt by what he saw there, but then he launched himself into the air and I heard myself cry out. *"Heath!"*

Pouring on the speed, I rounded into the room, only to find Sheriff Kogan bleeding and pale on the floor, his hands pushing hard on his belly as his feet kicked at his deputy, who was also on the floor, holding a knife and currently fighting for control over it with my boyfriend.

If I'd had the extra air in my lungs, I would've gasped. As it was, I reacted on instinct and threw myself at the two men, landing on the deputy's legs so that Heath could have the advantage of staying over him.

But one look at Heath told me he was in the fight of his life. The deputy was very strong and he had the most grotesque expression on his face. It was as if he'd shed all vestige of who he'd been three minutes earlier, and what was left was something more carnal. Dark. Evil.

"Damn you," Heath grunted as he struggled with the deputy. Then he yelled, "Em! Get out of here! Can't . . . hold . . . him!"

Panic-stricken, I saw the knife pushing toward Heath's chest even though my sweetheart was leaning all of his weight on the deputy's arm. I tried to think what to do and I looked around for a weapon and that's when I saw Kogan pulling his gun out of his holster with feeble fingers. In a move driven by desperation I let go of the deputy's legs and launched myself at Kogan, grabbing the gun right out of his hands, and turning with it to hold it by the muzzle, I brought it down with all my strength on the deputy's temple.

He went out like a light.

For long seconds Heath and I simply sat there, panting and unable to catch our breath. Still, I held the gun high, ready to strike again if the deputy fluttered so much as an eyelash.

"Beau," Kogan gasped, and I lifted my gaze to the doorway where Beau stood, pale and shaking again as his wide eyes surveyed the scene. He jerked at the sound of Kogan's voice, and his wide-eyed gaze focused on the sheriff. "Call for an ambulance."

Beau nodded as if in a daze and lifted his phone from his pocket, only to stare at it and say, "The battery's dead. How can that be? I just charged it in the car on the way over here." My attention was currently focused on the gravely wounded Kogan, and I ignored Beau and moved over to the sheriff, who panted out, "Use . . . your radio . . . boy!"

Out of the corner of my eye I saw Beau lift the mic of his radio to make the call, but it gave a loud squeal, as if it were getting feedback from something. Heath and I were fully loaded with magnets, but I suspected there was still evil afoot in the house, hovering at the edge of the room, trying to mess with us any way it could. "Beau, take that outside and make the call," I barked, while I tried to help Kogan. "If for some reason you can't get your radio to work, use Gilley's phone." Beau's footsteps clunked loudly out of the room.

Meanwhile I was pulling apart Kogan's shirt to get a look at his wounds. "Oh, God," I whispered, realizing he had more than one stab wound. "Sheriff, he got you good."

"I know," Kogan wheezed. It looked like he was having difficulty breathing. I wondered if Levi had nicked a lung. "I'm bleedin' like a stuck pig!"

I then searched around for something to cover the wounds and apply pressure, but there wasn't much in the room.

"Here," Heath said, and I looked up in time to catch his shirt. "Push hard on the wound, even if he doesn't like it, and don't let up until the paramedics get here."

"Okay," I told him, then nodded to his bare chest. "Put that vest back on."

"You . . . ," Kogan gasped weakly, and my attention was drawn back to him, "need . . . to . . . cuff . . ." I leaned forward to apply pressure to his wound when I saw that he was attempting to turn on his hip so that I could lift his handcuffs off his belt. I did so quickly and handed them to Heath before reapplying pressure to Kogan's wounds.

And then I thought of something. "Heath?"

"Yeah?"

"The deputy is still breathing, right?"

"Yeah, Em. You didn't kill him. Just knocked him out cold."

"That . . . son . . . of . . . a . . . ," Kogan rasped, a look of fury in his eyes.

"Shhhh, Sheriff," I told him. He winced as I pressed hard on the wound that was bleeding the most. "Don't talk, okay?"

He ignored me. "He just . . . turned on me," Kogan said. "I've known . . . that boy . . . all his life."

"Sheriff," I said a bit more firmly. "Don't talk. Save your strength. I mean it."

But Kogan merely turned his gaze to me and said, "Why . . . Mary Jane? Why?"

I knew he was asking me why Levi had turned on him, and I had my suspicions but didn't want to voice them at the moment. The sheriff really needed to focus on calming down and getting him excited with my theories was sure to be counterproductive. "We'll figure that out later, Sheriff. For now, you have to focus on just staying with me, okay?"

There was an alarming amount of blood still leaking out of the large man. My hands were covered in it and it'd started to form a small puddle on the floor. Kogan was also getting paler by the second. "Here," Heath said, coming up behind me. "Let me take over."

I waited for his hands to cover mine before letting up on the pressure and then I sat back on my haunches and surveyed the room.

The dead man who'd been nailed crucifixion-style on the opposite wall was now facedown on the floor, for which I was actually relieved. I didn't want to see his face, and I certainly didn't want to experience anything that Beau had suggested happened earlier.

And then, something on the opposite wall caught my eye. When the deputy had freed the dead man, a chunk of the drywall had come away with it, and now there was something silver and round sticking through the hole. I got up and edged closer to the wall, pulled by a gut feeling that I needed to take a closer look. "What's up?" Heath asked.

"Not sure," I said, edging closer still and mindful not to get too close to the body. I bent over at the waist to get a better look. When I realized what I was looking at, there came a slam from somewhere upstairs. I stood up rigid and tall again, waiting tensely as the seconds ticked by. But no other slamming door sounded, and I prayed that it was an isolated incident.

Heath said, "Let's hope there aren't any more of th—"

SLAM!

My breath caught, and Heath and I locked eyes. "Oh, no!" I whispered.

"Wha's tha?" Kogan asked, his words thick and slurred. He was losing too much blood.

"We have to get him out of here," I said to Heath.

My sweetheart looked pointedly at the sheriff, who had to weigh 250 pounds, or more. "How? I can't let up on this wound."

"I'll get Gilley and Beau," I said, and began to hurry toward the exit, but suddenly the door slammed shut right in my face.

I gripped the door handle and tried to turn it, but my hands were slick from all the blood still on them. Frantically I wiped them on my jeans and tried the handle again, but it wouldn't turn.

SLAM! came another door. *SLAM! SLAM! SLAM-SLAM-SLAM-SLAM-SLAM!*

"Can you open it?" Heath yelled, his voice rising above the noise.

I shook my head while I pulled on the handle again and again. Doors were slamming all over the house,

just like the day before, and my heart was beginning to race with fear.

Now, I've been in a lot of really scary situations, but for some reason this house came with an extra dose of spooky, and as the doors all over the manor continued to slam, all I could think about was getting the hell out. "What do we do?" I cried. "It won't open, Heath!"

"Come here!" he said. "Switch places with me and let me try!"

With a growl I let go of the handle and moved back toward Heath and the wounded sheriff. Meanwhile the entire manor was now shaking from all the slamming, and none of us could talk above the noise. Kogan's eyes were wide, but he looked like he was fading fast, and I had no doubt that increased stress was only making his condition even graver. *"We have to get him out of here!"* I shouted as loudly as I could, kneeling down on the other side of the sheriff.

When Heath looked at me like he didn't know how to make that happen, I pointed at the window. It was wide-open, as all the glass had been knocked out the day before. Heath eyed Kogan and his bleeding wounds, then bent close to him and spoke right into his ear. Kogan nodded weakly and lifted his own free hand to wind his arm around Heath's neck. I hurried over to help, but just as I got to them, something even spookier could be heard above the noise of the slamming doors.

There was a thumping sound coming from the far wall, right next to the dead body. I had Kogan's arm over my shoulder, ready to help him to his feet so that Heath and I could get him to the window, but all three

of us were stopped short by that bizarre sound. It was as if someone was behind the wall, trying to pound their way out.

"My gun," Kogan said into my ear. I looked at him and he dropped his gaze to the floor where I'd set down his firearm. I realized that he wanted me to get it and use it if necessary. What he didn't realize was that a gun wouldn't help us for what was about to crash through that hidden door behind the drywall. And I knew it was a door, because I'd seen the silver handle poking out of the Sheetrock.

So I shook my head at Kogan to let him know I wasn't going to pick up his weapon, and then I motioned with my chin to Heath. We had to get the sheriff out before whatever was behind that door could get free. "Ready?" Heath said loudly to the large man.

Before Kogan had a chance to answer, however, there was a sort of cracking sound, like wood being splintered, and it rose above the slamming doors still shaking the house. Heath and I looked over our shoulders and we could see that the door leading to the hallway was being kicked in. "Something is trying to get in!" I shouted.

Heath's expression became determined, and, still pressing firmly to the wound on Kogan's abdomen, he pushed up with his legs and lifted Kogan off the ground. I barely had time to get up myself and balance Kogan between us before Heath was pulling us toward the window.

For his part Kogan was hissing and cursing through his teeth, and I couldn't even imagine how painful it

must have been for him to shuffle across the room. I had no idea how we were going to ease him through the window, which might not even be wide enough for the large man to fit through.

All around us the crashing and the slamming and the thumping and the splintering continued, and then, all of a sudden, with one last explosion of sound, it all stopped. The three of us paused again and I glanced tentatively over my shoulder. Beau stood in the doorway, gun drawn, dripping with sweat and wearing Gilley's fishing vest.

Heath stopped pulling Kogan toward the window and we both craned our necks to take in the deputy, who was now rushing toward us. Before he got to us, however, he came up short and glanced at the wall where the hidden door had been.

I pulled my eyes forward too and nearly let go of my grip on Kogan when I saw the sight of the dead man littered with drywall and the secret door wide-open. And visible just inside the doorway was a skeletal hand.

Chapter 5

As we all stood there, staring at the open doorway and that skeletal hand, the sounds of sirens closing in reached our ears. "Em," Heath said to get my attention. "Let's set the sheriff down."

We eased Kogan to the floor and leaned him against the wall for support to help him breathe. "Beau," Heath said to the deputy, who was continuing to stand there slack-jawed, "Come here and put your hand over this wound."

Beau shuffled numbly over. Still he did seem to have enough sense to skirt the dead guy on the floor by a wide margin and he also avoided getting too close to the newly open door.

Once Heath was free to stand up, he walked cautiously over to the doorway and peeked in. All of a sudden there was a sort of *WHOOSH*, and cold air came rushing out of the doorway. I saw Heath's hair

flutter back and immediately he put up his arms defensively as the cold seemed to envelop him before circling the room, as if it had a mind of its own. I felt it circle me too, but it didn't linger and within another second or two it was out of the room by way of the smashed-in door to the corridor. As if it had never even entered, no lingering cold remained, and the room went back to feeling warm again.

Beau and Kogan looked at each other, then at me, as if to ask what the heck *that* was. I squeezed Kogan's arm gently to reassure him, then got up and moved over to Heath, making sure to keep clear of Scoffland and the handcuffed and still-unconscious deputy. Heath almost reached for my hand, but his were smeared with blood, as were mine, so I stood close to him instead and both of us stepped forward to look through the jagged opening where the drywall had been, to gaze on the interior of what looked like a hidden room.

"Ohmigod!" I whispered, pressing my shoulder against Heath's for comfort and reassurance. The skeletal hand belonged to the remains of what appeared to be a young man. He was still in his clothes—jeans and a striped shirt—and oddly, he still had some of his hair, a dust-coated ginger.

Beyond the skeletal remains was a small round table covered in pink cloth and in the center was a miniature porcelain tea set with little red roses. The table had been set for three.

Deeper into the room I saw dolls, games, and stuffed animals. The small room had obviously been a little girl's playroom.

I shivered violently, even though the chill had definitely left the room. There was something terribly familiar about the setting, and my mind went back to my out-of-body experience when I'd met DeeDee, my eight-year-old mother. The tea set was something an eight-year-old might play with.

"Holy Mother of God," came a voice behind us. Heath and I both turned to see two paramedics hovering in the doorway from the corridor. "Sheriff?" said the man on the right, hurrying toward the injured lawman. "What the hell happened?"

"Never mind that, Sam," Kogan said, his breathing now quite labored. "Just get me the hell out of here."

Heath and I stood close by the sheriff while the paramedics applied bandages, oxygen, and an IV before easing the sheriff flat onto a board. We then helped the paramedics and Beau get Kogan onto a stretcher. A second stretcher was brought in for the still-unconscious deputy, and I was starting to worry that I'd really hurt the man, but as he was being quickly put onto a gurney and wheeled away, his hands still cuffed behind him, Heath said, "You had no choice, Em. He would've killed me."

I sighed and nodded and just before the paramedics wheeled Kogan out of the room, he waved to Beau, who immediately went to the sheriff's side. Kogan seemed to be breathing a tiny bit better and he feebly removed the oxygen mask to say, "You're in charge. Call for backup, but you're running point on this." And then the sheriff surprised me by turning to me. "Mary Jane?"

"Yes, Sheriff?"

"You and your man, stay with him, would you?"

For being so terribly injured, the sheriff was showing remarkable clarity. In his eyes I saw the true meaning of his words; he wanted me and Heath to stay with Beau to help protect him against whatever evil was still lurking in these walls.

It was a tall order, but I couldn't abandon the poor deputy, who'd already had the worst scare of his life. And with two men clearly possessed by God knew what, there was no way I could leave him or any other lawmen who were going to show up to investigate the newly enlarged crime scene. "We'll stay with him," I vowed.

Kogan covered his mouth back up with the mask and closed his eyes. A moment later, he and the paramedics were gone.

Turning to Beau, I pointed to his vest. "That'll keep you safe enough while you're in here."

The deputy looked down at the fishing vest. "Gilley said the same thing to me. What's in these pockets anyway? This thing is heavy."

"Magnets," said Heath. "They screw with a spook's electromagnetic frequency. They hate to be around magnets."

Beau nodded, but I could see that he was still clearly rattled by all that'd taken place at the manor. "I called for backup," he said, "but there's an accident on I-eighty-four and dispatch has all other units out there. She's trying to route me someone on call, but it could

be a little while." Beau then let his nervous gaze travel
between the dead man on the floor and the playroom
with the skeleton.

I edged over to him. "We can help," I told him. I
hadn't been around a lot of murder scenes, but I'd seen
enough where I was a little more desensitized than
most people my age. Plus, dead bodies didn't much
scare me. Dead souls were a different story; some of
them had scared the pants off me.

Heath picked up a long black bag from the floor. I
realized it was a body bag and grimaced. Motioning to
Scoffland still lying facedown, Heath said, "We should
get him in the bag, Beau. That way, he can't cause us
any more trouble."

I liked the way Heath had said "us" over "you." It
was subtle, but it let Beau know that we believed his
story.

Beau nodded and moved over to a duffel bag with
the Valdosta sheriff's logo on it. I hadn't seen it in the
room earlier, and I suspected that sometime between
the paramedics loading Kogan and Deputy Cook into
the ambulance, Beau had brought it in from the hallway.
Unzipping the duffel, he pulled out two pairs of black
latex gloves, tossing one to Heath and the other to me.
"Try not to touch anything near the playroom, okay?"

Heath donned the gloves and moved toward the head
of the victim. Beau looked relieved that he wouldn't have
to be near the guy's face when they shuffled him into
the body bag. "Who is he anyway?" Heath asked as
they began to lay out the bag.

"Mike Scoffland," Beau said. "He's a contractor. Was a contractor. I knew him pretty well, actually. He was a good friend of my dad's, and after Dad got sick, Mike used to go visit him every day at the hospital, and he even kept on visiting when Dad went to hospice. I've never forgotten that."

Heath and Beau carefully rolled Scoffland onto his back, and I looked at the man's face. He seemed to have been healthy and in good shape for a man I'd guess was in his midsixties. Then I looked again at Beau, who was probably in his late thirties. He'd said Scoffland had been a good friend of his dad's. "How old was Scoffland?" I asked.

Beau glanced curiously at me. "I reckon he was the same age as Dad. They went to school together, so"— Beau paused to do the math—"probably around seventy-eight."

My jaw dropped. "He was *seventy-eight*?"

Beau grunted as he and Heath lifted Scoffland into the center of the open bag. "I know. He looked good, didn't he?" And then he seemed to realize he was looking directly at the elder man's face and he quickly averted his eyes by zipping up the bag.

"So what happened?" Heath asked.

"You mean to Scoffland?" Heath nodded. "Best we can tell, one of his workers killed him with a nail gun."

"The guy who was taken out on a stretcher?" I asked.

"Yeah," Beau said. "We got a call that some worker at the Porter house had snapped and killed Mike. When we got here, Cisco—that was the guy on the

stretcher, Ray Cisco—he was acting all crazy and poor Mike here was nailed to the wall."

"Was there any history of animosity between the two?" I asked.

The deputy shook his head. "No. Not that I know of. We interviewed most of the crew and they all said that Mike was like a father to Ray. It didn't make a lot of sense."

I couldn't tell if Beau was avoiding the fact that another deputy had basically done the same thing to the sheriff, without cause or provocation, and that maybe there was no reason other than that both men had become possessed by some kind of evil spirit.

I studied the deputy, who still appeared to be shaken by the day's events, and he caught my eye but then looked away toward the open door to the playroom. "And now I have another scene to process."

"How can we help?" I asked. I doubted we'd be allowed to participate in any way, given that we weren't deputized, but I underestimated just how badly Beau seemed to want to get the heck out of Porter Manor.

"You could take pictures," he said. "I have to document the scene and take a lot of notes. Whatever happened in that hidden room, it happened a long time ago by the looks of it." Bending down, he picked up the camera, but before he handed it to me, he studied it for a moment and swore under his breath. "The battery's dead."

I pulled out my iPhone and was relieved to see that it still had a charge. "I can use this if you want."

Beau nodded. "That'll work." Then he reached into

the duffel bag again and pulled out a series of yellow crime scene tags, each of them numbered. "Heath, can you set one of these down whenever I point to something and then Mary Jane can take a picture of it?"

Heath and I nodded and then we got to the business of heading inside the playroom. "Oh, now I see," I said, eyeing the architecture of the room. "It's a hidden corner. You don't realize there's a room here from the outside because of the curve of the exterior wall."

The first thing the deputy pointed to was the body. "We'll need lots of photos of that," he said. He then instructed me about how to frame the remains, and I began clicking away. The position of the skeleton was a bit odd, I thought. The young man was lying on the ground, his legs bent slightly, and one arm was tucked under the skull. I glanced toward the closest chair at the tea table, and walked to it, then looked back at the skeleton. If I didn't know any better, I would've said that the young man had fallen out of the chair and sprawled across the floor. I photographed that, even though Beau hadn't instructed me on that yet, and then I peered into the teacup at that place setting.

I saw nothing but dust in the bottom of the cup.

"Who do you think it could be?" I heard Heath ask Beau as the two of them moved slowly about the room, placing numbers and jotting notes.

Beau stared hard at the skeleton. "I have no idea," he admitted.

"Could it be Everett Sellers?" I asked.

Beau blinked at me. "Where'd you hear about Everett Sellers?"

"Mrs. Gillespie told . . ." At that moment I realized something and mentally smacked myself. "Gilley!"

Heath's eyes went wide. "We left him out by the car."

"He'll be worried sick!" Quickly I switched over to the phone function on my cell and dialed Gil.

"WHERE HAVE YOU BEEN?!!" he shouted by way of hello.

I winced, and was about to yell back when I realized he was crying. "Honey," I said. "I'm so sorry."

"I've been worried sick!" Gil wailed. "The paramedics left *hours* ago!"

I checked my watch. They'd maybe left fifteen minutes earlier, if that, but Gil was always one for theatrics.

"Honey," I tried again.

"I'm so scared out here, M.J.!" he said. "Beau took my vest and I have *nothing* to protect me!"

I was all set to go running out the door to give Gilley my vest when I heard the rustling of paper. My brow lowered. "Gilley?"

He sniffled. "What?"

"Was that a wrapper I heard?"

The scrunching of paper was a bit farther away, as if he knew he'd been caught red-meat-handed. "No," he said, but it was muffled, like he'd just stuffed his pie-hole with what remained of a burger.

"Are you even still out in the driveway? Or are you circling the parking lot of Burger King?"

"I'm in the driveway," he snapped. "I merely ran down the street to get a quick snack."

I didn't say anything—I just stood there shaking my head.

"You *know* I eat when I get stressed!" Gilley shouted.

I remained silent.

"Okay, I'm sorry! Will you please tell me what's going on?"

"We found another body."

"No way!"

"Way. We're helping Beau process the scene."

"Shouldn't there be other people doing that?"

"There's an accident on I-eighty-four and every other deputy is tied up. We're all that Beau has right now, so we're helping out."

"When are you coming out?"

I looked around the playroom. "Probably not for a bit." The sound of the engine starting came through the phone. "You're headed back to the burger joint, aren't you?"

"Might as well," Gil said. "Their apple pie looked good." Then he seemed to remember his manners. "Did you guys want anything?"

"No. I'll call you when we're through." I hung up the phone, and when Heath looked curiously at me, I rolled my eyes and said, "He's fine. Let's get on with this."

We spent an hour processing the scene, which, I almost hate to admit, was incredibly interesting. It was a bit like being in a time warp, because, save for the coating of dust, everything was in pristine condition. I had little doubt that almost immediately following that

young man's death, this room had been sealed and remained that way for the last fifty years.

And even though the day had been crazy stressful, I found myself actually intrigued by the crime scene. I wondered how the boy had died. I suspected that his end had involved something sinister, and that sinister had probably been at the hands of one of the Porters, because why else would the family have sealed him inside this room and pretended that he'd simply gone missing? It seemed likely that if the young man had had a seizure or had died of some other natural cause, or even by accident, the family would have reported it to the authorities. No, they'd sealed this room, and told the police that he'd wandered off, and as the Porters were such a well-respected family, of course the sheriff at the time had taken their word for it.

As I photographed every inch of that room, I was convincing myself that some older cousin or uncle had perhaps done something wicked to the poor young man, and perhaps he'd panicked and then he'd inadvertently killed Everett, and the wealthy family hadn't wanted the scandal, so they'd covered it up.

Yes, I had a nice tidy theory going when I began photographing the last corner of the room. I lifted my foot over a pile of stuffed animals and nearly stepped right onto a beautifully crafted Ouija board. For several seconds I simply stared at it. The board was coated in dust like everything else, but even through the layer of film, I could see the ornate hand-painted design.

It looked nothing like most Ouija boards out there, which were really quite simple creations with the

words "Yes" and "No" and the letters of the alphabet and numbers one through ten painted crisply on their surfaces.

This board had all the letters and numbers on it, but surrounding those was a dazzling nature scene with beautiful flowers, plants, and even a pair of birds.

Resting in the center of the board was a gleaming silver planchette, cast in the shape of a heart and with a beautiful light purple crystal set in the tip of the heart, which was clear enough to read a letter or number underneath.

After realizing exactly what I was looking at, I studied the board with caution. I don't like Ouija boards, and I personally think the major game manufacturer who peddles them should seriously reconsider giving children the opportunity to play with such a potentially dangerous and damaging thing.

A shiver traveled up my spine as I bent down to take a closer look. If someone had been playing with this board fifty years ago, I thought, it might explain why the house had taken on such sinister energy. Glancing over at Heath and Beau, I saw the deputy squatting down by the body, poking at the clothing on the skeleton with his pen. "Heath," I said softly.

He glanced up from looking over Beau's shoulder and gave me a questioning look.

"Come here," I mouthed. I didn't want to make Beau aware of the Ouija board yet. There was something about it being in here and out in the open that was unnerving me and I wanted Heath to take a look before I decided what to do about it.

"Whoa," my sweetheart whispered the moment he saw what I was kneeling next to. He looked over his shoulder at the deputy, who was still poking around the body. Heath squatted down too. "You found this just like this?"

I nodded. "It could mean nothing," I said. Plenty of children played with these things without a single thing happening; however, in some cases, the Ouija board was notorious for opening up avenues of communication to some of the lower realms, and every once in a while we'd hear about some poor kid who was in fact taken over by something evil after playing with a Ouija board.

If any parent knew the potential risk for that to happen, they'd never, ever let their kids within a hundred feet of the thing. "Do you think—," Heath began, but then his breath caught as he stared at the board.

I looked at it too and could hardly believe my eyes.

The planchette was moving.

Heath and I both stood up together and took a step back, transfixed by the fact that the little silver plank was tracing small lines in the dust on the board all by itself.

And, given that Heath and I were wearing enough magnets to make that insanely difficult for any spook, I was totally stunned and petrified. Something big, bad, and terrible was working to communicate with us.

The planchette moved at a snail's pace over toward the far end of the alphabet where the amethyst crystal hovered over the letter *T*. We waited for it to continue,

but it didn't and I felt a tiny wave of relief. Maybe that's all it was, just a small burst of negative energy that allowed the planchette to swerve over to the letter *T* before it lost steam.

"*T*," said Heath, and it was more of a question than a statement, but the second he said the letter out loud, the planchette began moving again.

My shoulders tensed. Whatever was moving the planchette hadn't run out of steam at all. In fact, it was now moving at breakneck speed and Heath was sounding it out, the planchette making it easier for him as it paused at the end of every word. "The . . . Sand . . . man . . . has . . . come . . . back . . . to . . . play . . . kiddos." I gripped his arm.

"M.J.? Heath?" we heard Beau say. "You guys okay?"

Neither of us answered. We just kept our eyes on the planchette, which kept moving.

Heath continued to sound out what it was saying. "Little . . . d . . . d . . . come . . . to . . . play?"

A terrible note of intuition burst into my mind and I knew the Sandman was referring to me, and not my mother.

"Guys?" Beau said.

I held up a hand to get him to stop talking, and Heath and I both focused on the planchette. "Sand . . . man . . . will . . . play . . . with . . . little . . . d . . . d . . . if . . . she . . . takes . . . off . . . her . . . coat," Heath whispered, and then he stiffened and turned to look at me. "He means *you*!"

I nodded. Heath turned his gaze back to the board,

and before I could stop him, he kicked the planchette with his boot and it skidded across the floor and under a bookshelf.

My attention went from Heath, to Beau—who was looking alarmed—to the bookshelf, then back to the board. "How did it connect me to my mom?" I asked Heath.

He gripped my arm, and he gave the crack under the bookshelf a furious glare. "Don't know, but we're leaving."

Beau's jaw dropped and he looked close to panic. "But I'm not done!"

Heath's grip on my arm remained firm. "I don't care," he said. "I'm getting M.J. out of here, and if you're smart, you'll pack it up and head out with us." And then he looked at me as if to see if I'd object, and I nodded to show him there was no way I wanted to stick around.

"Well, what the hell happened?" Beau asked, his voice going up an octave.

"I'll explain outside," Heath said, turning with me toward the door. But just as we took our first steps, a silver blur flew right at us and Heath and I both ducked just in the nick of time. A loud THUD sounded at the far wall and we glanced up from our crouched positions to see the planchette embedded in the wall.

From its position, I estimated that it'd missed Heath's head by a fraction of an inch, and if it'd been moving fast enough to embed itself in the wall, I shuddered at the thought of the damage it might've caused him had it made contact with his head.

"On second thought," Beau said, staring at the planchette, "maybe we should go."

Heath and Beau paused long enough to each grab one end of the body bag containing Mike Scoffland before the three of us made haste out of the house. As we moved through the front door, we nearly bumped right into two additional deputies. "Beau," said the first one up the steps with a nod to his comrade. "We came as soon as we could. There's a hell of a mess on Eighty-four. And what's this about Cook attacking Kogan?"

"I'll explain later," Beau said, still holding firm to Scoffland's feet. And then he seemed to realize both the new deputies were taking in the scene—the three of us in our colorful fishing vests and a body bag slung between us. Their expressions went from confused to barely veiled humor.

"You headin' to the lake after dropping that off at the morgue, Beau?" asked the first deputy. His name tag read WELLS.

Beau's face reddened, but after he motioned to Heath to set Scoffland down, he made no move to take off the vest. "Shut it, Matt. I ain't in the mood, and where the hell is the coroner?"

"Griswald has his hands full with that accident," Wells said. "Three dead at the scene and another died en route."

I felt a pang of sadness. That did sound like a bad accident.

"We hear there's a second body?" the other deputy, whose name tag read CARTER, said.

"Yeah, but I'm not going back in there to get it, Roy,"

Beau told him. This got him more funny looks from the newly arrived deputies.

"What's going on, Beau?" Wells said in that way that suggested he was wondering if Beau had lost his marbles.

"It's a long story, and I ain't talkin' 'bout it here." Beau glanced nervously over his shoulder before he added, "Roy, Matt, help me get this guy in the trunk. I ain't waitin' for the coroner."

Matt's eyes bugged wide. "Beau, what the hell's going on?" he demanded.

Suddenly the door behind us slammed shut so hard that the five of us jumped. For a moment there was silence, and then doors began to slam inside and all over the house. Wells and Carter looked toward the house and their faces drained of color, and they both put their hands on the guns at their side, ready to draw their weapons, but Beau had seen enough for one day to know there was no point in that and he grabbed Scoffland's feet again and motioned to Heath with his head. "Let's go!" he commanded.

Heath grabbed his end, and to help things along I took up the middle. Scoffland was heavy and we struggled with him over to Beau's patrol car. "Beau!" Wells said above the noise echoing from inside the mansion. But the deputy ignored him and wriggled his keys out of his pocket while awkwardly holding Scoffland with one hand and his hip.

"*Beau!*" Wells yelled again just as the lid opened and we half rolled, half shoved Scoffland into it.

Beau brought the lid of the trunk down hard and motioned to the backseat of his patrol car. "Get in," he

told us, and it suddenly dawned on me that Gilley and our rental car were nowhere in sight. Neither Heath nor I was about to argue—we both wanted badly to get the hell out of there—and we hopped into the back of the car, leaving the other two deputies to stare in shock after us.

Beau got into the driver's side, started the car, and pressed hard on the accelerator. The car bolted forward, spinning dirt and skidding slightly down the drive, but Beau didn't slow down. In fact, right before hitting the road, he turned on his light box and siren.

We hauled ass to the county morgue and on the way I called Gilley and told him where to meet us.

"You want me to come to *the morgue*?"

"If it's not too much trouble," I said drily.

There was a prolonged silence on the other end while Gilley debated the merits of leaving Heath and me to find an alternate way home, I imagined. Finally he grumbled, "Okay. See you in five."

Beau pulled up into the rear lot of the municipal building and we came to a stop outside two double doors, where, presumably, dead bodies were taken from the coroner's van inside to be dealt with. Once Beau had thrown the car into park, he turned in his seat to stare at us for a few moments before he spoke. "Can either of you tell me what the hell this is all about?"

"Not yet," Heath said honestly.

The deputy ran a trembling hand through his hair and shook his head as if he couldn't believe what he'd seen that day. "I feel like I'm going crazy."

I sat forward. "You're not."

He raised his eyes to me, and they looked so haunted and pained that I reached up to put my fingers on the cage separating us. "You're not," I repeated firmly. "Beau, Heath and I have seen stuff like this before, and it's not your imagination. Everything you saw and experienced today was real."

He swallowed hard before he said, "But, Mary Jane, I don't even believe in ghosts. How can *any* of this be real?"

I felt the corners of my mouth quirk. It must be really hard to remain skeptical in the face of what we'd all been through that afternoon. "I know it's hard to believe, but the sooner you accept that what you saw today was real, the sooner you'll be able to come to grips with it."

Beau nodded; then he shook his head, and went back to nodding again. "I need a drink," he confessed, and then he eyed me a little ruefully. "Too bad I gave up booze five years ago, huh?"

Heath and I both smiled at his attempt to lighten the mood. At that moment Gilley pulled up in the SUV. "Would you mind?" I asked Beau, pointing to the locked doors that could only be opened from the outside.

"Sure—sorry," Beau said, getting out to open my door for us. We shuffled out and stood for a moment in front of the deputy, but it seemed no one knew what else to say. "Oh, here," Beau said, shrugging out of Gilley's vest. "You guys should take this back."

"Thanks, Beau," I said, taking the vest.

Before we could turn away, the deputy added, "Is there someplace where I can buy one of those?"

I handed him back the vest. If he returned to the Porter house, he was going to need some protection. "Keep it," I said.

For an awkward moment the deputy looked like he was going to hug me, but then he sort of thrust out his hand and shook both mine and Heath's before turning to head up the ramp to the double doors, where, I suspected, he'd recruit someone to help him with Scoffland's body.

Heath shrugged out of his vest and helped me with mine. Then we headed over to Gilley, who seemed rather impatient to get a move on, if the little honks to the horn he kept sending us were any indication.

Chapter 6

Gilley was covered in crumbs and food wrappers. In fact, he looked bloated and uncomfortable sitting there, waiting impatiently for Heath and me to get into the car and buckle up. "Tell me everything," he said.

"Well—," I began, but Gil interrupted me.

"Wait. Hold that thought. We can't talk about this stuff without something to take the edge off."

Heath and I exchanged hopeful looks. Like the deputy, I could've gone for a drink, too.

Ten minutes later, however, Gil had pulled up to Lu-Lu's Ice Cream Shop. I exchanged another look with Heath. Clearly, the two of us had a different definition of "taking the edge off."

Gil bounded out the door like an anxious puppy and we had no choice but to follow him inside. At least he'd picked the best ice-cream parlor in all of Valdosta. LuLu

made her ice cream from scratch, and it was truly heaven in a bowl.

"I'll have one scoop of mint chocolate chip," Gil was saying to the young teen behind the counter when we caught up to him.

"Did you want that in a waffle cone or a bowl?"

"Bowl," Gil said, and I had to hand it to him. He was actually showing a little restraint. As the kid reached for the bowl, however, Gil said, "Cone! I'll take the cone." The kid moved over, got one of the big home-made waffle cones, and headed toward the barrel of mint chocolate chip. No sooner had she scooped out one round ball than Gil added, "Make that two scoops, please."

The double soon became a triple. With sprinkles. Whipped cream. And a freaking cherry on top. The towering concoction was so unsteady that the girl behind the counter offered Gilley a bowl should any of it topple over, which of course some of it did even before he reached the table. "He's a lotta work," Heath whispered in my ear, but he was chuckling when he said it, and it got me to laugh a little too, which I badly needed after the day we'd had.

Heath and I each got a double cone of chocolate chip cookie dough and joined Gil at the table. "Okay, spill it," Gil said, which I thought was hilariously ironic, as he said this while a big gob of whipped cream and sprinkles plopped onto the table, missing the bowl entirely.

While Heath got up to get Gilley more napkins, I started in, telling him everything that'd happened inside the house.

The more I talked, the faster Gilley ate, and I knew what I was telling him was likely stressing him out, but it was such a relief to get it off my chest, and he was bound to find out the details anyway. Valdosta was a relatively small town when it came to gossip.

When I got to the part about the planchette flying out from under the bookcase and nearly striking Heath, Gil stopped licking away furiously at his ice cream long enough to utter a frightened squeak. "Why'd it attack you?" he asked him.

Heath shrugged, but I could tell the near miss with the planchette had shaken him. "I was the one that kicked it under the bookcase. Maybe this Sandman was pissed off about that."

Gil then turned his wide eyes to me. "Do you have any idea what you're gonna tell Christine?"

I shook my head. "Not a clue."

"She can't keep hiring people to go work at that place," Heath said. Gilley pumped his head up and down.

"He's right. She'll get someone killed. I mean, someone *else* killed."

"After what happened today with Scoffland, and the fact that we've now just uncovered another murder, I doubt anybody's gonna be allowed back at that house for a long time," I said, a bit relieved by that fact, actually. I had no urge to get back to Porter Manor anytime soon. "Maybe I can talk her into letting it sit vacant and unattended for a while."

"Yeah, but what happens when the investigation is over?" Gil pressed. "I mean, at some point she's gonna

want to finish working on that house, right? She had to have forked over a ton of cash just to buy it, M.J. She's not gonna want to abandon it altogether, will she?"

I sighed. I hadn't been in town longer than a day and a half and already I was exhausted. This wasn't what I'd signed up for. When we'd agreed to find out what was happening at Porter Manor, I'd thought we were going to encounter some old cranky spook who just needed a kick in the proverbial pants to cross over. I'd never expected to encounter some sort of insanely powerful evil spirit whose origins were unknown, and who apparently had some sort of history with my mother.

And the truth was that I didn't want to deal with it. Whatever the Sandman was, he scared the hell out of me. There was something sneaky and sinister about him, and also something deadly. I knew he'd been at the root of possessing that construction worker who'd killed Scoffland, and also Deputy Cook, who'd stabbed the sheriff. What other minds could he take over and use to commit murder? Deep down I had another awful foreboding, and all I wanted to do was head back to Boston.

"He's got a point, Em," Heath said, while I silently debated what to do. "When the investigation is over, Christine is going to want to move forward with the renovation. And we either have to talk her into abandoning that place altogether, *and* convince her not to sell it to anybody else, or . . ."

Heath let the rest of that sentence hang, but I knew exactly what he was implying. So I finished the thought

for him. "Or we figure out how to shut down the Sandman."

We sat silently at the table for a few seconds, letting the weight of our responsibility sink in if I couldn't convince Christine to abandon Porter Manor.

And then Gilley slid his chair back from the table and said, "There's only one thing to do in a situation like this."

"What's that?" I asked him.

Without answering, Gilley turned away from me and headed back to the counter. "I'd like a double scoop of your peanut butter lover's with Reese's Pieces and Heath bar sprinkles, please. In a waffle cone. With a little chocolate syrup drizzled on top. Oh, and don't forget the whipped cream and cherry."

We left as soon as Gil's stomachache settled in, which was about midway through his second waffle cone, but the brave little soldier still managed to shove the rest of it into his piehole. "Ohhhhhhh," he moaned from the backseat while I drove us back to Mrs. G.'s.

"It's your own fault," I told him. "Going back for an extra helping of sprinkles when you were already complaining of an upset stomach didn't help your cause, buddy."

"Why didn't you stop me?" he moaned.

"For the same reason that, sometimes, even though it's really hard, you gotta allow a little kid to put his finger on a hot burner to find out that some stuff shouldn't be messed with."

Gilley whimpered and kept it up even after entering

his mother's house. Mrs. G. came out of the kitchen the second we returned. She took one look at Gilley's slouched posture and said, "What'd he eat?"

"What didn't he eat?" Heath replied, easing Gil over to the nearest chair.

"I think it was his second double-scoop ice-cream cone that did him in," I told her.

"Mama," Gil whimpered.

Mrs. G. frowned at her son. "I have half a mind to let that bellyache keep achin', Gilley. That or a diabetic coma is surely gonna do you in."

"I won't do it again," Gil lied.

Mrs. G. harrumphed and turned back to the kitchen muttering about getting her son some sodium bicarbonate. I stood by the door, eyeing it nervously.

"What's up?" Heath asked me.

"I think I should go talk to Christine."

"Have you heard from your dad since he left to go see her at the hospital?"

I slapped my forehead. "Ohmigod! I totally forgot about her panic attack."

"Did somebody say 'hospital'?" Gil groaned. I glanced over and saw that he'd managed to get himself from the chair over to the couch and was now lying back with one hand over his stomach and the other over his eyes, going for the most pathetic posture possible. Drama queen.

"No," Heath and I said together. The last thing we needed was for Gilley to insist on being taken away by ambulance, which he was likely to demand, given his current state of discomfort.

"What do you want to do?" Heath asked me.

I pulled out my cell and called Christine's phone, but it went straight to voice mail. I tried Daddy's cell next and he picked up right away. "Hello, Mary Jane," he said quietly.

"Hey, Daddy, how's Christine?"

"Oh, she's fine," he said, his voice barely above a whisper. "She's resting here at the house with me. Did the sheriff finish over at the Porter place?"

I bit my lip. "Daddy, there's something I need to tell you. . . ."

"Yes?" he asked when I lost my nerve.

I took a deep breath and chickened out for a second time. This just wasn't something I could explain over the phone. "I'm coming over, Daddy. I need to tell you and Christine what happened in person."

"What happened?" Daddy said, his voice a bit louder.

"I'm on my way. I'll be there in a few." With that, I hung up before he could grill me for details.

"Want me to drive?" Heath asked.

Before I could answer, Mrs. G. came out of the kitchen with a bubbling glass of milky liquid for Gilley. "Mary Jane, Heath," she said, her voice full of command. "Come over here and tell me exactly what put Gilley in the frame of mind to do this to himself."

I eyed Heath. "Can you stay and explain it to her while I head over to Daddy's?"

"You want to go alone?"

"I do. Christine might get upset again, and I feel like she won't want a lot of witnesses if that happens."

Heath's expression softened and he leaned in to kiss me sweetly. "Go. Text me later and tell me how it went, okay?"

"You got it," I said, giving him a hug before making haste toward the door. "Mrs. G., Heath is going to stay and explain everything. I've got to get over to Daddy's to talk to Christine."

"Will you be back by six?" she called after me. "I've got dinner in the oven and I'd hate for you to miss it."

"I'll do my best, ma'am," I promised.

"What's for dinner?" Gil asked meekly.

Mrs. G. leaned the glass toward Gil's lips. "Well, sugar, for us, it'll be eggplant parmigiana. For you, sodium bicarbonate and an early bedtime."

I got to Daddy's house and made my way inside without knocking. I found myself still coming up short in the front hall; it was just a shock to see how beautiful it had become since Christine had entered Daddy's life. "Hello?" I called out. "Daddy?"

He came out from the right side of the staircase, which would have put him in the parlor. He looked very different from the commanding presence I'd gone toe-to-toe with earlier in the day. I can't fully describe it, but there was a gentleness in his eyes and his expression, a touching sweetness that he'd hidden from me for so long that I hardly remembered him capable of such caring vulnerability. I realized he must've been sitting with Christine. It struck me that she brought that side out of him, when the only other person I'd ever known who could tame my father the lion had been my mother.

I had a flashback to a moment so eerily similar, a time when Mama had been complaining of pain in her lower back, and a feeling of fatigue. I'd been worried about her, and Daddy had come home early one afternoon because he'd been worried too. He'd doted on her all the rest of the day, and I'd caught him coming out of the parlor, where Mama was resting, and he'd looked just like he did now: a bit worried, but also so—I don't know—content for her company. He always softened around Mama. He never raised his voice or got angry when she was nearby. Instead, he was patient, and kind, and even loving. She'd had that effect on him. She'd had that effect on everyone.

After she was gone, I never saw that side of him again. It was like a light had gone out in our worlds, and for Daddy, things got very dark indeed. Until now. Until Christine.

"Daddy," I said as he paused to acknowledge me. For a moment that gentle vulnerability lingered as he took me in without saying a word, and I had the strongest urge to run to him and throw my arms around him. Something I hadn't done since Mama died. But then, I saw him square his shoulders and something shifted inside those eyes and he became the Daddy I'd known from the age of eleven on. Cool, commanding, and totally unapproachable.

I felt myself tense at the sudden change, and immediately squashed the urge to run over to him, but then, most unexpectedly, something else bubbled up from deep inside me. Something that I'd probably kept at bay for well over two decades. It started with my lower

lip, which began to quiver, and my eyes, which started to mist. I cleared my throat and blinked furiously, but caught sight of Daddy's now quizzical look in my direction. And then a tear slipped out and slid down my cheek. I blinked some more, shook my head, and swallowed hard, but then another tear leaked out. And another. And then I couldn't stop.

I ducked my chin to hide my face and wiped furiously at the tears. I opened my mouth to tell him that I was sorry for the emotional display, which was so unlike me, but a small sob escaped instead of words, and I quickly closed my mouth and covered it with my hand.

Turning away, I decided a hasty exit was in order, but then I found myself encircled by strong, steady arms, which were turning me back. "Mary Jane," Daddy said as he pulled me into a hug. "Whatever are you on about, baby girl?"

I tried to take a steadying breath, but got only a small lungful of air before more sobs forced their way out. I was crying and crying and I didn't think I could stop.

All the while Daddy held on to me, patting my back and telling me, "There, there, Mary Jane. There, there."

After what felt like an eternity, we heard a voice say, "Monty? Mary Jane? Is everything all right?"

I ducked my chin again as I pulled away from Daddy, and wiped at my cheeks with the backs of my hands. "I'm sorry," I managed to say, but it was a little choked.

"Oh, child!" Christine said when I lifted my chin,

and once again I was pulled into comforting arms and held tightly. "Honey love, tell me what's wrong!"

It was my undoing. Christine was not my mother, but she was so warm, and sweet, and lovely in her own right, and in that moment she reminded me so much of Mama that I felt myself tremble a little, then begin to sob all over again. And to my absolute horror, I was crying even harder and louder this time. Try as I might, I couldn't seem to hold it inside anymore.

It was as if all the years that I'd missed and longed for Mama were being compacted into one moment of anguish; and not just over her death, but for her entire absence from my life. The black hole created by her premature passing had sucked out so much joy, and love, and comfort, and stability, until her loss was the sum of all the things that she and I should've gotten to share with each other. As the years had passed, that loss hadn't gotten smaller; it'd gotten exponentially bigger until it was a giant gaping maw of sorrow and devastating sadness swirling in the center of my chest like a light-eating, life-diminishing, universe-destroying black hole. A hole that was now being filled with terrible, tearstained, gut-wrenching grief, and I couldn't seem to stop.

And all the while that Christine rocked me in her arms—all that time—I wished with everything I had that it could've been Mama who was there to comfort me instead. If only she'd lived. If only she'd stayed with us. If only she'd kept her sun shining and our world bright and that black hole at bay. What could I have been with Mama in my life? What struggles

would I have avoided? What triumphs would I have achieved? What would I have become other than something more whole, more courageous, more accomplished, and far more secure than the shell of a person left behind by her passing? What me could I have been with Mama that I could never, ever be without her?

So I let Christine rock me while Daddy hovered close by, and I cried tears of sadness, and bitterness, and anger, and loneliness, but mostly . . . mostly I cried tears of regret. For all of us. Because even Christine would've loved Mama.

Everyone did.

Later, I sat in Mama's old parlor on the new brown leather sofas with a bright tangerine angora throw tucked around my legs, and a warm cup of tea, which was doing its best to warm up my insides. Daddy was in his chair, pretending to read the paper, while Christine was sitting close to me, her arm curled through mine. She hadn't said a word to me since I'd stopped crying other than to ask if I'd like some tea. Since bringing me the cup, she'd been comforting me by sitting close and occasionally rubbing my arm, or tucking a stray strand of hair behind my ear.

Finally I felt like I'd be able to talk without losing it, so I said, "Sorry I was such a mess before."

I heard Daddy's paper rustle, but I didn't look at him. I focused on the bottom of my cup and keeping my fragile emotions in check.

"Want to tell us what happened?" Christine asked.

I nodded, but took my time replying. I needed to

choose my words carefully. "Christine, even aside from the murder that took place today, Porter Manor isn't the genteel old mansion that you thought it was."

"Oh?"

"No. It's got secrets. Bad, ugly, old secrets."

"What secrets?" Daddy said.

I looked up from my teacup. "You remember a story about a young boy from around these parts who went missing about fifty years ago, Daddy?"

My father's considerable brow furrowed. "You talking about that Sellers boy?"

I nodded.

Daddy scratched his head. "I recall that," he said. "That boy was a few years younger than me. Only met him twice. He was a cousin of the Porters or some such. Went missing back in nineteen seventy-one from what I recall. Search parties looked for him for weeks—hell, I was even part of one search in the first days after he disappeared. We looked for him everywhere, but he was never found."

"Actually, he's recently been located."

Daddy's brow shot up and Christine said, "He has? Where?"

I turned to her now. "Inside your house."

She gasped. "Inside . . . you mean . . . *in* Porter Manor?"

"Yes. I believe we discovered his remains shortly after Daddy left to check on you."

Daddy sat forward and laid his paper aside. Christine blinked furiously, as if she couldn't believe it. "But where inside, Mary Jane? I've been all through that

house with my real estate agent, an inspector, an architect, and construction workers. . . . Why, I've even personally opened every closet, pantry, and cabinet door myself!"

"There's a hidden room off the last door down the corridor to the right of the staircase," I said, and Christine pursed her lips, as if trying to locate the room in her memory.

"Oh, yes, I know which room you mean. The one with the large magnolia tree outside the window."

"Yes, that's the one."

"But what hidden room is there inside that one? I never saw any sign of another room, Mary Jane, and I must've been in there at least a dozen times."

"The door leading to it had been Sheetrocked over. Someone went to great lengths to cover it up."

"Was it a closet or something?" Daddy asked.

"No," I said. "From what we could tell, it was a playroom. It looked like a time capsule, actually, with dolls, and stuffed animals, and a tea set. . . ." My voice drifted off as I recalled the scene.

"And you say this young boy's remains were found *in* that room?" Daddy pressed.

"Yes. All that's left of him are his clothes and his skeleton, but he was lying pretty much as he must've lain when he was killed. He was next to the table with the tea set, lying on his side."

Christine's hand went to a small gold cross hung around her neck. She fiddled with it and said, "Oh, that poor boy!"

Meanwhile Daddy was glaring at the floor. "Now, why didn't Rusty call me and tell me about this?" he snapped.

I knew he was referring to Rusty Kogan, the sheriff, and that led me to tell him all about what'd happened to his old friend right after Daddy had left the premises.

"My God in heaven," Daddy said. He seemed truly stunned. "Has the whole world gone mad?"

"Not the whole world," I said. "Just the parts of it that come into contact with Porter Manor."

Christine eyed me with concern. "Mary Jane, tell me what is truly happening in that house, won't you? Is there an evil spirit at work?"

I took a deep breath and told Christine and Daddy most of what'd happened since Gilley, Heath, and I had first driven to Porter Manor. I filtered out the parts about my out-of-body experience where I'd met little DeeDee, because I knew that was way too weird for Daddy or even Christine to understand, so I kept mostly to the events that'd taken place that day, knowing that if either Daddy or Christine didn't believe me, I'd have some backup from the sheriff's department, and not even Daddy could doubt the word of our trusted sheriff and his deputy.

When I was at last finished, there was a protracted silence that filled the room. Christine had gone quite pale, but she'd held herself together throughout my story, so I figured she just needed time to take it all in.

It was Daddy who broke the silence when he reached for the telephone and made a call. "Olivia? Montgom-

ery Holliday. I just heard the news and I'm calling about Rusty. How's our boy?" Christine and I waited while Daddy listened. "I see," he said. Then another long pause. "So he's out of surgery and stable?" he said. "Oh, that's very good to hear, dear. Is there anything you need?" Another pause, then, "Well, you keep me posted, and if there's anything I can do for you, you just holler, you hear?"

Daddy then hung up the phone and looked at Christine. "It's all true," he said to her, his face registering the shock of it. "Rusty was attacked by Levi Cook."

"Levi Cook?!" Christine said. "That nice young man who let me out of a speeding ticket not a week ago?"

Daddy nodded. "Rusty's known Levi since he was sixteen and was heading down the wrong path. I had to represent Levi in juvenile court once, and it was Rusty who pulled him aside and set him straight. He mentored that boy through high school, encouraged him to enlist, and recruited him for the sheriff's department when he came home from Afghanistan. What could've happened to that boy to make him snap like that?"

I knew, of course, but I didn't think Daddy wanted to hear it.

Christine turned to me, however, and said, "Mary Jane, you suggested that there was something evil in my house. Something that got into the minds of these men and made them do those things?"

"Yes," I said bluntly. "I can't explain what it is, but something was lying dormant in your house, waiting for the right moment, and the right minds to take over.

I've seen possession firsthand," I added, pausing to suppress a shudder, "and it's nothing to be messed with. You can't go back there, and you can't send any more construction crews there either."

Her fingers trembled a little as they found their way to the cross at her neck again. "So what do we do?" she asked.

"Sell that damn house, Christine," Daddy said.

"Oh, Monty," Christine replied, but before she could continue, I interrupted.

"Daddy, there's no way you can sell that house to another unsuspecting buyer. What's loose in Porter Manor is dangerous. Deadly even." Turning to Christine again, I added, "I'm so sorry, but you're going to have to abandon the house altogether. Put a high fence around the whole property and don't let anyone near it ever again."

The color in Christine's face drained again and the trembling in her fingers spread to her limbs. "Oh, my," she said breathlessly. "Oh, Mary Jane, I don't know if I can do that! I paid an enormous amount for that home and the surrounding land, several million dollars in fact. My former husband developed golf courses, and taught me a great deal about the business, and I paid all of that money because the manor sits on thirty beautiful acres that I had planned to build a golf course on to help recoup some of the costs for the renovation. The manor sits mostly in the middle of the land at the very top of the highest hill, so there's no way to hide it from the golf course. Even if I break it up into smaller lots,

no one is going to want to have a view of a crumbling mansion in their backyard."

I didn't say anything, because what could I? Whatever was in that house was too powerful, too deadly, and honestly scared me too much for me to offer my services beyond what I'd already done. I wanted Christine to do what I'd said, but I couldn't imagine personally accepting the loss of several million dollars. I was asking her to simply walk away, and that had to be a terrible choice for her indeed.

And then Daddy said something that sort of stunned me. "Mary Jane," he said, "you work with all these people who deal with these things. Don't you know somebody, an exorcist or someone, who might be willing to come out here and sort this mess out?"

I wanted to laugh. My father understood so little of what I did for a living that it was shockingly funny. But then I wondered if I'd ever really tried to explain it to him, or if I'd simply walked away because it was easier. "I do happen to know some people in the business for something like this," I said, and both he and Christine looked encouraged. "In fact, I know a few of the very best ghostbusters in the world."

"Well, come on now," Daddy said, reaching for a pen and pad of paper. "Tell me who they are and we'll call them right up and see about retaining them."

I reached down for my purse and extracted a card, which I handed over to Daddy. He took it and studied it with interest before his brow furrowed again. "This is your card," he said.

"Yes."

And then it seemed to dawn on him. "*This* is what you've been dealing with over there in Europe?"

"Yes," I repeated. "And a few other places. And trust me when I tell you that we have dealt with some incredibly dangerous and scary things, but, Daddy, this one is particularly tricky. This one, more than all the others, scares me the most."

Daddy stared at me for a long moment before he asked, "Why?"

I took a deep breath and said, "Because this particularly dangerous spook knew Mama."

Chapter 7

"Mary Jane, you've got to stop talking in riddles here," Daddy said after my second attempt to explain it to him. "You're telling me you had some sort of dream about Madelyn as a young child, and she told you that she was haunted by some sort of ghost, and that same ghost was playing a board game with you today over at the Porter house?"

"Not a board game, Monty. A Ouija board," Christine corrected. She seemed to be taking this much better than Daddy was. "And it wasn't a dream—it was an out-of-body experience. I've had one of those. Scared me near to death!"

Daddy stared first at me, then at his fiancée, and then he sat back in his chair and simply shook his head. "I must be getting old. I don't understand any of this."

"You don't have to understand it, Daddy," I said. "You just need to see how dangerous this is. This spook

came after Mama when she was a little girl, and it seemed to know me personally."

"Could it come after you?" Christine asked, her fingers back to fiddling with the cross around her neck.

I sighed. "No. I think it's tied to the house, but where it came from I don't have a clue. The Porters have lived in that manor for nearly a hundred years, and they never seemed to be bothered by whatever was haunting their home."

Daddy grunted. "If they had been, we'd never have heard about it. That family is particularly tight-lipped—as the remains of that missing boy can attest to."

But I shook my head. "No, I don't think so. If anything as powerful and, frankly, as violent as that spook had been loose in that house, no way could they have continued to live there."

"So where did it come from?" Christine asked. "I mean, why did it suddenly show up in the house if it hadn't haunted the Porters before now?"

"I have no idea."

"Well, there has to be a way to get rid of it," Daddy insisted. "What if we hired a priest to sprinkle some holy water over there? Maybe if he walked through the place and blessed it, that'd do the trick—don't you think, Mary Jane?"

And then I realized that Daddy and Christine were never going to go for my idea to construct a fence and put it around the perimeter of the property. If I refused to take on this spook, then they'd look for someone who would be willing, and the two of them knew so little as to be completely trusting of some idiot who

claimed to be an expert at ridding houses of ghosts and then we'd probably have another murder on our hands.

"No, Daddy, that wouldn't do the trick. And under no circumstances should you attempt to hire or enlist anybody to investigate or bless that house."

"Then what should we do?" Daddy asked. "Christine can't just walk away from all that prime real estate, Mary Jane. She's got most of her money tied up in it."

I eyed the clock on the wall. It was getting late, and I'd long ago missed supper with Mrs. G., Gilley, and Heath. Daddy always ate a late supper, and I suspected he and Christine would ask me to share a meal with them in a few more minutes, but I didn't have the energy to sit with them any longer. I needed to go and be alone with my thoughts for a bit. I wanted the night to think about what to do.

Standing up, I said, "Let's talk about it tomorrow. I've had a long day, and all I want to do is head back to Mrs. Gillespie's and take a good soak in the tub."

"You won't stay for supper?" Daddy asked, standing as well, and I heard a small note of surprise in his voice. I eyed him curiously and wondered if there was perhaps the smallest trace of hurt there too.

"No, thank you, Daddy. I'm really not hungry, and I'd just like to go home."

Daddy pressed his lips together and I realized what I'd just said to him. Mrs. Gillespie's house had been more home to me than this house for a long time now, but I'd never, ever dared to say it out loud, especially not to Daddy. "I mean—"

"I know what you meant," Daddy said gruffly. "All right, Mary Jane, all right. You get on back to Minerva's and you tell her how much I appreciate her extensive hospitality to my little girl."

The words were right, but the sentiment was wrong, and before we fell into another familiar argument, I thought it best to leave.

I said my good-byes, but Christine wouldn't let me get away without another hug. She kissed my cheek and held me at arm's length for a moment, studying me. "Your mama would be so proud of you, Mary Jane," she said. "And I'm sure she's looking down from heaven right now, and beaming at you and the beautiful woman you've become."

Tears again welled in my eyes and I turned away before they leaked down my cheeks. That was my Achilles' heel. All you had to do was mention how Mama felt about me for me to dissolve into a puddle.

I wondered if the Sandman knew how strong our spiritual connection to each other was, and then I was racked by a violent shudder, because I felt quite firmly that he did know.

Driving the rental back toward Mrs. G.'s, I could almost feel the presence of an evil force at the very edge of my energy. I reached over and flipped on the heat. I couldn't get warm enough.

By now it was dark and I was feeling more and more anxious. Mrs. G. lived only ten minutes from Daddy, and yet the drive felt interminable. To make matters worse, I was having trouble concentrating. My thoughts were fuzzy and my lids were heavy. It was as if a sud-

den wave of exhaustion had snuck up on me and taken over.

I shook my head to clear it, and turned on the radio, hoping for a distraction. The station was playing an upbeat dance tune and I breathed a sigh of relief. It was just the kind of song to push the fogginess away.

Except that abruptly the song cut out and loud static filled the interior of the car. I reached for the knob and as I touched it, I got a tremendous burst of static electricity that had me pulling my hand back to shake it. "Ow!"

And then that same shiver traveled up my spine, because I realized that underneath that layer of static from the radio, someone was speaking.

My breath caught when I heard someone say, "Hello, little DeeDee. The Sandman wants to play."

Using the cuff of my sweater, I covered my hand and smacked the knob to turn off the radio, but my aim was off and instead of turning it off, I only managed to turn the volume up. "Little DeeDee," the Sandman taunted from the speakers. "Why don't we play a game of tag?"

I was about to punch the radio again when something huge came dashing out from the side of the road.

It all happened so fast that it felt like a blur. From the corner of my eye I saw a whisper of movement dart out from the bushes. My head snapped up and in the headlights I saw . . . a monster. There's really no other way to describe it. It was enormous, at least eight to ten feet tall, smoky gray, with long limbs and a ferociously hideous face. The eyes were red, the teeth sharp and bared, and the hands seemed to end in claws.

I let out a cry and stomped as hard as I could on the brakes while swerving to avoid the creature. There was a terrible THUD against the right quarter panel, and then the car was sent fishtailing into a full 180-degree spin. I lost sight of the road, felt the centrifugal force of the spinning car, which made it nearly impossible to hold on to the wheel and steer, and then there was a terrific jolt as the car dipped sideways down off the shoulder onto the embankment, where it finally . . . finally came to a stop.

For several moments all I could do was press my back firmly against the seat while my chest heaved and copious amounts of adrenaline coursed through my veins. My hands had a death grip on the steering wheel and my knee was locked under the dash as I continued to stomp down hard on the brakes. Dust swirled around the outside of the car, while inside, the radio had returned to that snappy dance number, but it sounded far away from me, and it barely registered that the static had ended and, with it, that horrible creepy voice.

At some point I came more fully to my senses and my gaze darted all around while I took in my surroundings. "Okay, M.J.," I whispered. "Get a grip here." Slowly I raised one finger at a time off the steering wheel just to loosen the tight squeeze I was giving it, and I took note of the fact that I'd ended up in a small ditch at the side of the road. There was only the fading glow of another car far down the road but no other cars in sight. The engine in my car was still running, which I took as a good sign, and I looked down

at the dash to see if there were any warning lights there.

Nothing seemed to be going haywire, so very carefully I eased my foot off the brake and over to the gas pedal. The car, still in drive, moved just a few feet of its own accord, and I didn't hear any rattling or bumping, so I pressed down on the gas just a bit and made my way over to the edge of the ditch. The slope back up to the road wasn't all that steep, so I pushed a little harder on the gas and the car lurched up and back onto the road. I sighed with relief and took a few extra deep breaths for good measure.

And then I remembered the monster.

My eyes darted to the rearview mirror, then to the two side mirrors, but there was nothing out of the ordinary to be seen behind me. I turned next to look toward the right side of the road, and then the left. Nothing unusual was hiding in the bushes, and I wiped my brow and took a few more deep breaths.

But then I saw something that nearly made me slam on the brakes again. Far off to the right and reflected in the moonlight was the faint outline of Porter Manor.

I blinked when I saw it, then blinked again. "How in the hell . . . ?" I muttered, looking around again to try to figure out where the heck I was. There was no way I should've been near that old mansion, as I'd specifically set off from Daddy's in a direction that would've taken me away from the Porter house on my way to Mrs. G.'s. I should've been at least three miles from it actually, so I couldn't figure out how I'd come to this side of town.

And then I remembered that fuzzy-headed feeling I'd had not ten minutes before. I glanced at the digital clock on the dash, and sure enough, the time was fifteen extra minutes ahead of where it should have been if I'd taken the direct way back to Mrs. G.'s.

Down the road I saw a gas station that was brightly lit, and I decided to head over to take a minute to get a grip and figure out what'd happened to me. I actually had half a mind to call Heath and ask him to borrow Mrs. G.'s car to come pick me up. I was shaking terribly with fright and rattled nerves.

I also knew I needed to inspect that right front quarter panel. Whatever had hit the rental car was sure to have left a dent.

Pulling up into the station, I was about to cut the engine when the radio suddenly cut out again and went to static. I tensed and debated quickly punching the knob or waiting to see if I'd get another warning before being struck by the monster again. "Tag, little DeeDee," the static-filled voice taunted. "You're it."

I never got out of the car at the gas station. Instead, I punched that knob hard enough to hurt my hand and peeled out back onto the road. Hovering over the steering wheel, I focused only on getting back to Mrs. G.'s, and without any further incident, I made it.

When I walked in the door, Heath took one look at me from the living room couch and sprang to my side. "What happened?"

"Remember how we were hoping the Sandman was confined to the manor?"

"Yeah?"

"Well, he's not."

Heath put his hands on my shoulders and looked me all over. "Are you hurt?"

"No, just shaken."

"Tell me," he said, leading me toward the kitchen.

We sat at the table and I said, "Where's Gil and Mrs. G.?"

"They went shopping," Heath said. "Gil wanted a new fishing vest since you gave his away, and I gave him a hundred bucks to bring back two for us that aren't as . . . bright."

I smirked. "That plaid is a little loud, huh?"

"It screams," Heath agreed. "Did you eat yet?"

I realized that the kitchen was still filled with the most delicious smells. "Nah. Daddy invited me to stay for supper, but I wanted to get back here and be with you."

Heath put a hand on my shoulder. "Sit," he said. "I'll get you a plate."

While Heath warmed up the leftovers, I told him about my conversation with Daddy and Christine.

"So you think that if we don't help them, they'll just find someone on their own to try to get rid of that spook?" he asked.

"I do. Christine has invested so much money in Porter Manor and the land around it that there's no way she'll just walk away from it. I don't think she's willing to give up on the idea of letting her dream go just yet."

"That's an attitude that could get somebody killed," Heath said, setting down a plate of steaming eggplant parm in front of me.

I took a huge whiff. God, it smelled good. "It's a point of view Daddy also shares," I told him.

"Which means, if we butt out, somebody else is gonna get hurt."

"Yep. Or worse than just hurt."

"Maybe we could try talking to them again. There's gotta be a way to convince them."

"Maybe there is," I said. "But I don't think that's a choice we have anymore."

"You don't want to try talking to them again?"

"No, I don't think we have the luxury of any other solution other than shutting down the Sandman, Heath. It came after me tonight."

"Tell me," he said.

Over dinner I told him everything that'd happened and his expression went from concern to outright fury. "If that car had hit a tree, you could've been killed," he said.

I nodded, because that was absolutely true.

Then he pushed back his chair, got up, and headed to the door. "Where're you going?" I called after him.

"To check something out. Stay put. I'll be back in a sec."

I still had the car keys in my purse, so I wasn't worried he'd take off in search of the Sandman, but I wondered what he was doing. I would've gone after him to find out, but I was so tired and chilled, and, yeah, maybe even a little afraid of the dark tonight. So, I focused on polishing off the last of my dinner before getting up to take my dish to the sink.

Heath returned just as I was setting it in the dish-washer.

"There's nothing on the car," he said. "No dents or scratches, and all four tires seem to be in good shape. But you did kick up a lot of dirt and dust. The SUV could use a bath."

"I'm telling you it hit the car, Heath," I said, more snappishly than I'd meant.

He seemed to understand that I'd been through a lot that day and he merely nodded and headed back to his seat at the table. "Then we can't just hide our heads in the sand, can we, Em?"

I sighed and joined him at the table. I was so weary of my life all of a sudden. That earlier moment when I'd wondered what I could've been had my mother still been alive came back to me, and I thought with no small amount of certainty that I would never have become a professional ghostbuster. I might've still become a medium, but that sometimes rash, slightly self-destructive streak that so often drove me to take on dangerous situations would've been tamed by her loving presence. And knowing that made me incredibly sad all over again, because that would've meant that I likely never would've met Heath. And Gilley and I might never have become best friends because he was the only kid in the class who'd taken pity on the sad, lonely girl on the playground whose mother was dying of cancer. And to bring me out of the state of muteness my mother's death had invoked, my paternal grandmother might never have gifted me with one of the greatest loves of my life, my parrot, Doc.

I realized then that thinking about what my life might have been was an impossible thing to consider, because in thinking about what my life would have been with Mama still in it, I would have to completely disregard the knowledge of what my life was now, with all its troubles and dangers but also all its miraculous gifts.

"I suppose," I said to Heath after taking up his hand, "what we need to do is to get a good night's sleep tonight, and tomorrow, we figure out how to kick some Sandman ass."

Chapter 8

I headed off to bed before Gilley and Mrs. G. had returned, and the night's rest did me a world of good. I was a little nervous about falling asleep, because I've been known to have out-of-body experiences when I slumber, but nothing unusual happened to me during the night. At least not that I remember.

I thought I was the first one up when I shuffled out to the kitchen, careful not to disturb Heath, who had been hogging the covers all night. The smell of coffee alerted me that I wasn't the earliest of birdies up at five a.m.

"Good morning, sweet pea," Mrs. G. said, greeting me warmly.

I gave her a hug and mumbled my good mornings before sitting down and reaching for a cup and the coffee carafe in the center of the table.

"What's gotten you up so bright and early?" I asked

her. The scent of another delicious baked good wafted up from the oven.

Mrs. G. lifted something out of her lap and I saw that it was a fishing vest. This one was all black. "Gilley kept insisting that the vests I got y'all were too bright for TV—he said they'd be too distracting for the audience to follow the action—so he and I went out to get you something in a better color, but we had such a time finding one of these in anything other than camel or army green, and you know how Gilley feels about camel and army green."

Sadly, I knew how Gilley felt about just about everything, including camel, which he dubbed the snooze color, and the much more volatile army green, which was a don't-ask-if-you-don't-want-a-lecture-from-Gil-about-everything-wrong-with-the-military's-policy-on-gays kind of color.

"Anyhoo, we got a few of the lightest camel ones I could find, and last night I dyed them. They turned out nice, don't you think?"

She held the vest up for me to look at and I marveled not only at what a great job she'd done dyeing them, but also at how truly wonderful Mrs. G. was. She wasn't hurt or put off in the slightest that the original vests she'd picked out for us weren't the best choice. "They look great," I said.

She beamed at me. "Well, they'll look even better once I'm done with them." Turning the vest around, she showed me the back and I had to work very hard at controlling my expression. "Oh! Wow! Would you look at that—sequins!"

Mrs. G. had spelled out *Ghoul Getters* in sparkling rhinestones on the back of the vest and it glimmered like something right out of Liberace's closet. "I couldn't let y'all go chasing after those ghosts without promoting the show," she gushed. "And you know how Gilley loves a little bling."

I couldn't help it. I had to smile. Gilley wasn't the only one who loved it. I'd seen Mrs. G. bedazzle her fair share of items in her own wardrobe.

"I'm going to put your names on the front," she said, setting down the vest to sort through a little box on the side of the table. Pulling up a small rhinestone, she said, "These are a good size for that, don't you think?"

I felt my eyes widen and I blinked to cover my surprise. "You know, Mrs. G., maybe we shouldn't have our names on our vests."

"Why not?" she asked.

"Well . . . um . . . you know . . . what if the spooks read our names and then try to follow us home?" I was reminded of the Sandman from the night before, and although I was fibbing slightly to Mrs. G. about spooks being able to read name tags, the thought did occur to me that I definitely didn't want to take the chance and give the Sandman the opportunity to know my given name. Names can be powerful things to those grounded spirits hungry for attention. Or revenge.

"Oh, my," she said, setting down the rhinestone. "Oh, Mary Jane, I never considered that! Well, maybe just sprucing up the back will be enough."

I smiled tightly. "Good plan. Say, did you guys get some more magnets?"

Mrs. G. reached down next to her and strained to lift a double bag filled with dozens and dozens of magnets. "Gilley insisted on cleaning out three stores of all their magnets."

My smile became genuine. "Awesome. That should totally hold us over."

"Oh, and we picked up two dozen spikes and a few other items that Gilley said you'll need for your ghost-busting at Porter Manor."

I squinted. "Gilley told you we'd be going back there?" And then I remembered that Heath hadn't followed me to bed. Maybe he'd told them.

"He did. And he also told me there was no sense in talking you out of it, because you could never let something so wicked roam your future stepmother's home. He said you'd figure out a way to shut that nasty spook down or your last name wasn't Holliday."

I blushed slightly. I came from a long line of rebels and was distantly related to Doc Holliday of O.K. Corral fame. Gilley also knew me better than just about anybody, and apparently he'd known what I'd do about the Sandman even before I did.

"He said the only thing we could do for you and Heath was to arm you to the teeth! So I stayed up half the night working on these vests, and look!" Mrs. G. took her butter knife and held it above the box of rhinestones. Several of them rose up and stuck to the knife. "I rubbed this whole load on the magnets to magnetize them too!"

I was quite touched by her thoughtfulness and reached out to squeeze her arm. She patted my hand in

return and at that moment there was a *bing* from the stove. "That'll be the muffins," she said, getting up. I watched her pull out a tray of mouthwatering blueberry muffins and my stomach gurgled.

She smiled brightly at me and turned over the pan before gingerly placing all but two muffins on steel racks to cool. The extra two she placed on plates and brought them back to the table with some homemade sweet butter and jam.

Neither one of us spoke while we carefully peeled off the wrappers on our muffins and slathered them with butter. I took a bite and moaned. "Oh . . . my . . . God . . . ," I said, closing my eyes to savor the flavor. There was just nothing like good old-fashioned country home cooking.

"Good?" she asked as I swallowed and chased the bite with coffee.

"Heaven," I said.

We chatted for a bit about all the delicious meals I'd missed from her kitchen—I'd practically been raised in Mrs. G.'s kitchen—and then she got around to asking me about the spook haunting Porter Manor. "I asked Gilley if this thing was really dangerous," she said to me. "But he wouldn't give me a straight answer, so I want you to look me in the eye, Mary Jane, and tell me what the heck you're dealing with over there."

I dropped my gaze. I couldn't lie to Mrs. G. She'd call me on the carpet the minute she thought I was fibbing, which was typically five seconds into the fib. "I don't really know at this point the full scope of what we're dealing with," I confessed.

"Did it really kill Mike Scoffland?"

I lifted my chin. "At this moment all we know is that he was murdered by one of his own crew," I told her. Perhaps not the whole truth, but not quite a lie either.

She bit her lip. "I knew Mike. He was always wantin' to work for me on the rentals, but he charged too much, and truth be told, I think what he was really after was a little piece of this Georgia peach." She pointed to herself and rolled her eyes. "Who has time for that nonsense?" She chuckled then and I did too. Mrs. G. had sworn off men from the time she'd kicked Gilley's dad to the curb. She always claimed men were too much work for her, and she had better things to do with her life. "Was there really another body found behind the wall?" she asked next.

Gilley had apparently given her the *Reader's Digest* version of events. "Yes. We found more human remains behind a hidden door in a room no one's been in for decades."

"Do they have any idea who the other remains belonged to?"

"Well, I can't be positive, but if I had to guess, I think, given that the skeleton was wearing a young man's clothing and was the size of a twelve- to fourteen-year-old, that it might have been Everett Sellers."

Mrs. G.'s hand flew to her mouth. "No! Really?"

"Really. The room where he was found appears to have been locked up for the past forty-five to fifty years. The timing and the clothing on the skeleton fit at least."

"Oh, that poor boy's parents!" she said, shaking her

head sadly. "I couldn't imagine if Gilley suddenly disappeared without a trace. I'd go out of my mind."

I nodded, then looked off out the window; the tea set on the table near the remains kept flashing in my mind and the most unsettling feeling wrapped itself around my shoulders.

"Mary Jane?" Mrs. G. said. "You look so troubled, sweet pea. What is it?"

"Did you ever meet my mother when she was a child?" I asked, unsure if I'd ever asked her that question before.

She cocked her head and squinted at me curiously. "Madelyn? Well, yes and no. Her mother, your grandmother, used to come to my mother's shop on occasion. Oh, your grandmother had such wonderful fashion sense, and, if you'll recall, my mother owned a small boutique on Conway Avenue.

"During the summer she'd practically force me to come help her at the shop, and I do remember one particular summer morning when Mrs. Bridgeport—your grandmother—came in to try on a dress she'd ordered and she brought along your mother." Mrs. G. paused to sigh wistfully. "Oh, Mary Jane, your mother was so lovely—even as a child she was just breathtaking. Everyone said she could have been Elizabeth Taylor's twin from *National Velvet*, and I can attest to that." Mrs. G. smiled and her gaze was far away. "Little DeeDee," she said. "She was quite shy, from what I remember. I smiled at her and tried to chat her up, but got barely more than the smallest smile in return."

I had to swallow hard to get my next question out.

"How old was she on that day that she came into the shop?"

Mrs. G. shrugged. "Oh, I don't know. Seven or eight, I suppose. For a time there were whispers that your mother was a troubled child. She heard voices, people said, and more than just the imaginary friends that most children make up. In fact, on that very day I even overheard your grandmother telling my mother that DeeDee heard voices all the time, and would sometimes have these long conversations with an empty chair, or a park bench. She was quite worried about her, or so she told Mama. She said that DeeDee hadn't been sleeping well, and she thought maybe that had something to do with it. I remember your mother looking so sad and tired that day. It's why I tried to cheer her up."

I bit my lip. The little girl I'd found suspended in midair in my out-of-body experience had been around seven or eight. "Do you remember the year?" I asked.

Mrs. G. made a funny face. "Oh, Lord, child, I can barely remember what day today is!"

I grinned but tried to look earnest. It was important to isolate when the Sandman had first shown up, because I was convinced that the reason my mother had looked so tired that day in the boutique had nothing to do with any conversation she might've had with some grounded spirit on a park bench—and as for that, I'd suspected for a long time that my mother had shared my psychic abilities but had kept hers hidden in her adult life.

Mrs. G. read my expression well, because she smiled back at me before putting a tapping finger to her lips.

"Well, now, let's see . . . ," she said. "It was sometime around the Fourth of July—of that I'm certain because my mother had been complaining that morning about all the litter left behind on the sidewalk by the people who'd watched the parade the day before—and I believe I was wearing a new pair of jeans with rainbows embroidered on the hem, and they made quite the statement that year at school, which would have been my junior . . . No, wait, my senior year. Yes, it was the summer between my junior and senior years of high school, so that would have been nineteen seventy-one!"

There was one more tricky question I needed to ask, but it wasn't something I wanted to. It took me a minute to work up the courage even. "Mrs. G.?"

"Yes?"

"What year did Everett Sellers disappear?"

Mrs. G.'s face pulled down in a frown. "Why, it was the end of that same summer, Mary Jane. I remember that morning the call came into the sheriff's office where I'd just gotten that new job which got me out of working at Mama's boutique. I started work for the sheriff the Monday after my eighteenth birthday, and the call came into the department on my second or third day on the job, so that would've made it August twenty-sixth or twenty-seventh, nineteen seventy-one."

I felt my stomach muscles clench. "Thank you," I said. "You've been really helpful."

She reached out to squeeze my hand. "Well, I don't know how, but I'm glad I was. Would you like another muffin?"

"No," I said, pushing back my chair and getting to

my feet. "Thank you, though. They're so good, and I'm tempted, but I think what I really need is a good run. Would you mind if I left you for an hour or so?"

Mrs. G. beamed up at me. "Of course not. But you just ate, shouldn't you wait a bit?"

I grinned at her. She was always looking out for me. "Nah, I'll be fine, Mrs. G. I always eat something before a long run. If you run enough, your body gets used to fueling and going."

"All right, if you're sure," she said. "Gilley told me that you and Heath were training for a marathon, and I'm so proud of you for taking such good care of yourself, Mary Jane. Now if you could just rub some of those good habits off on my son, I'd be most obliged!"

"Oh, I've been trying to do that for years. But you know Gilley. Stubborn as a mule and hardheaded as a rock."

She cocked an eyebrow and winked. "He got those qualities from his father."

A short time later I was running hard along a beautiful trail beside a lake about four miles from Mrs. G.'s. I figured coming out here and looping around the lake would give me a solid ten miles to work out the nagging clues that were the secret to figuring out what the hell I'd gotten myself into.

What bothered me most—and hogged most of those thought-filled miles—was the fact that my mother seemed to be inadvertently connected to all this. And I didn't for a second believe that my out-of-body experience with Mama had been a figment of my imagination. In

fact, I believed something that was hard even for me to wrap my head around.

The planes that expand beyond our physical world can be incredibly mysterious. I'd been a part of the paranormal community for most of my life, and I certainly didn't have all the answers as to how it was possible to have the consciousness travel outside of the body, but I'd had enough experiences to convince me that it was possible.

In fact, one of my first experiences being aware that I was out of my body was when I was quite young, and I'd woken up floating in midair, looking down at the back of my head. To make it even more confusing, when I'd woken up and was floating above myself, I'd been lying in midair in the exact same position I'd been sleeping in. It was crazy even now to contemplate that, but in a weird way it did make sense to me—especially because I'd experienced it firsthand.

So I'd known about the other planes of existence for a long time, and truthfully, they've always frightened me. There's a rather constant fear in the back of my mind about waking up out of my body—namely, what if I couldn't get back into my body? What if I ended up on a lower realm and couldn't make it back?

There are things that haunt the lower realm that are so frightening that they defy description. I know. I've not only encountered a few of them; I've personally sent some of them back to the lower realms, to be locked up there forever.

Somehow, this Sandman had escaped from that realm, not once, but twice. The first time to haunt my

mother, and the second time to commit murder at Porter Manor.

And then I nearly tripped when another thought occurred to me. What if the Sandman had been responsible for another death as well? What if that evil spook had killed Everett Sellers back in 1971?

That might explain why the Porter family had worked so hard to cover up Everett's death. Perhaps they thought they could lock up that room and its terrible evil spirit too. If they'd exposed Everett's murder, then they risked an investigation that might allow the spook to roam freely within their home, and also land them in the pool of suspicion, because who would believe that an evil spirit could kill a person?

Well, other than me, Heath, and Gilley of course.

Still, I believed that the Sandman had used that construction worker to carry out its evil act upon Mike Scoffland, and then it'd used Deputy Cook to try to kill Sheriff Kogan, so whom had it used to kill Everett Sellers?

An involuntary shudder traveled across my shoulders as I was rounding the lake. Something deep down made me feel like that was a question I really didn't want to have answered.

At least, not until I learned more about the Sandman. Figuring out where he had come from was going to be tricky—all I had for a clue was my mother's confession that Everett Sellers had been the one to call him forward, and he'd likely used that Ouija board to do it.

So the Ouija board could be the key to figuring all this out. I recalled it in my mind's eye, such a seem-

ingly beautiful board, hand-painted, well crafted, not at all like those terrible knockoffs sold on toy store shelves.

No, the Ouija board from the playroom had been crafted by a master. Someone who had taken great pains to make it beautiful. So where had it come from? Was the artist's name scrawled somewhere on the board? And that planchette was a pretty elaborate device as well. Most planchettes were made of wood, but this one looked like it'd been cast in sterling silver, and set with a semiprecious stone.

My pace picked up a little when I considered that, in order to answer the questions about the Ouija board and the planchette, I'd have to retrieve them, which meant I'd have to go back to Porter Manor. I hated the idea of ever setting foot in that place again, but it had to be done and I didn't see any other way around it. I also shuddered at the idea of having that board and planchette anywhere near me, but then forced myself to acknowledge that if I separated the board from its planchette, perhaps they would both become tame enough to handle.

I just had to hope that I didn't get attacked while inside the manor trying to retrieve them. I'd take Heath along, of course, but I didn't want him getting attacked either. Still, I didn't think I was brave enough to go it alone, and I knew he'd never let me head back there by myself. We'd have to be covered in magnets and ready for anything.

Around the eight-mile mark I realized that I'd probably have to get permission from the sheriff's depart-

ment to go back to the manor and retrieve the Ouija set.
I almost hoped that Beau said no. The more I thought
about it, the more I wondered how he could possibly
say yes. The board, after all, was an item found at the
crime scene of a murder. No way would he let me back
into the manor to take what could be evidence.

So then I debated some more about even asking permission. Better to ask for forgiveness than permission,
eh? Still, I wondered if I'd have to ask a judge for that
forgiveness right before he threw my butt in jail for ob-
struction. My pace picked up once again while I racked
my brain for a solution.

The answer came around mile nine and a half when
I concluded, with immense relief, that I held the answer on my person. My phone was filled with crime
scene photos, and I'd taken a few of the board itself. I
didn't need to return to the scene to take the board; I
merely needed to download the photos from my phone,
enlarge the images to hopefully reveal the name of the
artist, and do some additional research.

By the time I rounded the final corner to Mrs. G.'s, I
was practically sprinting. I felt euphoric from all those
glorious endorphins and the fact that I'd managed to
figure out a productive direction for our investigation that wouldn't put me, or Heath, or anyone else, in
harm's way.

All that changed the second I spotted the parked car
in Mrs. G.'s driveway.

Coming to a hard stop on the sidewalk, I paused
long enough to pant my way into a more regular
breathing pattern before heading through the gate and

up the steps. As I was about to pull on the handle, it opened on its own, and out stepped Deputy Breslow. "Mary Jane!" he said, looking surprised to see me.

"Beau," I replied, wiping my wet brow. "Everything okay?"

He looked me up and down—I imagined I was a sweaty mess after ten miles of hard running—and then he said, "You're just the person I was looking for."

I fidgeted nervously, even though I hadn't done anything wrong. At least not yet. "Oh?"

Before he could continue, Heath opened up the door. As typically happened when I had my first glimpse of him during the day, my breath caught. Heath was so incredibly sexy, with his long black hair, dark olive skin, deep brown eyes, masculine features, and gorgeous lean muscle everywhere you could see . . . and a few places you couldn't.

This morning he wore loose pajama bottoms and lots of sex appeal. It was my favorite look on him actually. "Hey, babe," he said, taking me in as hungrily as I was taking him in. "I heard you went running."

"Just got back."

"How far?"

"A hard ten."

"Pace?"

I glanced at my sport watch. "Seven thirty-seven."

Heath raised a hand to high-five me. He'd been the one to get me under an eight-minute mile.

"Excuse me," Beau said, stepping between our high five, "but can I talk to Mary Jane for a second?"

"I told you already, Beau," Heath said with an edge

to his voice. "We were nowhere near the Porter place last night."

My brow furrowed. What on earth was this about?

"Well," Beau said, clearly irritated that Heath had sabotaged his efforts to grill me without giving away details, "like I said to you inside, a black SUV was spotted going off the road last night not a quarter mile from the Porter house around nine p.m. and the license plate matches exactly to the rental you've got parked in your driveway."

Heath glared at Beau, but I knew there was no way to hide it. The tires on the SUV were covered in mud from the ditch I'd landed in, and of course the tread marks would match if they did a comparison.

I waved two fingers in the air. "That was me."

Heath's brow shot up. "You went to the Porter house?"

"No," I said quickly. "I was heading home from Daddy's, and, I don't know, I kinda got turned around. My mind was on other things last night, and somehow I ended up near Porter Manor."

"Were you drinking, Mary Jane?" Beau asked, and I swore I heard a note of apology in his voice.

I nearly laughed. "No, Beau. I'd had nothing but tea while I was at Daddy's, and I ended up in that ditch because something darted out from the side of the road and I swerved to avoid it."

"Ah," Beau said, and I was surprised to see that he seemed relieved by my explanation. "Lots of deer in that area."

I nodded because there was no way I was going to explain what'd *really* happened.

"So is that it?" I asked. "You were just checking up to make sure we weren't back over there? 'Cause you don't have to worry. We're not going anywhere near that place if we don't have to."

Beau pulled off his brimmed hat and began to slide the rim through his fingers. "See, that's just the thing, Mary Jane."

Heath crossed his arms and spread his legs, setting his mouth in a firm scowl. I had a feeling I'd missed a small argument between the two while I was out.

"What's just the thing?" I said.

Beau pulled his gaze from his hat and eyed me squarely. "I need your help."

I squinted at him. "With what?"

"The body's missing."

A cool morning breeze stirred the leaves on the trees overhead and I shivered. I'd completely cooled down by now and was still soaked from my run. "What body?"

"The young boy in the hidden playroom."

I looked at Heath and he shrugged his shoulders. Then I looked back at Beau to see if maybe he was kidding. His expression said he wasn't. "*How* could it be missing?"

"Matt, Roy, and me went back there this morning to get the boy's body, and when we went inside to the playroom, the body was gone."

I shook my head. "But . . . how could it be gone?"

"Somebody stole it," Beau said.

My jaw dropped. "It was *stolen*? Why would *anybody* steal an old skeleton from a haunted house?" Even saying it out loud, it sounded absurd.

"That's what I'd like to know," Beau said.

"You know who it could be," Heath said, rubbing his chin.

"Who?" Beau and I both asked.

"The killer."

I felt another chill and shuddered violently. "You cold?" Heath asked.

"I'm okay."

He turned around and went inside and I focused on Breslow. "I have no idea what happened to the boy's remains, Beau."

"Okay, but, see, here's the thing, Mary Jane. As you can probably tell, I'm a little over my head in this. Normally I'd turn this over to the state police, but I went to see Kogan this morning and he doesn't want them coming in here and taking over. He was planning on running for mayor next year, and he's all worried about the bad press. It'll make him look extra good, though, if he gets to claim that he ran the investigation from his hospital bed."

I rolled my eyes. "Okay, so, what'd he tell you to do?"

Heath came back out of the house again and wrapped his big sweatshirt around my shoulders. I looped an arm through his and squeezed it. Such a thoughtful man I had.

"Kogan wants me to deputize the two of you and ask you to help us out on the investigation."

I let out a small laugh. "He wants you to what?"

"Ask you for help."

"Would we get to wear a badge?" Heath asked, and I couldn't tell if he was making a joke or not.

"Well, no," Beau said, looking uncomfortable. "But I'd let people know you were working for us, and I'd be with you at all points along the way."

"How much does it pay?" Heath asked next, and that seemed to stump Beau.

"Uh . . . well, I think Sheriff Kogan was hoping that you'd volunteer your services and in return he'd be most appreciative."

Heath cocked a skeptical eyebrow. "Gratitude doesn't pay my cable bill, Beau."

The deputy nodded and twirled his hat a few more times, and that's when I stepped in. "Listen," I said, "before we agree to anything, I need to know why you're asking for our help. I mean, we don't know the first thing about investigating a murder." This wasn't exactly true, but I wasn't in the mood to add *Solve Murder* to my list of things to do when at the top of that list I already had *Kick Evil Spirit's Ass*.

"Like I said, I'd be right there with you two," Beau said. "Sort of directing things."

"But don't you already have several other deputies to assist you on this?" I pressed.

Beau sighed heavily. "Mary Jane, nobody—and I mean *nobody*—at the station knows how to deal with all

this occult stuff. I mean, Cook is still unconscious and they had to sedate Cisco with enough drugs to put an elephant to sleep, and none of the docs know why those two went nuts. On top of all that, I now have a dangerous haunted crime scene I haven't thoroughly investigated, a missing body, and another body in the morgue that I'm scared to death is some kind of zombie just waiting to come alive again and show up on my doorstep ready to eat my brains."

I couldn't help it; I gave in to a small smile. "Scoffland's no zombie, Beau," I told him. But that was all the reassurance I could offer. The rest of what he'd said remained both troublesome and true.

"Yeah, well, I'm still not gonna rest easy until whatever is going on gets figured out. And we've all heard about you, Mary Jane. I even watched one of your shows last night on demand. You've dealt with this kind of thing before. I mean, I haven't slept a wink and it wasn't just from what happened yesterday—your show could scare the warts off a toad."

It was Heath's turn to chuckle. We Southerners took pride in our toad metaphors. Beau wasn't trying to be funny, however. He still looked totally stressed-out. "You gotta help us out here, guys. Please? I'm beggin' here."

I frowned. The more I tried to skirt the edges of this thing, the more I got sucked down into the center of the storm. Beau read my hesitation and his shoulders sagged. I held up a finger to let him know I hadn't made up my mind yet and turned to Heath. He shrugged but added a nod. "I'm in if you are. I mean, as long as they're will-

ing to pay us." For added measure he eyed Beau again and said, "It's only fair, Deputy. You get paid, we get paid."

"I'll make that happen," he promised, looking hopeful. "So you'll do it?"

It was my turn to sigh. "Oh, fine." My conscience wasn't going to allow me to just let Beau head back to Porter Manor and keep on investigating blindly. It was far too dangerous. Plus, I reasoned that by helping him, we'd be helping ourselves to find out the source of the Sandman and figure out a way to shut his ass down.

"Oh, thank you, guys!" Beau gushed, pulling me back from my thoughts. "Thank you. Now, I don't mean to rush y'all, but I think we should get started right away."

I made a point to look down at myself. "Can I shower first?"

"Uh, sure! Sorry. Yeah. I'll just head to the car and talk to the sheriff and see if I can't get you guys on the payroll."

With that, he was hustling to his car and Heath and I were left to consider what we'd just agreed to. "Aren't you glad I talked you into coming down here?" I said, swinging his arm.

He lowered his lids, shook his head, and tried hard to stifle a laugh. "Trouble just has a way of finding you, doesn't it?"

"How do you know it's me? Maybe trouble's been looking for *you* and I'm just your plucky sidekick."

"Seems to me you were getting into trouble like this even before we met," Heath replied, sweeping me into a hug.

"Ah. Yeah. That's right. Okay, so you're the plucky sidekick."

He chuckled and gave me a sweet kiss. "Need help in that shower?"

"We can't!" I whispered. "Mrs. G. and Gil are inside."

"We can be quiet," Heath said, pressing himself against me and sliding his lips down to nibble my neck.

Behind us the door opened and I heard Gilley say, "Oh, jeez, you guys! Can you keep your hands off each other for two seconds? Seriously, you two are worse than a pair of oversexed rabbits."

Heath let his forehead fall to my shoulder. He then sighed. I was right there with him. "Morning, Gil," I said, waving over Heath's shoulder.

He frowned at me. For the record, Gilley had a knack for walking in on Heath and me at the most inopportune times. Mostly because he thought knocking was something you did *as* you opened the door.

"I heard Beau was back," he said, shoveling the remains of a muffin into his mouth. "What's he want?"

Heath let go of me and muttered, "I'll bring you some coffee, Em." I noticed that he maybe shut the door a little more firmly than usual.

"What's his problem?" Gil said, looking toward the door.

"He's worried the Kardashians aren't getting enough exposure."

Gil lowered his lids and pursed his lips at me before waving a hand in my direction. "Sweaty just isn't your color, sugar."

I rolled my eyes and pointed to the deputy still in his

car talking on the phone. "Beau came by to recruit us for the murder investigation."

Gilley squinted hard at me. "He came by to what with who for what, now?"

I knew he'd heard me and I was itching for a shower, so, rather than elaborate, all I said was, "Yes." Then I began moving toward the door.

Gilley stepped in front of me. "Wait. Hold on there. Recruit you how, M.J.?"

I sighed again, trying to put on my patience hat. "He wants to deputize us and have us work with him on the investigation of the second body we found at Porter Manor yesterday."

"He wants to *deputize* us?"

"Sorry. Not 'us' as in you, 'us' as in Heath and me."

Gilley's squint narrowed just a tad more. "Is that legal?"

"Is what legal?"

"Him deputizing you guys. I mean, don't you have to go through some sort of training or sheriff's academy or something?"

"I guess not. Now, if you don't mind, I'd really like to take a shower."

But Gil wasn't budging. "Wait, wait, wait," he said. "Why can't I get deputized?"

My brow lifted. "You want to get involved in this investigation? This investigation that involves whatever spook is haunting the Porter mansion and may be responsible for the murder of that young boy and that construction owner?"

"Well, no," Gil admitted. "But I would like a badge."

"We don't get badges."

"A star to pin to my shirt?"

"Nope."

"A certificate?"

"Sorry, pal. We're deputies in name only."

"What does that mean exactly?"

"It means we get to tell people we're deputies, but we can't prove it unless they call the sheriff's department and they confirm it."

"Hey," I heard behind me, and I glanced over my shoulder to see Beau there. "So, it's all set. Sheriff Kogan has authorized a temporary salary for you and Heath. It's equal to first-year cadet pay, which isn't a lot, but it's something. Oh, and when we stop by the station, I'll give you some temporary badges to carry in case anybody wants to see proof you're legit."

"I thought we weren't getting those?"

"Yeah, Kogan had a chance to rethink that, and as long as you're gonna be on the payroll, we sort of have to give you a badge."

"I'm in!" Gil practically shouted.

Uh-oh.

"Gil," I said, ready to talk some sense into him. "Do you really think that's a good idea?"

"Yes!" he said confidently. "I mean, who else is gonna do all your research for you, M.J.? You'll need background checks, verification of alibis, etc., etc."

I eyed him keenly. I was onto him. Gilley could do all of that from the safety of his mother's house. There was no need to deputize him. "It's up to Deputy Breslow," I said with no small measure of confidence. No

way was Beau gonna authorize yet another addition to
the payroll. Not when he had deputies and staff that
could also do everything Gilley had just mentioned.

"That'd be great, Gilley," Beau said with enthusi-
asm. "Thanks for volunteering."

I wanted to smack Breslow. Didn't he know what a
pain in the butt Gilley could be? Oh, wait. How could
he know? Well, judging by the way they were both
beaming at each other, he'd find out pretty quick.

"You're welcome, but just to be clear, I get the same
salary and a badge, right?"

"Uh, sure. Yeah. No problem," Breslow said.

"Good. And of course I'll need an hour lunch and
maybe time off to get a coffee here and there. Oh, and I
can't possibly start work until ten a.m. I mean, I'm a
wreck if I don't get my beauty sleep. Plus I'll need
weekends and nights off."

I smiled sweetly at Beau. "Welcome to my world,
Deputy."

His brow furrowed, but he didn't comment further
on Gilley's demands. "So, you ready to go?" he asked
me, probably just to change the subject.

I made a point of looking down at myself. "I still
haven't showered or changed yet, Deputy."

"Uh, right," Breslow said, a touch of color heating
his cheeks. "Sorry. Take your time. Just not too much
time. We've got a lot of ground to cover."

Chapter 9

I left Gilley and Breslow to work out the details of Gil's temporary employment with the sheriff's department of Valdosta, and managed to take a quick shower (sans boyfriend), change, and be back on the front porch within twenty minutes.

Mrs. G. was in the front yard tending to her garden and looking worried. I wanted to reassure her that there was nothing to worry about, but like I said before, that woman could sniff out a lie like no one else I knew.

We drove behind Deputy Breslow to the station, where we all filled out some paperwork and were sworn in as deputies. That part was pretty cool, actually, and then Beau fished around in one of the desk drawers and came up with three badges for us. "Do we get guns?" Gilley asked.

Beau looked like he was beginning to regret his de-

cision to put Gil on the payroll. I knew just how he felt. *"No!"* the deputy said. "No guns, Gilley."

Gil pouted, but then he flashed his badge at me and said, "Deputy Gillespie, ma'am. Do you know how fast you were going?" Before I could say anything, he lit up and turned back to Breslow. "Ooooo, can we write tickets?"

I noticed a nice sheen forming on the deputy's forehead. Served him right. He should've checked with me before agreeing to give Gilley a badge. Still, I felt a little sorry for him. "Gil," I said, pulling him to the side and retrieving my cell from the pocket of my fishing vest. I'd managed to squirrel the vest away from Mrs. G. before she had a chance to bedazzle the back. "I have some research I need you to look into."

"Oh?"

I opened up the photo tab on my cell and flipped through the photos I'd taken of the crime scene the day before to the Ouija board. "I need to know where this came from."

Gil lifted the cell out of my hand and studied it. "That's the coolest-looking Ouija board I've ever seen."

"I thought so too until the planchette started moving on its own."

"The Sandman?"

"Yeah. I was thinking about the board while I was out on my run, and it occurred to me that this thing had to have cost a pretty penny. I mean, look at the detail."

Gil enlarged the image with his fingers. "It is super elaborate."

"Exactly. So, I'm wondering if the board is responsible

for the Sandman's appearance. If I can find the origin of the board, I might be able to come up with some history about the Sandman and find a way to shut him down."

Gil eyed me curiously. "Why don't you just jam a spike through the board?"

I blinked. What he was saying was so obvious, and I hadn't even thought of it. "The board is the portal," I whispered. "Of course!"

Gil fiddled with my cell for a minute before handing it back. "I just texted the pic to my phone. I'll see what I can find out about the board, but busting that spook's ass might be a whole lot easier than we thought."

"Do we have spikes in the car?"

"A whole duffel bag full," Gil assured me.

"Awesome," I said, beaming at him. Okay, so maybe I'd been a little quick to judge his joining us in the investigation. If we could shut down the Sandman, we could at least help Breslow with the investigation without the threat of a dangerous spook on our tails. "Heath," I called. He and Beau were currently in a conversation over a file.

"What's up?"

"We need to head over to Porter Manor."

"Why?" the deputy chimed in.

"There's something Heath and I need to do there. Actually, there's something I need to take care of. There's an item at the crime scene that I need to drive a spike through."

Heath gave me a thumbs-up. He knew I was talking about the Ouija board.

Beau looked at me like I had to be making a joke.

"You want to put a spike through a piece of evidence at my crime scene?"

"I'll explain on the way," I assured him, anxious to get to Porter Manor and put a spike into that board before the Sandman could inflict any more damage. "Would you mind driving us over there?"

Breslow agreed to drive us, but he told me there'd be no way he'd give me permission to put a spike into anything before he saw what I was talking about. I thought I could wait to show him how harmless it would be to his crime scene until we got to the playroom and I pointed out the board and its connection to the dangerous spook we were all so worried about.

We arrived at Porter Manor and Heath and I zipped up our fishing vests, loading a few extra magnets for good measure, and checked the duffel bag for spikes. Gil had prepared us well; the bag weighed a ton from the two dozen spikes rattling around on the bottom. I took a few out to hand-carry, just in case, and Heath tucked two into his waistband.

My sweetheart carried the duffel, and Beau—wearing Gilley's plaid vest—led the way up the steps. He moved cautiously, with his right hand hovering over his sidearm while with his left hand he slid a knife through the crime scene seal over the door. Before he had a chance to open the door, I slipped one of the spikes I was carrying into his right hand. He looked down at it in surprise and I said, "Your gun isn't going to help you here, Deputy. But that spike could save your life. Hold on to it, and if anything spectral jumps out at you, jab it with that and run like hell."

Breslow paled a bit and swallowed loudly. "Maybe Heath should go first?"

I would've smiled if we'd been anywhere else, but I knew that as nervous as I was to be back at Porter Manor, Deputy Breslow had to be ten times more so, and still he'd driven us here and was willing to go inside.

Heath stepped forward and put a tentative hand on the handle. It turned without resistance and he opened the door wide.

Peering into the darkened hallway, he said to Breslow, "You were here today?"

"This morning," the deputy answered. "I came with Deputy Wells and Carter and made them carry a few magnets when we went inside to retrieve the remains from the playroom."

"Anything weird happen to you this morning?"

Breslow shook his head. "No. It was quiet. We weren't here long, though. Just a few minutes to go in, look for the body, find it was missing, and get the heck out."

"Okay," Heath said, and I saw him square his shoulders and step across the threshold. "Let's do this thing fast. I don't want to give the spook a chance to get creative."

I followed Heath through the door and Breslow brought up the rear. We traveled down the corridor and made our way to the room at the end, which seemed to be the center of all the activity in the house. There was more tape across the doorway, and Beau indicated that we should simply duck under it. "When did you put that up?" I asked.

"This morning," he replied. "I also resealed the front door."

I paused before ducking under the tape. "You *re*-sealed the front door? When did you seal it the first time?"

"Last night," he said. "I told Carter and Wells to do it before they left."

"Did they come inside?" I asked.

He scoffed. "Nope. They gave me a bunch of flak about sticking around long enough to put that seal up too. Those doors were still slamming long after we left."

"Ah," I said, not surprised, but then something else occurred to me and again I paused before ducking under the tape. "Beau, you said that you resealed the door this morning. Was it broken when you came here to retrieve the body?"

He shook his head. "No, but sealing the door was probably a dumb idea anyway. I mean, the window leading into this room is broken, and anybody could've come in through the back door. I never thought to have the guys check it and seal it last night, but this morning when we looked, it was unlocked. I sealed it up, but anybody could get in here and take a skeleton out through that window. No way was I gonna get some boards and board it over this morning. Not without you two around."

I noticed that the deputy was shaking slightly, but trying to hide it. I put a reassuring hand on his arm to let him know we'd be okay; then I moved under the tape and headed over to Heath, who was standing in front of

the playroom door holding tightly to the duffel bag. He seemed to be waiting for something to alert us to the Sandman's presence, but the house remained quiet.

Maybe a little too quiet.

I came up beside Heath and he pointed to the faint outline of darkened wood that perfectly matched the body of the young boy whose remains had lain there for over four decades. "Why would you steal a skeleton?" he asked.

"The only reason I can think of," Beau said, "is because you're trying to hide some key piece of evidence. And, as evidence goes, bodies, even old bodies, can reveal a whole lot about the murderer."

I noticed that the deputy's shoulders sagged a bit, and I thought he was probably upset with himself for not taking Everett's remains at the same time we'd taken Scoffland's. "It's not your fault that it's gone, Beau," I said to him.

But he merely shook his head. "Try telling that to Kogan."

"I'd be happy to." The house had been going crazy at the time we'd made a run for it. No way could Kogan fault us for getting the hell out—especially not after what he'd been through in here himself.

"So where did you want to put that spike?" Beau asked, looking nervously around.

I pointed to the other side of the small table with the tea set. "On the other side of there."

We walked around the table and the floor came into view and the second it did, my breath caught. "Where . . . ? Where is it?!"

The Ouija board was gone. All that was left behind was a dark-stained patch of wood similar to that where Everett's body had lain, but this one was in the shape of a rectangle.

"The planchette is gone too," Heath said, motioning with his chin to the wall, where we could all see a dark slash cut into the drywall.

"Maybe it got kicked aside or something," I said, feeling my heart begin to race, because if someone had taken that Ouija board, and the planchette, and if the board was in fact the Sandman's portal, then he could pop up anywhere in the county. Like at Mrs. G.'s, for instance.

"What're we talking about?" Beau asked.

"There was a board here," I said, distracted by the thought that the Ouija board was now gone. "We have to find it."

"What kind of a board?"

"A Ouija board. But it wasn't your typical Ouija board—this one was pretty elaborate and artistic."

"A Ouija board?" he said. "My sister had one of those when she was little. It freaked her out one night at a sleepover and my parents got rid of it."

I nodded because I heard that kind of story a lot from unwitting parents. "This board would've been about a thousand times more powerful than your sister's board," I said.

Beau gulped. "Then we'd best find it and put a stake through it," he said simply.

We searched the room for several minutes, but there was no sign of the board or the planchette. "This is bad," I whispered to Heath.

"Why didn't we think to strap a magnet to it when we had the chance yesterday?" he replied, his face riddled with guilt.

"The house was going crazy and we weren't at our best," I said.

"If the board isn't here," Beau said, "what does that mean?"

I stopped fishing around on the floor to sit back on my haunches. "It means the spook who possessed Cisco and Cook, and manipulated Scoffland's dead body, and slammed all the doors in this house at once, and threw a planchette across the room hard enough to embed it in a wall . . . is on the move."

Beau's face went the whitest I'd seen it. "What the heck was painted on that thing, anyway?"

"Access to our realm," I said. Beau's brow furrowed, but I didn't explain more. I was too frantic to find any trace of the board and went back again to pull up the skirt of the table to look under it.

"Who would've taken it?" Beau asked.

"Everett's killer," said Heath, and I lifted my chin to stare at him. "It's the only thing that makes sense," he explained. "The killer took Everett's body, and the board and the planchette. No body, no murder, and the killer gets to manipulate the Sandman any way he wants."

I shuddered. "He could use it to murder someone else."

Beau's wide eyes got even wider. "We have to figure out who murdered that boy before that happens."

"We do," I agreed.

"Where do you want to start?" Heath asked.

Beau blinked and stared at the floor as if trying to decide on a direction. After several long moments where he didn't offer anything, I said, "You know where I think we should start?"

"Where?" Heath and Beau said together.

"With Sheriff Kogan. I want to know exactly what happened to him in the moments after we left the room, before Deputy Cook attacked him."

Beau nodded enthusiastically and was already moving toward the exit. "That's just what I was gonna suggest. Come on, let's go talk to the sheriff."

A short time later we arrived at the hospital and Beau asked us to wait while he went in and made sure the sheriff was up for a short interview. A minute or two after he disappeared into Kogan's room, he stuck his head out and motioned us over.

We found the sheriff alert but very pale with lots of tubes coming out of him. "Mary Jane," he said hoarsely. "Mr. Whitefeather."

"Sir," Heath replied with a nod. "Please call me Heath."

"You got it. And thanks for agreeing to work on this, Mary Jane. I hope your daddy isn't too uptight about my recruitin' you?"

"He's not upset at all," I assured him. He didn't really need to know that Daddy knew nothing of my new title, or that I intended to keep him completely in the dark. I doubted that he'd allow me to continue if he knew what I was up to. I mean, it was fine if I wanted to go off and explore old abandoned castles and such,

but he'd have a cow if he discovered I was working on an actual murder investigation. "How're you doing, Sheriff?" I asked, hardly able to believe a man so gravely wounded could be up and talking so soon after nearly being stabbed to death.

"Aw, I'm okay," the older man said with a dismissive wave. "He stuck me pretty good, but didn't do any major damage other than nicking my lung. The docs patched that up and they say that as soon as my blood count is back up to normal, they'll release me and send me home."

I always knew that Kogan was a tough old guy, but he was certainly proving that now in spades.

"So," Kogan continued. "Beau here says y'all wanted to ask me about yesterday; that right?"

"It is, Sheriff," I said, taking a seat in the only chair in the room, which was to the side of the bed.

"Well, I don't know that there's much to tell. See, y'all left the room and it was just me and Levi, and we were gonna put Scoffland in that body bag when all of a sudden there was this weird noise—"

"What kind of noise?" I interrupted.

Kogan frowned. "I don't know, some kind of compression sound. Like a pop but not a high-pitched pop like when a gun goes off. This was kinda deeper, and maybe even a little muffled."

"We know exactly what you're talking about," Heath said. And we did.

Sometimes a spook will literally pop into our realm from one of the lower realms, and when that happens, it makes a sort of deep *POW*. It's not crazy loud, and

I've only heard the sound a few times, but it can be quite eerie to experience.

"Then what happened?" I asked.

"Well, Levi and I stopped loadin' Scoffland into the bag, and we were lookin' around to see where the noise came from, and that's when I looked over at him and he'd changed."

"Changed how?" I said.

Kogan lifted his hand weakly and let it fall like he was frustrated by my questions. "I don't know, Mary Jane. He just wasn't himself, and I could tell right away I was about to have some trouble."

"What happened next?"

"He pulled out a knife and he stuck me in the gut."

"Did he say anything?" Heath asked him.

Kogan seemed to think on that for a moment. "No," he said. "No, he mostly just started growling and waving the knife at me."

"You mentioned a popping sound," I said. "From which direction did you hear that noise?"

Kogan considered that for a second. "You know," he said, "now that you're asking, I remember that it was coming from behind that wall. The one where the hidden playroom was."

"Do you think it could have come from the playroom itself?" I asked.

"Yeah," Kogan said. "I think it might've."

"And you're sure Deputy Cook didn't say anything before attacking you?"

Kogan started to shake his head, but then he stopped. "Wait a sec. You know what? I think he did say some-

thin'. It was right before I turned to see him pull his knife. We were both starin' at the wall where the noise had come from and Levi says, 'You know, Sheriff, I don't feel so good.' I forgot all about that once the knife showed up."

I dug a little deeper with my next question. "And when you saw him with the knife, other than acting different, did he also look different?"

Kogan fiddled with the bedsheet. "Now that you mention it, Mary Jane, he did look different. He looked plumb crazy . . . like, psycho or somethin'."

"Can you elaborate?" I pressed.

"Well, I guess he just looked unrecognizable. I mean, his face seemed like it belonged on someone else. It was Levi, but it wasn't Levi. I ain't never seen nothin' like it. I asked the docs here to check him for drugs, and so far everything's come back negative, but he hasn't woken up and they also told me they've done a full MRI and PET scan and there doesn't seem to be a reason for either the sudden mental break or for him to remain unconscious. You knocked him out, Mary Jane, but he's really only got a slight concussion from that, and nobody here knows why he hasn't come to yet."

"Can we see him, Sheriff?" I still carried a bit of guilt for being the one to knock Cook into unconsciousness, and maybe I did want to see him to make sure he was okay.

"I don't see why not," Kogan said. "He's out like a light and handcuffed to the bed. You should be safe enough."

"I think I also want to see Cisco," I said.

"Why you want to see him for?" the sheriff barked.

"Well, sir, because from what we've learned so far, there is a very powerful evil spirit who possessed Cisco and probably Cook too. If we can't speak to Cook because he seems to be in some sort of coma, then we need to try to figure out what happened to Cisco."

"He's been sedated," Beau reminded me.

"Well, maybe we can convince his doctors to wake him up so we can talk to him," I said.

"What would that solve?" Kogan asked me. "I mean, great if you get him clearheaded enough to start talking to you, Mary Jane, but he still murdered a man and no judge in the world is going to accept the evil-spirit-made-me-do-it defense."

"You're probably right, Sheriff," I said, simply to placate him. "And yet I still feel like trying to talk to him is a good idea."

"You might get more answers from the coroner," Kogan muttered.

"Why's that?" Heath asked.

Kogan eyed Beau, who shook his head slightly. "I didn't tell them yet, sir."

"Tell us what?" I asked.

Kogan said, "The coroner finished the autopsy on Scoffland early this morning. He says that Scoffland was killed several hours before Cisco went crazy and nailed his hands to the wall."

"He was killed sometime in the middle of the night?" I said. "How can that be?"

"Don't know," Beau admitted. "That's why the sheriff thinks we should talk to the coroner."

"But I thought there were witnesses?" I said, unable to let it go. "I thought the other construction workers saw Cisco kill Scoffland?"

"No," Beau said. "Cisco and the other workers all got there around the same time that morning. Between eight and eight forty-five. They claim that Scoffland's truck was already there and the boys split up to go look for him. When they heard the sound of a nail gun, they found Cisco with it in hand, and Scoffland nailed to the wall."

"If Scoffland was killed sometime earlier, then how was he killed?"

"A nail through the heart," Kogan said.

"So he was killed with the nail gun," I said.

"Yep. Helluva way to go too. I mean, that had to hurt." The sheriff gingerly touched his chest just above where he'd been stabbed. He knew better than most what a sharp object to the chest felt like.

"But now you're thinking that Cisco didn't do it?" Heath asked the sheriff.

Kogan sighed, and I could tell he was beginning to fatigue. We had to be wearing him out after what he'd been through. "I don't know what to think," he said. "Which is why I asked Beau to talk the two of you into helping us figure out what the hell is going on here. Is this some kind of demonic possession? Or just a big hoax? What I can't get my head around is the fact that I've known Levi almost half his life. The boy's like a son to me, and why he'd attack me like that I just can't figure."

"You know what this means, don't you?" Heath said, and I realized his question was directed at me.

"What?"

"It means we now have *two* murders to solve. Scoffland's and Sellers's."

The room went silent except for the sounds from the machines pumping strength and health back into Kogan. He was the first to break the silence. Turning to Beau, he said, "One of the things they teach you as a detective is that when you discover two separate crimes at one scene, there's almost always a connection."

"You think the murders were related?" I asked.

"I think it might be smart to approach it from that angle," he replied.

"So we'll need to keep our focus on Everett Sellers's murder."

"If it was Everett's skeleton we found in the playroom," Beau said. "With the body missing, I don't know how we can be sure it was him."

"There might be a way to narrow the likelihood down, though," Kogan said, motioning for Beau to hand him a folder on the table to his right. "I had Wells bring over the missing-persons file on Sellers. He had to dig it out of storage, but there's a photo in there I want you three to look at."

We all came forward and gathered round Kogan's bed. His hand shook as he opened the folder and began to sort through the contents. It was a thick file filled with witness statements, maps, and at least a dozen photos. "Ah, here we go," Kogan said, lifting one out

of the folder to show us. In the picture was a freckle-faced, redheaded youth of about fourteen, holding a croquet mallet and displaying a forced smile. He was also wearing the exact same clothing as the body we'd found in the playroom. "This was taken the morning Everett disappeared," Kogan said. "In fact, not long after he and his cousins finished playing croquet, Everett was seen heading off into the woods, never to be heard from again."

Heath nudged me and said, "Em, show the sheriff the photos you took on your phone. I think we'll convince him it was Everett's body we found."

I pulled out my cell and sorted through the images until I found the best picture of the remains of Everett Sellers. Seeing the photo, I was just as convinced as Heath that we were looking at the missing boy.

"Same outfit," Kogan said, looking from my cell to the photo he was holding.

"Same hair too," Beau said, noting the ginger hair on the skull.

"It's him," I told them, knowing it in my heart.

And then Beau focused on me intently. "Is he speaking to you?"

I blinked. "I'm sorry?"

"Everett. Is he talking to you? You know, from beyond the grave?"

"Oh," I laughed. "No, Beau. I'm not sensing his spirit. I just feel it in my gut that it's him."

Kogan seemed to focus on me intently too. "No, no, Mary Jane, I think you're missing Beau's point. You talk

to dead people. Can you . . . you know, talk to Everett and see if he can point the finger at his killer?"

I shook my head. "It doesn't work that way, Beau, and besides, I haven't felt a whisper of that boy's spirit. Granted, I've been wearing a vest full of magnets, which alters the magnetic field around me and isolates me from any spectral energy, but even when Heath and I were first at the house, we didn't pick up on the spirit of a young boy, and certainly not one who'd been murdered."

"Do we know if it even was a murder?" Heath asked suddenly.

We all switched our focus to him, and it was Beau who answered him. "We do. I know we no longer have a body, but when I was studying the skeleton yesterday, I saw that the back of the boy's skull had a big, round dent in it." Beau then lifted the photo of Everett out of Kogan's hands. "The dent was big enough to have been made by one of these," he said, pointing to the mallet in Everett's hands. Then he tapped at my phone a little and said, "And if you look carefully here at this photo that Mary Jane took of the body, you can see this oblong dark stain which moves outward from the boy's skull. If I had to guess, I'd say that was the blood pool from the blow, which seeped into the wood."

I made a face, glad I hadn't noticed that. Then I had another thought and motioned for Beau to give me the phone. When he did, I began to tap through the images myself.

"What're you looking for?" Heath asked.

"A croquet mallet."

Beau moved to stand behind me and peer over my shoulder. "Wouldn't that be some good luck if it were still in the playroom?"

I sighed as I reached the last picture, which was the one I'd given Gilley of the Ouija board. "No sign of the mallet," I said, but Beau had put a hand on my arm.

"Hey, is that the board you were talking about?" he said, pointing to the image on my screen.

"Yes. That's the Ouija board."

He nodded and then the dawn of understanding lit up in his eyes. "You think that's how that demon showed up in my picture of Scoffland? Like, maybe it was called there by that Ouija board?"

"I do, Beau. And I think it's also how that same demon showed up forty-five years ago."

"Forty-five years ago?" the deputy said. "You think there's been some demon living in that house for forty-five years?"

I nodded, then shook my head. I wasn't sure. I only had my out-of-body experience with my mother to go on, but I suspected the Sandman had made at least two appearances in the last half century. "All evil spirits need a portal to travel through," I explained, and by the wide-eyed expressions of both Beau and Sheriff Kogan, I knew I had their full attention. "A portal is a small window made of electromagnetic energy which can thin the veil between our plane of existence—the physical world—and a realm that's . . . well . . . lower than ours."

Beau gulped audibly. "You mean like . . . hell?"

"Well, yes, maybe. The lower realms can house truly demonic energies, and they should never be trifled with. Ouija boards have the ability to create a sort of peephole by using the energy of the user, or users, to create a focused opening between the two realms. Energies that haunt the lower realms know this, and they often hunt for these peepholes to send scary messages, because fear can amplify the energy being pumped into the planchette, and that can then be used to create a bigger hole.

"If that focused energy becomes large enough, then the peephole can turn into a window big enough for the evil energy to climb through. It's incredibly dangerous for children to play with Ouija boards for exactly that reason. They're too easily scared and too naive to know when to let go of the planchette and step away from the board. Often, they don't think to back away from the board until well after the portal has been formed and the evil spirit is let loose to wreak whatever havoc it wants to. And once it's out, it's very hard to put the genie back in the bottle."

"So—so—so—," Beau said, stuttering now because he seemed quite frightened by what I was telling him. "You mean to tell me that this board"—and he tapped my cell phone for good measure—"is the way that *thing* is coming and going?"

"Yes. We think so," I admitted. "And this particular evil spirit is one of the most powerful I've ever encountered, and if you knew what Heath and I have been through in the last few years, you'd know that is saying a lot."

The room fell silent while Beau and Kogan pondered that with nervous expressions. Finally, Kogan said, "How do we destroy it?"

My gaze fell to the floor. I couldn't believe I'd had such a good opportunity to drive a magnetic spike through the board the day before and missed it. Then again, when Heath and I first encountered the board, we hadn't had any stakes on us, and projectiles were being lobbed at our heads, so perhaps I could give myself a break. Lifting my gaze, I said, "First we have to find the Ouija board."

Kogan's mouth fell open. "It's missing?"

I nodded. "Along with Everett's body, the board and the planchette are both gone."

"Sweet Jesus," Kogan whispered. I noticed his arms were lined with goose pimples. "Y'all have to hunt that thing down, Mary Jane."

"We know, Sheriff."

At that moment a nurse came into the room. "Are you all still in here?" she asked a bit tersely. "Deputy, I told you not to stay too long. Sheriff Kogan needs his rest!"

Breslow, Heath, and I all adopted guilt-ridden faces. But Kogan said, "Now, now, Brenda, don't be too hard on them. I'm the one keepin' them."

Nurse Ratched crossed her arms and looked at us sternly.

"I think she means business," Heath muttered. Turning to Kogan, he said, "You get some rest, Sheriff, and we'll keep at it."

Kogan laid a hand on his arm and said, "Thank you,

Heath. Take the Sellers file with you, though. You'll need to review who was there on the day that boy went missing. And especially who was playing croquet."

We waved our farewells to Kogan and headed quickly past the irritated nurse. Once in the hallway, Beau said, "Levi is down this way."

Heath and I walked solemnly behind the deputy to a room way on the other end of the hospital. I don't know what I expected, a guard at the door maybe? But the corridor was empty, and when we stepped into Deputy Cook's room, he lay there alone and pale with an IV in his arm and his eyes closed.

I was about to ask Beau why there was no guard posted, because, to my mind, Cook could wake up at any moment and start attacking people, but then I noticed that both his wrists were strapped to the bed, and just under the covers, I saw another strap securing his chest. He wasn't going anywhere.

While Beau hung back with a pained look on his face, Heath and I stepped forward. I opened up my senses and tried to feel if there was any evil spirit hovering close to Cook, but I sensed nothing. With a nod to Heath I unzipped my fishing vest and handed it to Beau. "Hold that, will you? And if he does anything freaky, throw that to me."

Heath did the same and then the two of us approached Levi, again very cautiously, and again I opened up my senses. I felt that Heath was doing the same, because the energy around us sort of expanded and became charged.

This is a technique that my sweetheart and I had all

but perfected. When two psychics work together, their joined forces can act as a booster to the kinetic energy that surrounds them. It can make the act of reaching out to the other side, or even to grounded spirits, that much easier. We'd been using it a lot together on our most recent ghostbusts, but it also came in handy for the occasional joint readings we gave to clients, and Heath and I had actually talked about doing some group readings using this technique, just to give it some good exercise.

"You want to take the lead?" Heath asked me, and I smiled because I could sense the energy of a woman who'd sort of been alerted to the shift in energy of the room, and she'd stepped forward to look first at Heath, then me, as if deciding whom to communicate with. I'd felt her make her decision and approach me. "Sure," I said. Then I addressed the spirit directly when I felt her introduce herself. Her name came to me in two parts that sounded like "Sill" and "Vee" and I extrapolated to put the name together. "Hello, Sylvia," I said aloud. "I'm Mary Jane, and that's Heath. Are you connected to Levi?"

I felt rather than heard her affirmation that she was connected to the deputy, and she showed me a tree with several branches, moving up to the second tier. "She's his grandmother," I said. Sylvia then tapped me on the left shoulder, which is where I've always put the male side of the family. "She's his paternal grandmother," I said.

"Oh my God," Beau whispered. "Are you talking to his grandma Sylvie?"

I smiled at Beau. I'd missed on the name a little. "Yes, Beau. She's indicating that she knows you too."

"That's true!" he said.

"She's showing me lemon cakes," I told him.

"Whoa!" he said. "When Levi first joined the department, Sylvie used to bring by her famous lemon cakes. They were so good," he sighed. "Will you tell her I always thought she baked the best lemon cake in Valdosta?"

I felt Sylvie laugh. "She says thank you," I told him. Sylvie had heard him quite clearly, but I understood how he assumed I'd need to relay the message.

Sylvie then pointed to her grandson, and I felt her leave my side and move over to hug him. "She's very worried about him," I said, wincing a little because I could see the bruise at his temple where I'd clocked him with Kogan's gun.

"Does he still have that evil spirit inside of him?" Beau asked.

I focused intently on Sylvie. If anyone would be able to sense that, it would be her. Her answer greatly troubled me. "She says not entirely, but there's a remnant of it that's keeping him asleep."

"It's okay, Beau," I heard Heath say, and I looked up at him only to find him staring at Breslow. When I glanced at the deputy, I could see he'd gone pale and was holding our vests close to his already fully protected chest.

"How do you know he's not gonna wake up and start actin' all possessed again?" Beau said.

I focused again on Levi and Sylvie. "He's in a dor-

mant state," I said. It was the best translation I could find. His grandmother was indicating that Levi was still in danger from being taken over by the Sandman, but at the moment he really was totally unconscious. And then Sylvie helped me to understand the demon himself. "Oh, my God," I said. "That's why he calls himself the Sandman."

"Wait. What'd I miss?" Heath asked.

I pointed to Levi but looked to Beau. My next question would be aimed at him. "The doctors can't figure, out why he won't wake up, right?"

"That's right. They say they can't see any brain bleeding or damage from the knock to his head you gave him."

I grimaced at the reminder, but went on to explain. "The Sandman from childhood fables goes around at night and puts sand in your eyes while you sleep, right? Supposedly helping you get a better night's sleep, if I'm not mistaken."

"Yeah, somethin' like that," Beau agreed.

"Well, this Sandman will keep you asleep until he's ready to take your body over again," I said, and I couldn't suppress the shudder that snaked its way up my spine.

"Whoa," Heath and Beau said together. "That's bad, Em," Heath added.

"Yep," I agreed. Again I felt Sylvie come close to me and she all but implored me to help her grandson. For several seconds I communicated with her silently, letting her know I'd do my best, but I could still sense the worry she had for him as she drifted back to Levi's

side, and it left me feeling unsettled. At last I felt her energy begin to fade, and in a wink, she was gone again.

A moment later I heard Heath say, "Did she give you any ideas about how to fight the Sandman before she left?"

I shook my head. "No. She was trying to pump a lot of energy into her grandson to help him resist the next possession, assuming there is one, and she ran out of energy before she could tell me more."

Beau's phone rang and the ringtone made us all jump. "Sorry," he said, lifting it from his belt to look at the display. "I'll take this outside," he added, setting our vests on the floor and ducking out to the hallway.

Heath and I walked over to our vests and started to shrug into them. Mine felt very heavy, but maybe that was because I was just so weary.

"You okay?" Heath asked.

I realized he'd been studying me as I got into my vest. "Yeah. I guess. I'm just tired. It's been a long three days."

He nodded and reached over to pull me into his arms for a supportive hug. I loved how well Heath seemed to read me. Sometimes I needed him to be close and sometimes I needed my personal space, and he always seemed to intuitively know, at any given moment, which way I was leaning. I sighed into his chest and he rocked me from side to side. "We'll be okay," he said, giving the top of my head a kiss.

I so wanted to believe him, but I was facing Levi Cook, lying unconscious in that bed, and I couldn't

help but worry. With another sigh I forced my gaze to move away from the deputy. As Heath continued to rock me, my eyes drifted over to the bedside table. There was a pitcher there with a cup next to it, and I thought it was so stupid to put those next to an unconscious man who was currently strapped to the bed . . . but then something about the pitcher caught my eye.

It was a simple plastic pitcher with a small red rose on the side, and it felt so familiar in the way that reminded me of something. . . .

"Ohmigod!" I gasped.

Heath stood back but held my shoulders. "What's the matter? Are you okay?"

My breath was coming in short bursts and I moved out of his arms and over to the side table to pick up the pitcher and study the red flower. "The tea set in the playroom," I began, chills running up and down my spine. Quickly, I set down the pitcher and pulled out my cell, flipping through the photos, hunting for a particular sequence of images. I wanted to be wrong, but I knew that I wasn't. "The second I first saw that tea set," I explained to Heath while I searched, "something about it seemed so weirdly familiar, but I couldn't figure out where I'd seen it before. I just realized I haven't seen it before. I've only seen a small piece of it."

"I'm not sure I follow," Heath said, coming over to me.

At last my finger landed on an image of the tea set and I bit my lip, because displayed there was exactly the thing that had been troubling me. Or rather, the absence of the thing that had been troubling me. "The

tea set on this table is missing its sugar bowl," I told him, and turned the image around so that he could see the tea set, with its three cups, saucers, teapot, and creamer. But no sugar bowl, which I knew would've completed the set. And just to make sure I wasn't wrong, I expanded the image a little with my fingers to note the fourth cup and saucer on the bookshelf right behind the table. All the pieces of the tea set were visible in the image except the sugar bowl.

"Why is a missing sugar bowl important, Em?"

"Because I know exactly where it is. Was. Or at least, I think I know."

"Where?"

"On the vanity in my mother's dressing room."

Chapter 10

Heath considered me for a long moment before he spoke. "What would the missing sugar bowl be doing on your mother's vanity?"

I bit my lip, feeling I'd just discovered something about my mother that I wished I hadn't. "She used to keep our ponytail holders in it. Mama had very long hair—well, until the chemo made it all fall out—but she used to keep this little dish on her vanity with our elastics in it and she'd braid my hair, then pull hers back into a ponytail. I loved that little dish, because it was small and delicate, and while she braided my hair, I used to hold it up and admire it. It had two little handles and a pink rose on the side and gold around the rim and along the bottom."

"Maybe it came from a similar set," Heath said, but I could tell he thought it was really odd that my mother had a little sugar bowl on her vanity and the tea set

from the playroom was missing only one thing—its sugar bowl.

I looked up at the ceiling, feeling like I wanted to cry. "I wish I thought it was only a coincidence, Heath," I whispered.

"Em," he said, taking my hands and pulling my attention back to him. "It probably is. I mean, there had to have been lots of those tea sets sold around the time your mom was a little girl, right? Maybe she and someone at the Porters' had the exact same tea set. Maybe it's just a crazy fluke that there's no sugar bowl in this photo, and one on your mom's vanity."

I nodded, but I was worried all the same. I didn't want my mother to have a connection to any of this mess, and the fact that I'd encountered her as a little girl being haunted by the Sandman was still really bothering me.

"Hey," Heath said when my gaze began to travel back up to the ceiling again. "Did your mom even know the Porters? I mean, it sounds like they were pretty snobby, right? Maybe they hung with their own crowd and she and they never even met."

"It's possible," I said, but I still felt a terrible nagging in the pit of my stomach. "We've got to find out for sure, though, Heath. We've got to make sure Mama was nowhere near any of this."

At that moment the door swung open and Beau came into the room. He saw us huddled over in the corner and said, "You guys okay?"

I pocketed my cell. "Yeah. Fine. Everything okay on your end?"

Beau blushed slightly. "Yeah. My sister is eight months pregnant and her husband is overseas on his second tour of duty, so my two brothers and I are filling in if Carrie needs anything. This week it's my turn and she wants me to bring her some onion rings and a cupcake."

Heath and I both smiled. "Cravings, huh?" I asked.

Beau nodded. "She can't get enough of that combo. Anyway, speaking of cravings, y'all hungry? I figure we can grab lunch and pick up my sister's order in one shot. Two birds and one stone, you know?"

"Sounds good to me," I said, a little shocked by how hungry I suddenly was.

"Great," he said. We can talk about strategy over lunch."

Beau drove us to Patsy's, a delicious Southern-home-cooking-style restaurant that was an old favorite of mine. Heath and I ordered the battered tilapia with grits and collard greens, and Beau ordered a slab of ribs. Over the meal we talked mostly about the missing-persons file on Everett Sellers. "This is the list of guests at the Porter house on the day he went missing?" I asked. There were at least twenty names on the list, with their corresponding ages. I breathed a huge sigh of relief when I didn't see the name of my mother there.

"Yep," Beau said. "If you look at that first witness testimony, you'll see that Regina Porter was throwing a luncheon for the society ladies that afternoon. Many of them had brought their children over to play, and it turned into a small party."

I skimmed several statements only to realize that most of the ladies who'd attended the luncheon had left about an hour before Everett was last seen. I pointed this out to Heath and Beau. "And besides all of that, we now know that the room where Everett was killed was intentionally boarded up, meaning someone in the Porter family had to know that Everett was murdered inside the house and likely by whom."

"The Porters had four kids," Beau said, obviously more familiar with the Porters than I was. "Jack, the oldest, died in a car accident when he was seventeen. He was Regina's favorite, and from what I hear, she never got over it. She spent most of her later years locked up in that big ol' house wearing black till the day she died.

"The next oldest was Molly. She went to work for her daddy, who was one of the meanest sons of bitches you'd ever want to meet. My own mama worked for him as a secretary for a few years, and he wore her down to a nub. She finally got the courage to quit on him, and he made sure nobody in town would hire her. For a lot of years after that, it was lean times at our house."

I noted the hint of bitterness in Beau's voice as he spoke about Winston Porter III, who I'd also heard was as mean and vindictive an old coot as ever there was one. Daddy had once had a run-in with him, and the two spat at each other for months afterward.

"Things got a little better when old man Porter died," Beau continued. "I wasn't on the force back then, but Kogan was. Some sort of accident at the home,

from what I remember. Porter liked to drink and he ended up falling down that big ol' staircase. Made a hell of a mess from what Kogan told me."

I scowled, wishing Beau hadn't been quite so descriptive while we were eating lunch.

"Molly Porter was close in age to Everett—she was fifteen when he went missing—but she was off at some friend's house that day, and only heard about it when she got home and saw all the police cars at her house."

"Still, she's someone we may want to interview," I said.

Beau shook his head. "Well, you can interview her if you want, but I can't."

"Why not?" Heath asked.

"Because she's dead. She killed herself a few years before her daddy died. It was Kogan's first case, actually. He'll tell you about it if you ask him, but I got the lowdown from another source."

"Who?"

"Mama. Like I said, Porter was a mean son of a bitch and Mama said he was always hardest on Molly. She was still working for him the day it happened. Mama told me that Molly and old man Porter had a hell of a fight that day and then Molly locked herself in her office. An hour or so later, there was this loud crash outside and everybody ran out of the building to find the poor girl had thrown herself out the window and landed on her daddy's car."

"That's one way to make a statement," Heath said with a wince.

"What was his reaction?" I asked.

Beau paused and looked down. Wearing a bitter scowl, he said, "He called her a dumb bitch and yelled at her dead body until Kogan showed up and pulled him away from there. Mama said he was more upset about the car than he was about his own daughter commitin' suicide."

The pit of my stomach was filled with fury for poor Molly. "What a horrible man."

"He was," Beau agreed. "Mama quit a week afterward. He just disgusted her."

"Okay, so Molly and Jack aren't around, and neither is old man Porter or his wife. Who does that leave?"

"Well, Glenn Porter is still alive. He handled the sale of the house to Mrs. Bigelow, but from what I hear, the house was in a trust left to him and his sister Sarah."

I lit up when Beau mentioned her. "And how old was she at the time of Everett's murder?"

"Should be in the file," Beau said, wiping his sticky hands on his napkin and about to reach for the thick folder.

I was afraid he'd get barbecue sauce all over it, so I grabbed it first and began to look through the papers. "She was eight," I said, and again that tickle of unsettling energy pricked its way up my spine.

"Would an eight-year-old still be playing with a tea set?" Heath asked. I knew where he was going. He thought the playroom might've belonged to Sarah.

"With a set as gorgeous as the one we found in the playroom?" I said. "Definitely."

"Could she have killed Everett?" Heath asked no one in particular.

We all considered that. "It's possible," I said. "And it would explain why the family covered up the playroom and directed the investigation away from the house."

"Who was it that saw Everett walking away into the woods?" Heath asked next.

I flipped through more of the file. "It says here that it was Glenn Porter who was the last person to see Everett alive."

"So he's lying," Heath said.

"Could be," said Beau. "And he's still around to interview."

"We should talk to the sister Sarah too," I said. I felt an almost urgent need to speak with her about a few things, like why my mother possibly had the sugar bowl from her tea set. Try as I might, I simply couldn't dismiss the coincidence.

Beau opened his mouth to say something, but at that moment his phone rang and he took one look at the screen and answered it. "Breslow," he said briskly. And then I saw the shocked and alarmed expression on his face and a moment later he was on his feet, yanking out bills from his pocket to throw onto the table. "We gotta go," he said, motioning for us to run with him to the car.

Heath and I didn't hesitate, but on the way I said, "What's happened?"

"There's an incident at the state psychiatric hospital," he said, reaching his car door and throwing it open. "One dead and several others injured."

Heath and I both stopped short before getting into

the car, stunned by the announcement. "A shooting?" Heath asked.

Breslow waved at us impatiently. "No! Now would you get in?"

We obeyed, but before I closed the door, I said, "Beau, what kind of an incident is happening over there?"

"That's just it, Mary Jane. No one really knows. Cisco is dead, two nurses are being rushed to the hospital, and three other patients have had serious injuries."

"If it's not a shooter, what is it?" I pressed, closing the door when Breslow threw the car into reverse and shot us backward out of the parking space.

"Nobody knows," he said. "Wells is over there right now, and he says it's pandemonium. He says patients all over the place are going berserk, attacking nurses, workers . . . anybody who moves. He also said that when he got there, all the doors were slamming all over the hospital, just like at Porter Manor yesterday."

"The Sandman," I said breathlessly.

"Shit," Heath swore, leaning down to pick up his duffel bag of spikes. I took a few from him when he handed them to me.

As we were getting prepared, Breslow's radio crackled with sound. He picked up the mic and spoke rapidly into it. I didn't understand a word of it as it was mostly in police code.

Very shortly thereafter we arrived at the hospital and came to an abrupt halt behind several other cruisers. Wells popped up from behind one of the cars and

hurried over to us, huddling down next to Breslow's window. "I don't know what the hell is going on in there, Beau, but it's bad!"

Even from inside the cruiser we could hear the sound of doors slamming on all three floors of the building. They were slamming in rhythm, a four-four beat, and it was so creepy that I wanted to cover my ears and block out the sound.

"Who's still in there?" Breslow said, pulling out his sidearm and checking the chamber.

"I'd say at least a half dozen patients. We got most of the staff out, but Debra said that she's still getting calls from folks stuck in the building. They're hiding under desks and in cabinets."

"Do we know if anybody's armed?"

"Not that we can tell. Mostly they've been picking up the furniture and throwing it around."

I looked toward the building and my gaze fell on something out of place on top of an industrial-sized air-conditioning unit. "Ohmigod, is that . . . ?" I said, pointing.

"Don't look," Wells told me. "That's Cisco. He threw himself out the third-floor window. Crashed right through the glass." The deputy paused to shake his head as if he couldn't believe it. "I mean, that glass is triple paned. You're not supposed to be able to go through it!"

"Why is he still on the unit?" Breslow snapped, pointing to the air conditioner. "You guys just left him there?"

"Beau," Wells said, "you gotta understand. This is like a scene out of a zombie movie or something—I

mean, wait until you see some of these guys in there! Their eyes are all buggy and most of them are foaming at the mouth and growling like some kinda rabid coyote!"

Wells looked totally freaked-out, and I knew he didn't want to go anywhere near the building with its mysterious slamming doors and possibly possessed patients.

And, judging by the way Breslow's pistol-wielding hand was shaking, he didn't want to go in there either. That's when Heath squeezed my hand, then motioned for Wells to open the back door for us, and we got out. "Breslow," he said to Beau. "You got a Taser I can borrow?"

The deputy reached inside his glove box and pulled out a wicked-looking instrument. He then pressed the yellow button on the side, which ignited a loud spark of electricity between two metal points at the top, before handing it to Heath. "If one of them comes within three feet of you, hold that up under their neck until they drop. You got it?"

"Got it," Heath said, taking the Taser. Then he turned to me. "Let me take point," he said, shoving several spikes into his waistband with one hand while holding tight to the Taser with the other. "You stick close behind and if anything happens to me, you run like hell."

"Right," I agreed, but no way would I ever leave Heath behind. If we were going in together, we were coming out together.

Breslow surprised us when he got out of the car with

Gilley's fishing vest, which he put on before stepping forward to stand next to me. "You're coming with us?" I asked him, a bit surprised.

He nodded, his lips pressed together in a firm line. "Can't let you two go in there without some backup," he said, patting the top of his firearm. Then he turned to Wells. "You coming?"

Wells paled and looked toward the building. Several of the patients still inside were screaming in the most horrific fashion. It was as if they were being tortured but also as if they were enjoying the terrible pain. I shuddered and I wasn't the only one who did, right before Wells reluctantly agreed and we headed off toward the chaos.

Moving at a cautious trot, the four of us made our way to the front door, which, thank God, was a sliding door and not a swinging door. It opened automatically for us, and the second we crossed the threshold amidst all the screams and slamming, the terrible racket abruptly stopped.

It was as if a switch had suddenly been thrown and the two deputies and Heath and I were now standing in a deserted building. Nothing moved. No one spoke. Not a door slammed. And no one screamed.

We came to a dead stop, and I barely allowed myself to breathe while we all listened for any hint of movement or trouble.

But the only sound that came to me was from Wells, who had stuck close to me on the left side. He was breathing and sweating so hard that I was afraid he

was having a panic attack. "Hey!" I whispered, and he turned big wide eyes on me. "You okay?"

"Why did it suddenly go quiet?" he whispered back. "Like, how did that even *happen*?"

I knew what he meant. The screams from the patients had been coming from all over the building; it would've been virtually impossible for them to coordinate their abrupt silence at the moment we entered the building. Not to mention the equally abrupt end to all those slamming doors. It just didn't seem possible without something supernatural at play.

"Listen to me," I said, grabbing his arm and moving close to hiss in his ear, because there was no way I was going to let him lose his shit in here when the situation was so dangerous. "You need to hold it together, Matt. Do you hear me?"

He nodded absently, but his wide eyes were roving all over the lobby area like he expected the boogeyman to jump out at him at any moment. "What if that thing tries to get into my head?" he said in a shaky whisper. "I mean, it got into Levi's head. What if it comes after me?"

I clenched my jaw and dug into my pockets. Pulling out several magnets, I began to stuff them into the top of his Kevlar vest. "These are magnets. No spook can get into your head when you wear them. They'll keep you safe from being overtaken, okay?"

For whatever reason, Wells seemed to relax a fraction. "They will?"

I held up two fingers. "Scout's honor."

"You guys ready?" Heath asked us over his shoulder. He didn't seem impatient, just focused on moving us forward when Matt had collected himself.

I cocked my head at the deputy. "We're good," he told Heath, as he adjusted his grip on his pistol.

Heath nodded at me, then squared his shoulders and moved forward slowly and cautiously. Breslow followed him, I followed Breslow, and Wells followed me as we made our way through the lobby to the main corridor and began to head down it. Along the way we heard the faint sounds of sobbing, and I squinted at what appeared to be a gurney with a sheet tossed over it.

I pointed to the floor under the gurney, where I could just see a set of tennis shoes poking out from under the sheet, and we moved over to it. Stepping forward, Heath and I squatted down and I carefully pulled up the sheet. A woman in a set of flowered scrubs jumped slightly when I pulled aside the sheet. She was sobbing and biting her fist to try to keep the noise down. "Hey, there," I said softly, reaching a hand out to her, but she jumped again, so I pulled it back. "I'm M.J."

She was trembling so violently, I wondered if she was able to take in anything I said.

"I know you're scared," I said, trying to keep my voice light. "But we're here to help. If you take my hand, we'll walk you right out of here." Again I reached my hand out to her, but she merely looked at it without taking it.

"What's your name, honey?" Heath tried.

She wouldn't answer him.

"I'm Heath," he said. "I promise you that we can

keep you safe. If you want to come out from under there, we'll get you out of this building in no time."

The woman made a whimpering sound, then sniffled, and then, like magic, she seemed to pull it together. The violent trembling stopped, no more tears leaked out of her eyes, and instead she took a deep, calming breath. I smiled at her. "That a girl," I said. "See? You can do it. Now come on, honey. Come with us and we'll get you to safety."

She eyed me for a long moment, and then the corners of her mouth quirked and just like that, something shifted inside her eyes. I felt the warning a microsecond before she leaped at me.

Scrambling backward, I tried to dodge her outstretched hands, but she got my vest and began pounding away at me. She was strong as hell too. I put my arms up to block her blows, and Heath was doing his best to grab her and pull her off me, but then she started kicking too and she caught me right in the chest.

I went flying backward and for several seconds I struggled to take a full breath, but I also heard the sound of crackling electricity right before a loud thud shook the ground. A moment later Heath was at my side. "Em? *Em?*"

I held up my hand. I just needed a second so that I could get my diaphragm to cooperate. Closing my eyes, I forced myself to think calm thoughts—no easy task when you're in a haunted crazy ward, and at last I was able to suck in some air. "I'm fine," I said weakly as Heath and Breslow helped me sit up.

"What the hell was *that*?" Wells barked. I looked

over at him and saw that he was standing over the woman, who was out like a light.

"Cuff her," Breslow ordered.

"But she's one of the employees!" he said, as if he couldn't believe what'd just happened.

"Do it, Matt," Beau told him, and his tone brooked no further argument.

Wells cuffed the nurse to a safety railing along the side of the corridor and we set off again, but this time I was right behind Heath.

"I'm sorry," he whispered to me over his shoulder.

"For what?"

"I should've blocked her."

I put a hand on his back. "It wasn't your fault, babe."

Heath turned his head as if he was about to say something but was immediately silenced by the sound of laughter filling the corridor. It wasn't nice laughter either.

The four of us froze, staring straight ahead, ready to run, fight, or stand our ground. From out of one of the rooms stepped a tall, skinny man in his mid- to late forties, or thereabouts. His features were long and gaunt, and his eyes were too big and buggy for his face. He was dressed in a loose sweater and baggy pants and his feet were bare.

After stepping into the middle of the corridor, he eyed each of us in turn with a sort of cunning look—as if he had the measure of us immediately. "Little DeeDee has come back to play?" he said, his voice so filled with evil that it made my blood run cold.

"Put your hands above your head!" Breslow shouted, pointing his weapon right at the man.

"The Sandman has missed his DeeDee," he said, completely ignoring Breslow. "She's gone on, hasn't she?" he taunted. I tried not to appear rattled, but it was very, very hard. "DeeDee played a trick on the Sandman," he continued. "She should have known that wasn't smart. Now I'll have to play a trick on DeeDee's little DeeDee. Even the score. Won't that make DeeDee learn her lesson?" he said, cackling with delight.

"*I said, put your hands above your head!*" Breslow roared. He moved a few steps closer to the man and Heath moved with him, the stun gun and a spike clutched in his hands.

The possessed man at last seemed to focus on the advancing threat coming toward him. He eyed them warily at first, and then he simply grinned, held up his fingers, and gave a loud *SNAP*.

In the next instant every single door in the hospital began to open and slam, open and slam. The noise had been loud when we were outside. It was downright deafening inside.

Breslow and Heath flinched at the sudden eruption of sound, but they also kept advancing.

Wells, who'd been next to me the whole time, put a hand on my shoulder and said, "Stay put!" Then he moved forward too, trotting down the hall to catch up to Heath and Breslow.

The guy currently possessed by the Sandman shifted his gaze back to me, and we locked eyes. I started to

shiver, and I didn't think I could stop. The Sandman knew my mother. And he knew I was her daughter. And by the speech he'd just given, I knew that she'd gotten the best of him at some point in her past, but how and in what context I couldn't be sure.

What was certain was that if I didn't figure out how to send that son of a bitch spook back to hell, he'd take me with him. There was murder in the eyes of that mental patient, and I knew it was murder inspired by the Sandman.

"Screw you," I mouthed at him, hoping he could read my lips. He smiled wickedly. He'd read them perfectly. I gripped my spikes and began walking toward him. There was no way I was going down without a fight.

His smile got even more sinister and he held up both hands, preparing to snap his fingers again, but then he held them in the air as if he wanted to draw the moment out.

Heath picked up his pace, and then so did Breslow and Wells. They were closing the gap as if they sensed that with the snap of those fingers, something even more terrible would happen.

I picked up my pace too. The air was filled with tension and malice. Heath and Breslow were side by side, closing the gap, rushing a little bit faster with each step, but I knew . . . I *knew* they wouldn't tackle him in time.

Ten feet from them, the mental patient snapped his fingers and seemingly from every doorway emerged a wildly crazy person. Screams and howls filled the hallway, and I realized too late that I was too far away from my three companions for my own good.

Two men came out from opposite sides of the hall-way and lunged at me. I shrieked and raised my spikes, turning them in my hands to use the flat top side to pummel one in the shoulder, and the other in the ribs. Both of them backed off immediately, but then they seemed to recover and they came at me again.

Somehow I stayed clear and spun around just out of their reach. I thought to run out of the building, but I took only two steps before more doors opened and several more howling mental patients came rushing at me. I spun yet again, weaving and dodging and hitting at anything that got too close.

There was such chaos in the corridor that it was impossible to see Heath, Breslow, and Wells. I was lost in a sea of snarling faces, foaming mouths, wild eyes, and clawing hands. I felt like I was in a zombie horror movie, especially when my face was scratched by sharp nails, and my ankle nearly kicked out from under me.

I reeled, and twisted, and spun and darted, trying in vain to dodge all the hands trying to grab me. *"Heath!"* I screamed. *"HEATH!"*

And suddenly the hands stopped grabbing for me, and the blows subsided, and in an instant my path seemed to clear. I looked up expecting to see the love of my life there to rescue me, but instead I found myself in front of the possessed patient. My mind reeled. How had he gotten around Heath, Breslow, and Wells?

His appearance threw me and the shock of it caused me to pause.

In that split second, he smiled so evilly that I felt my blood run cold. And then he grabbed me by the sides of

the head with both hands, cocked his own head slightly before opening his jaws wide to reveal unnaturally sharp teeth, and in an instant I knew he was going to bite my face off.

I closed my eyes reflexively and tried to pull away, but he was far too strong. I screamed and then something hit me in the shoulder hard enough to send me flying backward for the second time that day. There was the sharp sound of an electrical current, a blood-curdling scream, and then the whole place went absolutely silent again.

Chapter 11

I rolled around on the floor for a few seconds, trying to get my bearings, when I felt a hand on my arm. I shrieked and struck at it, but then I heard Heath say, "Em! Em, it's me!"

I blinked and looked up at him, forcing myself to focus on his beautiful face. This time I reached for his hand and let him pull me to my feet, then threw my arms around his neck and let out a pathetic sob.

"Hey," he said gently. "Babe, it's okay. You're okay."

I realized this was so *not* the time to lose it, and swallowed hard several times before backing away from him and looking around, ready to battle anything that moved.

But all around us were the prone bodies of fallen mental patients. "Are they dead?" I gasped. I hadn't registered any shots being fired, but I'd been a little preoccupied with trying not to have my face bitten off.

Heath held up his stun gun and gave the trigger a good push. It zapped with energy. "Remind me to get one of these," he said.

"You did all this?"

"He had help," Breslow said from down the hallway. I realized then that he was holding a baton and Wells had his own stun gun in hand.

I turned back to Heath, pointed to his Taser, and said, "We're *both* getting one of those."

A bit later we had twelve patients plus the nurse in handcuffs and zip ties, and we'd cleared the building. All of the people who'd been possessed were then taken to the hospital for evaluation, because none of them had come to. The paramedics who tended to them at the scene kept commenting that they couldn't understand how a couple of stun guns had put thirteen people into a perpetual state of unconsciousness, but then, they'd had no experience with the Sandman.

It was such a frightening thing to consider that one evil spirit could possess the wills of so many people all at once. I mean, I'd heard of a couple of cases where up to three people had been possessed by the same spook before—but never more than that. This spook had taken over the minds of thirteen people. *Thirteen.* It made me tremble to think of the power that would take.

I was told by one of the nurses that several of the patients who'd attacked us in force were some of the most docile patients in the hospital. "It just doesn't make sense!" she'd said. "Why would they all turn on us so suddenly like that?"

I had the answer, but I didn't have the energy to tell her specifically what'd happened. Instead, Heath had taken one long look at me, marched over to Breslow, and told him he was taking me home for the day.

"You're leaving us?" the deputy said nervously as Heath led me over to a bench.

"Yep. I've already called for a ride so you don't have to worry about getting us home."

I leaned back on the bench and winced. It felt like I was bruised all over.

"But what if that thing comes back?" Beau asked.

Heath hefted the duffel bag he'd pulled out of the back of Beau's squad car and handed over several spikes and magnets. "Have your other deputies wear these flat magnets under their Kevlar and carry the spikes in their belts," he instructed. "I doubt that spook will be back today, but just in case, you should be safe enough with those on you and your team while you work the scene."

"Uh, okay," Breslow said, taking the bag and looking none too enthused about Heath's instructions. "Will you two be back tomorrow?"

Heath looked at me to see what I thought. I nodded dully. "We'll pick it up in the morning, Deputy," I said.

That seemed to set him a little more at ease. "Great. Thanks, Mary Jane. Heath, take care of her and I'll pick you up tomorrow around nine a.m."

"We'll be ready," he promised.

Gilley arrived a short time later and he took one look at me and said, "What the hell happened to you?"

"The paparazzi heard I was in town and they mobbed me for a picture."

Gil graced me with his most well-aren't-you-funny expression. "There are days, M.J., when you are just *so* much fun."

"It's a gift," I said, limping my way to the car and getting in.

"Heath?" Gil said when my sweetheart got into the backseat.

"She got roughed up," Heath said.

Gilley reached over and touched the side of my cheek. I winced because it felt raw and sore. "What roughed her up? A mountain lion?"

"Polar bear," I said, and felt a small smile at the edge of my lips. It actually felt good to joke about it.

"Come on, tell me!" Gil said impatiently. "Who or what roughed you up?"

"A bunch of possessed mental patients," Heath told him.

Gil glared hard at Heath in the rearview mirror. "Fine! Don't tell me! God, you two are impossible— you know that?"

I glanced over my shoulder and winked at Heath, who reached out and put a reassuring hand on my shoulder.

We drove in silence for a long while and I thought that I couldn't wait to get home and have a good hot soak in the tub, but then Gilley took a familiar shortcut down a residential street and I suddenly called out, "Hey, would you pull over next to that house on the right, Gil?"

"Mrs. Chadwick's?" he asked.

I should've figured he'd remember. "Yeah," I said,

pulling down the visor to take a look at myself. I looked frightful. "Can I borrow this?" I asked Gil, pointing to his water bottle in the cup holder.

"Have at it," he said.

I dabbed the end of my shirt in the water and patted away some of the blood on my face, then smoothed out my hair. "Where are we?" Heath asked.

Gilley answered for me. "We're at Linda Chadwick's house. She was M.J.'s mom's best friend, and she's like an aunt to M.J."

I felt Heath study me, but I didn't want to waste time filling him in on what I was about to do. Instead, once Gil pulled over, I got out of the car, poked my head through the window, and said, "Would you mind if I did this alone?"

"Sure," they both said, even though I knew they didn't have a clue what I was up to.

"Thanks. I'll try to make it quick," I promised.

"We'll be right here," Heath vowed.

"Or at the ice-cream parlor," Gil said with a bounce to his eyebrows.

I rolled my eyes and hurried off to see if Linda was home. I walked nervously up the drive, and shook my hands to steady my nerves. I hadn't seen Linda in almost five years, although we did keep in touch through e-mail and a phone call every few months.

Linda had been one of the angels in my life who'd helped me during that awful time right after Mama died. She used to come pick me up almost every Saturday to go to the movies. I didn't speak for a long time

after Mama's funeral . . . like, not even a word. The heartbreak I felt had pushed me into muteness and I spent about a year as silent as a mouse.

Linda had also been grieving terribly at the time. She and Mama had been best friends since grade school, and they'd been the maid or matron of honor at each other's wedding. I never got the sense that Linda cared for Daddy much, but she made a special effort to be kind to him in the months following Mama's passing. I think she did that solely for me, because she knew that if she argued with him, he'd never let her take me out on those precious Saturdays.

And we always went to the movies, never to a place where I'd feel pressured to talk. We used to see two or even three shows in a row, and it was the most wonderfully comforting thing anyone could have done for me.

It still choked me up to consider that kindness, that Linda could have cared so much about me, as to put aside her own grief and give me what I needed with such a selfless act. One that truly humbled me.

I got to her back door and hesitated, running a hand through my hair one last time and hoping I didn't look too scary, and then I rang the doorbell. "Just a minute!" I heard from inside, and I closed my eyes to keep them from misting up. I realized suddenly that I'd missed Linda far more than I'd first thought.

A moment later the door was flung open and there she stood, my mama's best friend in the world and my honorary aunt. She was a beautiful woman—always had been, with perfectly coiffed blond hair, sparkling green eyes, and a smile as big as Georgia. "Why, land

sakes!" she cried, opening her arms wide and throwing them around me. "Mary Jane! Oh, my baby girl! Is this really you?!"

I laughed and squeezed back, and those damn tears flooded my eyes again. "Hi, Linda," I said, my voice cracking. "I've missed you."

"Oh!" she said, squeezing even tighter. "You can't imagine how much I've missed you, my darling girl! Now let me step back and take a look at you!"

Before I could warn her, she'd let go of me enough to look at my face and I saw her whole expression change. Cupping the side of my cheek where I'd been scratched, she said, "My God! Mary Jane! Who did this to you?!"

"Linda, I promise, it's nothing," I tried, but she was looking at me so tenderly, and with such concern, and in that moment I just missed her so much that I found myself crying big, wet, sloppy tears.

"Oh, honey!" she said, pulling me inside and shutting the door with her foot. "Now don't you worry! We're gonna take care of you—just let me get the phone and call the sheriff! Do you need to go to the hospital? Oh my God, were you . . . were you . . . ?"

I shook my head and pulled on her arm. Wiping my cheeks, I said, "Linda, I promise you, I'm okay. And the sheriff already knows. I was helping with an investigation and things got a little rough."

Linda stood there blinking for a long minute. "You were helping who with what and it what?"

I smiled at her. She'd just mimicked Gil from the day before. Then I took a deep breath and gave her the

shortest version I could of the afternoon's events. By the end of it we were sitting in her cozy living room and she was practically forcing me to drink the water with cucumber slices she'd had chilling in her fridge. "Does your daddy know you're doing all this work for the sheriff's department?"

I shook my head. "No, and don't you tell him, neither."

She leveled a look at me. "And if he finds out I knew and didn't tell him, what do you think he'll say?"

"I expect he'll say a great deal, Linda, which is why we won't tell him that either."

She threw her head back and let go her rich, throaty laugh. No one laughed like Linda. It was such a beautiful sound. It made me really homesick all of a sudden. Then I remembered what I came here for. "Listen," I began, "there's something I need to ask you."

She cocked her head like a curious puppy. "What's that, baby?"

"It's about Mama."

"Okay," she said, sitting forward and lacing her hands together. "Shoot."

"Mama used to have a small porcelain cup on her vanity. It held all of our ponytail holders. Do you remember it?"

Linda looked at me like I'd asked the oddest question she'd ever heard. Still, she must have guessed by my earnestness that I wasn't joking around. "I don't believe I remember it, Mary Jane. I'm so sorry. Did your daddy lose it or something? I know he had some of

your mama's things moved to storage when he took up with that Mrs. Bigelow."

"No," I said. "No, it's nothing like that. I just . . . I just needed to know where it came from."

"Did she not tell you?"

"No."

"Why is it important?"

"I think it's connected to a tea set that was owned by someone else."

"Who?"

"Sarah Porter."

Linda's brow shot up. "Oh, well, that's quite possible. DeeDee and Sarah used to be best friends before DeeDee and I became best friends."

My back went rigid. "They were?"

"Oh yeah. See, your grandmama was a bit of a social climber, and I don't usually speak ill of the dead, but you knew your grandmama, always puttin' on airs when she had no cause for it.

"Anyway, when she found out that your mama and Sarah Porter were in the same kindergarten class together, well, she practically forced them into a friendship. She was always encouraging your mama to go over to Sarah's house. You know I suspect that your grandmama thought that eventually she'd get invited to one of those fabulous parties Regina Porter was always throwing.

"But the joke ended up being on her, because Regina only had the patience and liking for your mama. But then, DeeDee was so beautiful—even as a child she

was the spitting image of Elizabeth Taylor—and Regina loved beautiful people, as she considered herself to be a great Southern beauty—even though she was the only one who was willing to consider that."

Linda made her brows dance and she shimmied her shoulders a little to indicate she was making fun of Regina Porter, and I couldn't help but laugh. "So, at what point did you and Mama become best friends?"

Linda pressed her lips together and squinted, her gaze far away. "Well, now, I suspect it was right at the beginning of third grade. DeeDee came into the first day of class, sat down next to me, and said, 'Listen here, Linda S. Walters. You and I are gonna be best friends. Forever. And by the way, your grampy says hello, and to stop hiding under your bed.'"

She then threw her head back and laughed uproariously and I felt my heart swell with longing to have been there on that day with the two of them in that moment.

"Now, what I should also say about that day, Mary Jane, is that not two weeks earlier, my grandpappy had in fact died, and he was my favorite person in the whole wide world, and I'd spent the next two weeks before school started hiding under my bed, crying my little heart out! That's how I knew that when your mama told me that you were starting to talk to people who'd died, she'd passed on her talents to you."

It took me a few seconds to be able to talk after that. I was always so moved by stories of my mother. Still, I was after information and I tried to focus back on that.

"So, you guys became friends in third grade—how old were you?"

"Oh," Linda said, taking a moment to think about it. "I believe we were eight going on nine."

"What happened between Mama and Sarah Porter?" I asked.

Linda waved her hand. "Oh, hell, honey, I don't know. At that age you're making friends and unmaking them in the bat of an eye. From what I remember, though, Regina Porter found some fault with your mother, and banned her from ever speaking to her daughter again. It was probably that DeeDee had said something passed on from a dead relative or something. Back in those days people were so spooked by those kinds of things."

"Linda?" I asked next.

"Yes, buttercup?"

I had a hard time meeting Linda's gaze for my next question. "Did Mama ever mention someone called the Sandman?"

Linda's sharp intake of breath told me I was right to be worried. "How did you find out about him?" she asked carefully.

"It's not important," I said. "What did Mama say about him?"

Linda's entire demeanor had changed dramatically, and for the first time ever in the entire time I'd known her, she seemed to eye me angrily. "I made a promise to your mother, Mary Jane, a promise that I swore I would take with me to my grave, and I have no intention of discussing that with you, now or ever!"

I was so stunned by the forcefulness of her statement that for a moment all I could do was sit there and stare at her.

To Linda's credit, she appeared to be rather alarmed by her outburst too, and really neither of us knew what to say next. The entire atmosphere had changed and what had been a lovely reunion had suddenly turned into an awkward encounter.

Getting to my feet, I said, "Thank you for your time, Linda. It's getting late and I left Gilley and Heath waiting in the car."

Linda got to her feet too. "Oh! Oh, my, Mary Jane, they've been waiting for you in the car? Why didn't you—"

"I've got to go," I said. Now that the shock was over, I was beginning to feel the full sting of Linda's outburst and all I wanted to do was run out of there.

Linda's hands attempted to reach out to me, but I turned away from her and headed straight for the door. Pausing only for a moment, I said, "Thank you again, Linda. It was great seeing you." And then I was out the door and running down the block, searching frantically for the rental car, which wasn't in the spot where I'd left Gilley and Heath, and they were nowhere else in sight.

Feeling even more desperate, I began to run down the street in the direction of Mrs. G.'s. She lived only a mile and a half from Linda and I focused on getting there as quickly as possible.

About a quarter mile into the mad dash away, a car pulled up alongside me. "M.J.!" Gil shouted.

I took several more steps, on the fence about stop-

ping to get in the car, or whether to keep running and work off some of the hurt I felt at Linda's rebuke. "M.J.!" Gil shouted again.

I slowed down, then stopped, but I didn't immediately move to the SUV. I heard a car door open and in the next moment I was drawn up into a hug. "What happened?" Heath asked me.

I shook my head. "It's nothing. I'm sorry. I think I'm just tired."

Heath lifted my chin and forced me to look at him. "You don't want to tell me?"

"Not really."

"Okay," he said, stroking my hair. "I'd run with you, ya know, but I think you're worn-out and could use a lift home."

"Yeah, okay," I said, allowing him to lead me by the hand to the car. He opened the passenger door for me and I scooted in next to Gil.

"What happened?" Gilley asked the second he saw my tearstained face.

It was odd, but there were things I could say to Gilley that I knew he'd understand instantly because of our shared history, which made it much harder to explain to Heath. "She yelled at me."

Gilley was holding a large, double-scoop chocolate–peanut butter ice-cream cone. By the amount of chocolate smeared around his mouth, it was an easy call to say that it'd started out as a triple. "She did not!" he said.

"She did."

"Why?"

"I asked her if Mama had ever mentioned the Sand-

man. She told me she'd sworn an oath never to speak about it to anybody, including me. Actually, she yelled it at me."

Gil adopted a sympathetic expression. He knew how much Linda meant to me, and how kind she'd always been to me. Of course he'd also know how being unfairly yelled at by someone I loved so much might feel. He looked down at his cone, seemed to think about something, and then he offered it to me. "Here," he said. "This'll make you feel better."

That small gesture went a long way to doing just that. "I couldn't take your cone, honey," I told him, although my mouth watered a little.

"We got a pint of pistachio," Heath said from the backseat. I'd once told Heath that my favorite flavor ice cream was pistachio, and I'd done that because his mother had told me that it was his favorite flavor and I wanted him to think we shared something sweet in common.

And while I do love pistachio, my favorite flavor was the one currently being offered to me. Chocolate peanut butter. It was Gil's favorite too. "Go on," he said with a wink, knowing I'd been a big fat fibber to Heath. Over his shoulder he said, "I think she needs some of LuLu's comfort now rather than waiting until we get back to Mama's."

I cleared my throat, and eyed Heath apologetically. "I am kinda hungry."

"Then go for it," he said easily and with a knowing grin. "I hear that's your real favorite anyway."

"What? Who told you?"

Gil shoved the cone in my hand and put the car into drive. "That's not important. What *is* important is that we get you home and have Mama take care of you tonight. You look like you've gone a few rounds with Mike Tyson's polar bear."

Mrs. G. took one look at me and ushered me into the house with a great deal of fuss. "I saw it all on the news!" she said. "I hoped y'all weren't involved, but then they played some footage of you and Heath coming out of that building where those mental patients went nuts and I knew you two were in the thick of things."

"Wait," Gil said, looking wide-eyed at us. "That really happened?"

I let Heath tell him the story while I polished off Gilley's cone. Gil stared at his disappearing dessert with more than a hint of regret in his hungry eyes, but then Heath broke out the pistachio and added some hot fudge, and that set Gilley back to rights again.

Meanwhile, Mrs. G. drew me a nice hot bath, which I soaked in for about an hour, letting the healing fragrance of the bath salts work their magic.

Toward the middle of my soak Heath popped his head in and said, "Want some company?"

I smiled. "Come on in, baby, but I'm afraid we're all out of bubbles."

Heath stripped down quickly and I marveled at the exquisiteness of his physique. He was so beautifully proportioned and wonderfully well toned that he constantly took my breath away. He slid into the tub, careful not to jostle or splash me, and I sighed when he

settled in and picked up my foot to rub the sole. "How's the tendinitis?" he asked.

I'd developed a mild case of posterior tibial tendinitis on the inside of my right foot, just below the anklebone, and while it wasn't getting any worse, it wasn't exactly getting any better. "The same," I said, laying my head back and relishing the feel of Heath's strong hands.

"You should ice it after each run," he told me.

"I have been, except today there wasn't time."

"Crazy day, wasn't it?"

"Insane. On so many levels," I agreed.

Heath was silent for a moment before he said, "Em?"

"Yeah?"

"What aren't you telling me about your mom and the Sandman?"

I tensed, but then I sighed and lifted my head up to look at Heath. "I'm not keeping anything from you."

Heath cocked a skeptical eyebrow and worked his thumbs into the center of my sole. It was so pleasurable that I moaned. "You sure there isn't something else bothering you?"

"You mean besides the fact that we have an insanely powerful spook able to possess the minds of a dozen people while slamming every door in a ten-thousand-square-foot building, and we have no idea how to shut his ass down or where his portal might be hiding? On top of which we somehow got roped into helping to solve a set of murders forty-five years apart and we have very few leads and even fewer suspects?"

Heath chuckled as he set my right foot back down in

the tub. He then lifted the other foot and worked his magic on it. "Yeah, besides all that."

I looked away from Heath and inhaled deeply. There was a terrible thought currently running rampant in my mind that threatened to cause so much havoc that I didn't know if I could voice it out loud. But if I held it in, it might still destroy me. "I have this fear . . . ," I began.

"Of?"

Lifting my foot out of Heath's hands, I set it down and sat up toward him, taking up both of his hands in mine. I needed to whisper this and look into his eyes, because I didn't think I'd have the courage otherwise. "I think Mama may have played a part in Everett's death."

Heath kept his expression neutral, but he squeezed my hands to reassure me. "The sugar bowl?"

"Yes. Linda confirmed that it likely came from Sarah Porter's tea set. She and Mama were best friends right up until the third grade. There was some sort of falling-out over that summer, and Mama became best friends with Linda."

"Was it the same summer that Everett was murdered?"

I nodded. "The timing matches."

Heath sat back but held on to my hands. "We need to know what happened in that playroom."

I dropped my gaze. "But what if what happened in that playroom isn't something I can handle?"

"Hey," Heath said, sitting forward again. When I kept my gaze averted, he lifted my chin with his finger.

"There isn't anything you can't handle, babe. Don't you know that by now? You're the strongest person I ever met. The most courageous. The most loyal. And . . . ," he added, leaning in to hover his lips above mine, "the most beautiful."

A moment later we were intertwined, and soon after that, we were making a wet mess of the bathroom floor.

Later, as he and I were lying in bed, whispering to each other, he said, "Em?"

"Yeah?"

"Do you want me to try to reach out to your mom and ask her about Everett?"

Heath asked the question I'd been silently debating for much of that day. And, as much as I thought I might want answers, I didn't know if I could face what might come directly from my mother. "I don't know," I said, because I really didn't.

"If she was there that day, babe, she could tell us what happened, and assuming Everett didn't die because of anything she did, she might be able to point to the killer."

I trailed my finger along Heath's arm, starting at the top of his shoulder, moving across the bulging muscle of his upper arm along the curl of his biceps and over to the smooth part of his forearm. I loved every beautiful square inch of him and found the tactile connection tonight so comforting. "What if she won't tell us?" I asked, snaking my finger back up the way it'd come.

"Then she won't," he said simply.

My finger stopped its languid stroll. "What if she does and I can't handle it?"

"Like I said before, you'll handle it."

"What if handling it means seeing her differently?" I asked next, barely able to get those words out.

"Would anything she told you affect how much you love her?"

I thought about that for a minute. "No," I said at last. "Nothing could change how much I love her."

"Then it's okay to ask."

I sighed. "Have I told you how much I love *you*, Heath?"

A sly grin formed on his lips. "A couple of times, but for me, it never gets old." I moved in and kissed him, so deeply in love at that moment that I felt he was right. I could handle anything. "Now, how 'bout it?" he asked me when I released him from the kiss. "You wanna reach out to her now?"

I sat up and Heath did too. "Can we light a candle?" There was a white scented candle in the room. I loved the symbolism of a white candle, how it promoted peace and harmony especially during spiritual endeavors.

We found a box of matches next to the candle and lit it; then Heath and I sat cross-legged on the bed, facing each other. I opened my senses wide and felt him do the same.

He quickly adopted a faraway stare and suddenly smiled. "What?" I asked.

"Grampa," he said. Heath's grandfather, Sam White-feather, was one of my spirit guides, and the second Heath mentioned him, I felt a calm come over me. I adored that old man something fierce. "He's talking

about how we got beat up today," Heath said. "He says this Sandman spirit is nothing to fuck with."

I burst out laughing. "He did not say 'fuck'!"

Heath tried to look serious, but the corners of his mouth were quirking. "Yeah, well, you know a lot of this is left up to interpretation."

I giggled. "Nice."

"Anyway, he says the Sandman is really dangerous. He's superpowerful and he has a vendetta against . . ."

"Against?"

Heath's faraway focus switched to looking directly at me. "Against you."

"Well, that was sort of obvious from what happened today at the mental hospital."

"Yep," Heath said, his eyes becoming unfocused again. "Now I'm asking him if he would bring your mom forward."

I waited with my nerves fluttering in my chest, and I watched as Heath's blank face morphed into a lowered brow. "He says he won't bring her forward."

"Why not?"

"The Sandman has gained some power and right now he's too fixated on her energy. If Gramps brings her into this room, or anywhere around you, it'll draw him like a magnet. He says she's doing her best on the other side to keep him guessing where she is, distracted, and away from you, but to do that, she also has to keep her distance from you until this is over."

My hopes fell. As much as I was afraid of the truth, I so wanted to hear from Mama right now that it almost physically hurt. I needed reassurances that she was

close, even if that was the most she could offer me. And then I thought I had a better idea. "Can you ask Sam to bring Everett Sellers forward?"

Heath's eyes cut to me again. "That's what I was just asking."

I tapped my temple. "Great minds . . ."

Heath began to smile, but it quickly faded and his gaze went over my shoulder again. I knew he was listening to what Sam was saying. "He won't be able to bring Everett forward," he said.

"Can't find him?" I guessed.

"No," said Heath. "Everett didn't make it to the other side. He went another way." And then Heath made a point of looking down and I let out a breath. "No way!"

But Heath was nodding. "It was Everett's choice. He turned away from the light and ducked through to the lower realms. That's all the history Gramps is able to get. He says the records for Everett on his side close with his turning away from the light."

"Whoa."

"Says something about Everett, doesn't it?" Heath said.

"It does," I agreed, a bit disturbed by the revelation. It was incredibly rare for a child to turn away from the light and head to the lower realms instead. I mean, I could've seen Everett remaining grounded, but Sam was telling us that wasn't what happened. Everett had chosen the dark, evil energy of the lower realm, and that let both Heath and me know that there must have been something dark and perhaps even evil within Everett.

After a moment I worked up my courage a bit more and said, "Ask Sam if he can ask Mama what happened on that day that Everett died."

Heath adopted that faraway expression again, and I knew by the way he pursed his lips in a frown that we weren't going to get an answer we liked. "He says she won't tell him."

"Then she knows what did happen that day," I said softly.

"I think she does, Em."

I fell backward onto the bed and stared up at the ceiling. I was starting to feel lost and abandoned by the most precious spirit I'd ever known, and it hurt like hell.

Then Heath said, "Sam says Gilley might turn up a clue tomorrow."

That got my attention and I sat up again. "Can he see how this will play out?"

The future can be a bit murky to souls on the other side. Sometimes it's clear as day and they make wonderful fortune-tellers. Other times, the future is riddled with possibilities, and no one way looks clear enough to be able to predict. I had a feeling we were currently wading in waters more murky than clear. "He says he sees answers coming, but they're from unusual sources. He says he thinks we'll have everything we need to put the puzzle pieces together, but throughout all of it, we need to be careful of the Sandman."

"Does he have anything else to tell us that isn't obvious?" I joked.

"Nah, he's pretty much sticking to that. Except that

he's pointing to your foot and telling you to take care of that."

I knew what Sam meant. I'd had this tendinitis issue for a couple of months and I was a bit worried that I might be doing lasting damage to the tendon. I knew what I had to do to fix the issue too, namely, adjust my stride, change my running shoes to ones with more arch support, and soak my foot in an ice bath after every run, but that hurt something awful, and I tended to skip it more than I should. "Got it, Sam," I said, vowing to take better care of myself.

"He's pulling back," Heath told me, and a second later I felt the energy in the room shift, as if someone had closed a window.

After Sam left, Heath and I talked late into the night. I was quite tired but not sleepy and I suspected that it was the same for Heath. I think we finally nodded off around three a.m. and I was in a very deep sleep when I heard the sound of loud knocking. I struggled to come fully awake as the knock sounded again and I half fell, half clambered out of bed to see who was at our bedroom door.

"Who is it?" Heath groused, his face in the pillow. From the sound of his voice I thought what he meant to say was, "Make them go away!"

I grabbed my robe from a chair, threw it on quickly, and opened the door to find Mrs. G. standing there. "Oh, Mary Jane, I'm so sorry to disturb you, but Linda Chadwick is here to see you. Did you want me to offer her some coffee and a piece of Danish while you pull yourself together?"

My eyes were blinking rapidly as I tried to come up

to speed. Linda was here? Now? Why? And there were Danishes? "Uh, yes, please, Mrs. G. Thank you. Tell her I'll be right out."

She smiled kindly at me and was gone; then I hustled around to my suitcase to fish out a clean pair of jeans. I glanced over at Heath; he and Linda had never met, but I'd told her all about him. I had a fleeting thought to introduce them now, but my sweetheart was already back asleep, snoring softly.

I paused in the bathroom long enough to quickly brush my teeth and comb out my hair. It refused to cooperate without a proper shower, so I settled for sweeping it back into a ponytail.

When I arrived in the kitchen, I saw that the clock on the wall read eight o'clock. No wonder I was tired. "Hi, Linda," I said shyly.

She was sitting next to Mrs. G., a steaming cup of coffee and a half-eaten, delicious-looking homemade raspberry Danish in front of each lady. "Good morning, Mary Jane," Linda said, pushing a smile to her lips. Her eyes betrayed her nervousness, however, and I hated that we were in this awkward state with each other.

"Well! I'll leave the two of you to your visit," Mrs. G. said, scooting back her chair. "I must get out to water my garden before it gets too hot out."

Before she left, Mrs. G. poured me a cup of coffee from the carafe in the center of the table and plated me one of her Danishes. My stomach gurgled hungrily. I'd skipped dinner the night before, and wished I'd had a sensible meal instead of that ice-cream cone.

"I went by your daddy's place this morning," Linda

said, as if yesterday's outburst had never happened. "He told me you were staying over here with Gilley."

"Daddy and I get along better if we're not under the same roof."

"Oh, you don't have to tell me, honey," she said with a laugh. "I know how your daddy can be."

From anyone else, that statement would've gotten my dander up, but from Linda it wasn't in the least bit offensive. Daddy *could* be ornery and hardheaded. "So what brings you by?" I asked as I took a sip of coffee.

Linda had been picking at the edge of her pastry. "I wanted to apologize."

"Oh?" I said lightly.

Linda rolled her eyes. "Don't you dare be coy with me, Mary Jane. I *invented* that sweet little 'Oh?' and don't you forget it."

I smiled. "Sorry. Force of habit."

"Yes, well, I really *do* want to apologize, buttercup. You see, your mention of the . . . of the . . ."

"Sandman?"

Linda shuddered. "Yes, that, well, it just threw me, is all. I had no idea you knew about him."

"How do *you* know about him, Linda?" I knew it was bold of me to ask, but I figured the worst she could do was yell at me again, and I thought I was better braced for that reaction this time.

She eyed me in that way that said I was a wicked, mischievous child who ought to know better. "I can't tell you anything," she said to me.

I set down my coffee cup. "He's come back, you know."

Linda's back stiffened. "Who?"

"The Sandman."

She blinked. "That's impossible."

"Impossible because Mama somehow managed to banish him to the lower realms?"

Linda's mouth opened and closed, but she offered me no further insight. "Mary Jane," she said, wrapping her hand around mine, her face now pinched with concern. "You must swear to me that you won't try to communicate with this evil spirit. He's dangerous, baby."

"It's too late, Linda," I said to her. "I've already had two encounters with him and he knows I'm DeeDee's daughter."

My mother's best friend put a hand to her mouth. "Oh, please tell me that's not true!"

"It's true, Linda," I said. "You must've heard about the incident at the mental hospital yesterday. That was the Sandman, and that's how I got roughed up enough for you to notice when I showed up at your back door yesterday."

For several seconds Linda simply stared at me in disbelief, and then I saw her gaze travel to my cheek where the scratches and the bruises were, and even more scratches on my forearms. And suddenly, she was in motion. "I have to go," she said, pushing back her chair and making haste to grab her purse.

"Linda," I said, jumping to my feet. "What's going on? Come on, you have to tell me!"

But she wasn't having any of it. She practically ran to the door, pausing only to say, "Promise me you won't go looking for the Sandman," she said. "Please?"

"I may not have a choice. And if you don't tell me what you know, Linda, he may have the advantage against me."

She stared hard at me and I could see the wavering in her eyes, but then she simply shook her head and went out the door, barely pausing as she passed Mrs. G.

"Hey, honey," I heard Heath say while I watched her drive away. "Everything okay?"

I shut the door and turned to him. "We have to figure out who this Sandman is, and how to shut him down, and we have to do that *today*, Heath. Today."

Chapter 12

While I showered, I gave Heath a brief summary of what'd happened with Linda. "She knows something about how your mom is linked to all this," he said from his place at the sink, where he was shaving.

"She definitely knows something."

"How do we get her to tell us?"

I turned off the faucet and wrapped myself in a towel. Pulling back the shower curtain, I said, "We don't. I know Linda, and when she promises to keep a secret, it's as good as locked up in Fort Knox."

Heath wiped the remnants of shaving cream from his face and said, "Then what do we do?"

Before I could answer, the bathroom door flew open and Gilley stood there with a big fat Danish in his hand. "Aww, jeez, you two! You're half-naked! Get a room, would you?"

I glared at Heath. "What'd we say about locking the door?"

"You said to lock it, and I forgot," he replied sheepishly.

"Gil," I snapped, pulling the towel tighter around me and waving at him to shut the door. But Gilley was currently ogling my boyfriend and stuffing his piehole with breakfast. "*Gil!*"

"Yeah, yeah," he said, finally tearing his gaze away from Heath's bare chest and scantily covered rear. "Breslow is here to pick you guys up, so y'all better get a move on."

I reached for my phone on the counter. "He's early!"

"Well, how about I feed him a bagel and coffee and stall him?"

Heath squinted at the last few bites of pastry resting on Gilley's napkin. "Didn't your mom make Danishes?"

Gil shoved the last bite into his mouth and gave a muffled, "We're all out."

With that, he closed the door and I made sure to walk over and lock it behind him.

When I turned back around, Heath was pouting. "I was looking forward to one of those Danishes. They smelled awesome."

I didn't have the heart to tell him they tasted even better. Instead I rushed through a quick blow-dry and got dressed while Heath headed out to fish around for some breakfast.

I found Breslow in the kitchen with a mug in his

hand and his back to the corner as Mrs. G. did her best to grill him for information about what we'd all gotten ourselves into.

As Gilley's mom tended to worry a lot, we'd done our best to keep the explanations brief and skip many of the more troubling details, but she was a wily one, that Mrs. G., and she knew there was more to the story.

"Ready to go?" I said loudly when I entered the kitchen, and Breslow jumped to his feet.

"Yep!" he said, setting his cup in the sink and tipping his hat to Mrs. G. "Thank you kindly, ma'am."

She frowned at me. I suspected she'd been getting close to having Breslow tell her what she wanted to know. Heath was already waiting on the front porch, nibbling on a banana and a power bar. Sloppy seconds to the homemade Danishes.

For his part, Gilley was lying on the porch swing, rubbing his belly and looking as lazy and happy as a well-fed tomcat. I tapped his foot and said, "Hey. Have you done any research on that Ouija board like I asked?"

"Oh, yeah," he said with a yawn. "I'm all over it."

"Gil," I said levelly.

"M.J.," he replied, mocking my tone.

"I'm serious. I need to know where that board came from. We have to trace the roots of the Sandman and look for a weakness or something."

Gil sat up and rubbed his eyes. "He comes from Louisiana."

That took me by surprise, and I couldn't tell whether Gil was making a joke or being serious. "Are you playing with me?"

Gil rolled his head around on his neck, which made several unsettling popping sounds. "No, I'm not. I was up most of last night searching and finally found a pretty obscure reference to the Sandman and that Ouija board from Louisiana back in the nineteen twenties."

"How obscure?"

Gil went back to lying down. "An article in the *Times-Picayune* from nineteen twenty-two described how police were called to the scene of a house in the Garden District. A wealthy eccentric widow named Olivia Baumgarden had hosted a séance that night, and she'd invited a few friends over for cocktails and a bit of adventure.

"According to the article, Baumgarden had hired a spirit medium named Lady Madelyn." I tensed. Madelyn was my mother's full name. My father and her mother were the only ones who ever called her that, however. The rest of the time she'd gone by DeeDee. "Lady M. claimed to be able to call up not just dead people, but powerful forces capable of leaving no skeptics in the room," Gil continued.

"What happened?" Heath said over my shoulder, and I realized he'd come up behind me and was listening to Gilley.

"Things went south shortly after ten p.m. One of the party guests, a retired general of some note, had apparently snapped, and he'd attacked several of the patrons including the host, Mrs. Baumgarden, who'd, tragically, suffered a broken neck."

"He killed her?"

"Yep. Witnesses claimed that something weird had

happened to the general as Lady Madelyn manipulated her planchette over her elaborately painted Ouija board. He suddenly started growling, foaming at the mouth, and he was quoted as saying, 'The Sandman cometh for you!'"

"Then what?" I asked when Gilley didn't continue.

"Then nothing. That's where the article ends. The general was tried for murder, convicted, and hung a year later."

"So what happened to Lady Madelyn and the board?"

"That's where the trail ends, sugar. I looked late into the night for another reference to her, but so far, nada."

"So, somehow the Ouija board made it from New Orleans in the nineteen twenties to Valdosta in the nineteen seventies," Breslow said over my other shoulder. Apparently everyone had come to gather around Gil while he told us what he knew.

"Wait a minute," Heath said, and he disappeared back inside only to come out a minute later with Everett Sellers's missing-persons file. "I was reading this in the car yesterday while you were in with Linda, Em, and . . ." Heath paused to flip through several pages of the file. "Where was that? Oh, here. Okay, so look at this."

He handed me the file and I looked down at the sheet of paper, which appeared to be a summary of Mr. Owen Sellers's business practices. "Everett's dad owned a shipping company based in New Orleans," Heath told Gilley and Breslow while I scanned the sheet.

I stared at the summary and wondered, "Could the board have belonged not to the Porters but to Everett Sellers?"

"It's possible," Breslow said.

Turning to Gil, I said, "Uh, Gilley?"

"Yeah, yeah, you want me to research the Porters and see if they had any ties to New Orleans. Got it. Right after my nap."

I was tempted to insist that Gil get off his duff and do the research, but then I remembered he'd said he'd been up most of the night trying to find a reference to the Sandman, so I let it go. "Thanks," I told him.

With that, we left Mrs. G.'s and Breslow talked about which leads we should focus on. "Today we definitely need to stop by Glenn Porter's," he said.

"I think it's more important to talk to Sarah than Glenn," I said.

"It's not as easy to talk to Sarah as you'd think," Breslow told me, and he seemed uncomfortable about something.

"She's not dead, is she?" Heath said from the back, and I thought he was only half kidding.

"No, no, she's alive. She's just not quite all there, if you get my drift."

I glanced over my shoulder at Heath and he shrugged. "We're not getting your drift, Beau. How about filling us in?"

"A few years back Sarah Porter had a nervous breakdown. She's a sweet lady, but she's not all there," Beau said, tapping his temple. "She startles super easy too, so we'll have to tread lightly with her."

"Okay," I agreed. "But we still need to talk to her about that playroom. If she didn't witness or wasn't involved with the crime, she had to have known about the body in the playroom. I mean, all those toys in there belonged to a little girl, and she was the only little girl in the house at the time."

"I hear ya," Beau said. "But let's tackle Glenn Porter first."

A bit later we had come to a stop in front of an old home that'd been converted into an office building, which sat atop a hill overlooking lovely manicured lawns and well-kept gardens and was ringed by a fleur-de-lis capped wrought iron fence. The exterior of the building appeared freshly painted a light gray-blue with gleaming white trim and as a whole it represented a most charming facade.

The sign at the front read GLENN PORTER, LLC.

"What does Porter do?" I asked as we got out of the car and headed up the first set of stairs leading us to the front door.

"Mostly real estate investments," Breslow told me. "At least that's what I read in the paper about him a few years ago."

"Have you ever met him?" Heath asked.

"Oh, yeah. Stopped him for a speeding ticket a year ago. He fought it in court and won. He was pretty smug about it too, the bastard."

I squared my shoulders. "Well, let's see if he's as smug about a forty-five-year-old body showing up in his old house."

We entered the building and I took note of the rather

dim interior, the creaking floors, and the smell of a very old house.

"Hello, Deputy," said a husky female voice. We all turned toward the sound and discovered a gorgeous woman with ebony black hair, bright blue eyes, and a porcelain white complexion. I took one look at her and wished I'd put on a little more makeup. Heath took one look at her and turned away, pinning his eyes on anything in the room but her.

Great. He thought she was crazy beautiful too; otherwise, he wouldn't have made such a show of averting his eyes.

"Uh, hello," said Breslow, quickly pulling off his hat. "How're . . . uh . . . how're you today, ma'am?"

She stifled a smile. The deputy was clearly also a bit thrown by her beauty. "I'm fine. What can we do for you today, sir?"

Breslow's face went blank. It was like a switch was flipped and he lost the ability to think. I stepped forward and said, "Hi, I'm Deputy Holliday, and these are my associates, Deputy Whitefeather and Deputy Breslow. We're here on a matter of some urgency. Is Mr. Porter in?"

"Oh! Of course, let me just go in and tell him you're here. Won't you please have a seat?" She made a motion for us to sit in the small area near her desk, which held a fainting couch and two wing chairs. The boys took the wing chairs, and I was left with the couch. It wasn't lost on me that the chairs faced the gorgeous woman's "desk, while the couch was angled away from it.

We'd barely gotten comfortable when the woman came back and smiled sweetly at us. "Mr. Porter is just finishing up a phone call. May I interest you in a cup of coffee, or water, or maybe a soda?"

"I could go for a cola," Breslow said.

"I'm good," Heath said, again keeping his eyes trained on anything in the room but her. His gaze landed on me and I gave him a pointed look. "Okay, maybe a cup of coffee?" he said, misinterpreting my expression.

I rolled my eyes before turning to her and saying, "I'm sorry—what was your name?"

"Chloe," she said. "And I'm the one who should be sorry. I should've introduced myself to y'all."

"Don't worry about it, Chloe. I'd love a water. Either bottled or tap is fine."

She moved over to a small credenza at the opposite end of the room and got our drinks ready before placing them on a tray and bringing them to us. She moved with a beautiful fluidity, and Breslow practically swooned when she handed him his soda can and accompanying glass.

"You look very pretty today," Heath said to me immediately after he lifted his drink off the tray.

I did my best not to give in to the temptation to roll my eyes. "Thank you, Heath."

"Your water, ma'am?" Chloe said.

After taking the water and thanking her, I hoped like hell Porter wrapped up his phone call soon.

I got my wish a very short time later when the office door Chloe had disappeared through earlier opened

and out stepped a very handsome man in an impeccably tailored suit. "Sorry to keep you waiting," he said, brushing a hand through his dark blond locks and flashing the most winning smile at us.

I turned to Heath. "You look pretty today."

He chose to ignore me and focused on standing up without spilling his coffee. Breslow and I also got to our feet and Porter said, "Deputy, won't you and your associates please come in?"

Breslow took a step forward but then seemed to hesitate, unsure what to do with his glass of soda.

"Would you like me to hold on to that for you?" Chloe asked.

Beau's cheeks went scarlet red. "That'd be great!" he said with a bit too much enthusiasm. He seemed to realize it because he immediately cleared his throat and added, "Thank you, Zoe."

Her solicitude never faded and I had to hand it to the girl for keeping nothing but a pleasant smile on her lips. As we headed toward Porter's office, I nudged Breslow. "By the way, if you work up the courage to ask her out later, you really should get her name right."

He looked almost panicked. "What? Why? Isn't her name Chloe?"

"Yes, Deputy, but you just called her Zoe."

He rather subtly slapped his forehead right before turning into Porter's office. I glanced at Heath, who was behind me, and he grinned and shook his head. He'd caught the deputy's slipup too.

When I turned to face forward again, however, I nearly walked right into Breslow, who'd stopped unex-

pectedly just inside the doorway. "Beau?" I said, tapping his shoulder.

But he wasn't moving. And then it hit me why he'd stopped dead in his tracks. "What the . . . ," I heard him whisper, perfectly mirroring my thoughts as I took in the interior of Glenn Porter's office.

"Holy shit," Heath whispered from behind me. He'd seen it too.

"Come in, come in," Porter told us, waving his hand enthusiastically as he took a seat behind an enormous desk covered in folders and paper.

I eyed him more keenly now and dismissed the initial thought I'd had at such a handsome man. "It's okay, Beau," I whispered. "Heath and I have enough magnets on us to stop any spook in its tracks."

This may or may not have been true, because all Heath and I had on us were our fishing vests, and considering that we were up against a room where every single square inch of wall space was occupied with a hanging planchette, I wasn't especially confident in anything except my ability to run . . . very, very fast if necessary.

"Do you like my collection?" Porter said, sitting down rather elaborately and waving to the walls.

Breslow took three tentative steps forward into the room and Heath and I stuck close on either side of him. "Is this some kind of a joke, Mr. Porter?" Beau managed in a horse voice.

Porter adopted a confused look. "Joke? What joke would that be, Deputy . . . ah . . . ?"

"Breslow."

"Deputy Breslow. What kind of joke do you believe I'm trying to make?"

He was toying with us, the son of a bitch. "Maybe you think you can outsmart the investigators on a forty-five-year-old murder?" I suggested. "That'd be a great joke, wouldn't it, Mr. Porter?"

Porter turned his steely blue eyes on me. "Forty-five-year-old murder?" he said with forced surprise. "What are you people going on about?"

"We found the remains of a young man in your home," Breslow said bluntly.

Porter put a hand to his chest and widened his eyes. "In *my* home?" The deputy nodded. "Well, first, I will repeat that I have no idea what you're talking about, and second, I hope you obtained a warrant to search my residence?"

"We didn't need one," Heath said, but Porter talked over him.

"Well, I can't possibly think that you would enter my home without my permission or a warrant. Furthermore, as I've only owned my house for the past six months, I can't possibly imagine why you would think I had anything to do with anything suspicious dating back to that property from forty-five years ago. If there was a murder committed on my premises, it was well before my time there."

I wanted to smack him. He knew damn well what we were talking about and he seemed to be enjoying playing semantics with us and forcing us to explain ourselves.

"The skeletal remains were found in the hidden

playroom inside Porter Manor," Heath growled. He didn't much care for Glenn's antics either.

"Inside Porter Manor?" Glenn repeated. "Well, I sold that home several months ago. . . . Er . . . who did you say you were?"

"Deputy Whitefeather," Heath said, and for emphasis, he coolly flashed the badge Beau had given him.

Porter merely smirked at him. "I didn't know the Valdosta sheriff's department was keeping its deputies in plain clothes these days."

"We think the remains belong to Everett Sellers," I said.

"You think?" Porter said, his cunning eyes shifting to me. "The coroner hasn't confirmed to whom they belong?"

"Not yet," I said, without elaborating.

"So, how can you possibly know that these remains aren't far older than forty-five years?" Porter said, his amused and overly dramatic antics starting to really irritate me. "I mean, that house was in our family for seven generations! Those remains could have been anyone's, including another one of my relatives who died of natural causes and was, for whatever reason, stored in the house in this hidden room you claim to have found."

"We don't think so," Breslow said.

Porter picked up the receiver on his phone, dangling it in one hand. "Yes, well, assuming I'm about to be accused of something, I'll call my attorney and have him head down to the morgue to see this body for himself and tell me what he thinks."

"It ain't at the morgue," Breslow told him, a bit anxious to have Porter set down his phone.

"Why not?"

"The remains were stolen," Breslow admitted. I was a little irritated that he'd done that, but then I realized that if Porter had killed Everett, then he most likely would've snuck back into the house to remove the remains and he'd know already that they weren't at the morgue. "Do you know somethin' about that, Mr. Porter?"

"Stolen?" Porter said, a wicked smile lifting the edges of his mouth. "From the morgue?"

Breslow was quiet, and that seemed to be all that Porter needed to set down the receiver and settle smugly back into his chair. "I see," he said, barely keeping back a snicker. "Well, if you don't have a body, Deputy, then you don't have a murder."

"So you're claiming that you knew nothing of the fact that your cousin was murdered in your home back in nineteen seventy-one and left in your sister's playroom, which was then covered over with drywall and hidden from the rest of the world?" I said. I wanted to get Porter's lie on the record.

"On the contrary. My cousin Everett walked off into the woods one afternoon and never returned. My family and I searched tirelessly for him for weeks and months, but no trace of him was ever found. Furthermore, I am not now, nor was I ever, aware of this 'playroom' you keep mentioning. My sisters didn't have playrooms. They had closets."

"Okay, so maybe one of the closets was converted

over into a playroom and you just didn't realize it," Heath said.

Porter rolled his eyes. "I wouldn't know about that either. My mother was very strict about our placement in that house. The boys were assigned bedrooms on the third floor and my sisters were assigned rooms on the first. We were not allowed in each other's rooms. My mother thought that inappropriate."

"And yet the room in question had a door that was covered over with drywall," I said. "Assuming Everett met an unfortunate demise in your sister's converted closet—who covered over the door with drywall?"

Porter eyed me dully. "I've no idea, Miss . . ."

"Holliday," I said when he refused to go on without knowing my name.

But instead of elaborating on how he'd happened to miss the reconfiguration of his sister's room, Porter focused intently on me. "Did you say Holliday?"

"Yes."

"As in Montgomery Holliday's daughter?"

I nodded and was about to direct the conversation back to the topic at hand when Porter said, "So you're DeeDee's daughter." I felt a chill ignite my spine and the room suddenly got very quiet. "I knew your mother quite well, you know," he said, his eyes never leaving mine. "She was such a beauty, even back then. Mother was always thrusting the two of us together, you know, hoping that sparks would catch fire even at an early age."

I felt my skin crawl. The thought of this man having such inappropriate thoughts about my mother, who was

only eight at the time to his twelve, disgusted me. "What happened in that playroom, Glenn?" I asked, refusing to look away.

Porter smiled. "Why don't you ask your mother, Mary Jane?" he said. "Oh, but that's right. DeeDee passed away some time ago, didn't she? But, from what I gather, you two still chat from time to time, don't you? And you don't even seem to need a planchette."

Heath took a threatening step toward Porter's desk, his hands balled up into fists, and I grabbed for his arm to stop him.

Porter laughed like he thought it was hilarious that we were so offended. Then he set his hands on his desk and stood up. "Now, don't let me keep the three of you. I'm sure you have much to do to see about finding that lost body. Can't very well proceed without that, now, can you?"

I let go of Heath's arm and took the short steps to his desk myself. Porter stood and leaned forward over the desk to meet my unspoken challenge. Unperturbed, I stuck my face right into his and said, "Somehow, someway, we're going to prove that you killed your cousin, Glenn."

He narrowed his eyes at me. "Oh, but *I* didn't, Mary Jane Holliday. And your mother knows it."

A flood of angry heat seared my cheeks and for several seconds I had a hell of a time holding back the punch to the face I desperately wanted to inflict on Glenn Porter. I felt Heath's hand on my shoulder just as I was really close to losing my cool, and he said, "Come on, Em. He's not worth it."

I let myself be tugged backward, but I continued to snarl at Porter. Just before we made it through the door, however, something in Glenn's eyes sparked and in an instant all the planchettes in the room began to vibrate and rattle. Alerted by the odd noise, Heath and Breslow paused and turned back to look, while I stood rooted to the spot. We watched as the wall behind Porter came alive with movement. The planchettes rattled on their nails and began tapping out a rhythm against the wall.

With dread I noticed that they began keeping four-four time. Porter smiled his most wicked smile, then sat back down, leaned back in his chair, and waved lazily at the planchettes. And then he snapped his fingers and all the planchettes were once again still and silent.

"Neat party trick," he said to us, "isn't it?"

That's when I turned away from him and grabbed Heath and Beau by the arms, pulling them out of the room. "See you around, Mary Jane," Porter called after me.

It took everything I had not to run from the building.

Chapter 13

We bypassed Chloe without even stopping to say good-bye. I made a beeline for the car and took my frustration out on the door, which I slammed after I got in.

Heath got quietly into the backseat, and Breslow slid in as well. We sat there for a few beats in silence, and I did my best to rein in my temper, but I still had the urge to go back into Porter's office and sock him in the nose.

Breslow started the car and pulled out from the curb and still no one spoke. At the first red light we came to, however, he turned to me and said, "Wanna fill me in on what Porter meant by your mama knowing what happened in that playroom?"

I froze. "I have no idea."

"Well, you seemed to know," he insisted.

"Beau, will you drop it, please?"

"No, I won't drop it, Mary Jane!" he yelled, and behind us a car tapped its horn ever so lightly. The light had turned green and we were holding up traffic.

Breslow punched the gas and I turned away from him, so angry and troubled, and confused. "We need to go see Sarah," I said after several more minutes of silence.

Nobody answered me, so I turned to Breslow. "Beau. We have to go interview Sarah. She was there that day. I know she was."

"That's where I'm heading right now," he said through clenched teeth.

I didn't fault him for being angry with me. I would've been ticked off too, but I couldn't offer him anything other than the fact that my mother used to spend time at the Porters' and she had on her vanity a small porcelain sugar bowl that looked very similar to the tea set in the playroom. That was it. That was really all I knew.

Except that wasn't really *all* I knew.

Linda's reaction to my question about the Sandman, the spook who'd been torturing my mother as a child, witnessed by me in my out-of-body experience; the way DeeDee had told me that Everett and Glenn had called up the Sandman; and the fact that Glenn Porter had craftily implied that my mother was there, in that playroom, the day Everett Sellers supposedly went missing. All of it suggested that Mama was involved, but to what extent I couldn't say.

And how involved could she have been anyway? She was only a child herself! Just eight years old at the time.

True, she probably could've swung that mallet, but murder was an act that I found my mother completely incapable of. There was no way, just *no way*, she could've been the one to kill Everett.

That's what I told myself over and over at least all the way across town. "There," Breslow said. "She lives there."

The house was hard to see, hidden behind so much overgrown foliage, but I caught sight of a two-story redbrick colonial with black shutters.

We got out and approached the house, and as we headed up the walkway, Heath took up my hand. "You okay?" he mouthed.

"Yeah. Thanks," I whispered back. Heath gave another good squeeze to my hand. He knew I was fibbing.

We got to the front steps and Breslow's phone rang. He took it from his holster and eyed the screen. It must've been important because he answered it. "Breslow. Yeah. Yeah. When? Where? What hospital?"

Heath and I had paused beside Breslow to wait for him to finish the call, but alarm bells were going off in my head and I had a terrible feeling about that call.

"What happened?" Heath and I both asked the second he hung up the phone.

"Linda Chadwick was attacked. She lost consciousness right after Matt arrived on scene, but she managed to say your name and told him to warn you. Then she blacked out."

My knees buckled. Heath caught me before I sank to the ground, and Beau reached down to help steady me.

"I know you two are tight, Mary Jane. She's been taken to South Georgia," he said, referring to Valdosta's main hospital. "I can take us there right now if you want."

"Yes, yes, please!"

Heath wrapped his arm around my waist and we hustled back to the squad car. Breslow drove like a madman, zooming down side streets, switching on his siren and the lights.

We made it to the hospital in no time, but I still didn't wait for the car to stop before I was out of it and running for the emergency room. A panic so fierce it wrecked my ability to think clearly took hold and refused to let go. Linda and Mrs. G. were my surrogate mothers. If anything happened to either one of them, I'd be undone. I just couldn't imagine losing one of them, not now. Not yet.

"Linda Chadwick!" I shouted at the nurse behind the check-in desk.

She pulled her head back. I'd startled her. "Is that you or someone who's come through here?" she said calmly.

"Someone who came through here. Deputy Wells might've come with her." I was fishing for information to give the nurse so that she could cut through the identification process and just tell me how Linda was.

"Are you a relative?"

Before I could answer, Heath and Breslow stepped up next to me. "She's her niece," Heath said.

The nurse didn't even question the statement. Instead she began to type on her keyboard before pausing to tap the screen. "She's in surgery."

My eyes flooded with tears. "What happened to her?" I asked.

The nurse adopted a sympathetic expression. "I don't know, ma'am. That's all this screen will tell me. If you'd like to take a seat in the lobby, though, I promise to come out and update you just as soon as there's more information."

My breathing was coming in short, quick pants and I was having trouble keeping my knees from buckling. Heath took hold of my waist again and guided me over to the waiting area. "Ohmigod!" I cried. "Ohmigod!"

"Shhhh," he said, cradling me close to him. "Em, she'll pull through. She will. You heard what Beau said. She was conscious right up until Wells got there. That's a good sign."

I wept into Heath's chest and prayed as hard as I'd ever prayed for Linda to be okay. At some point I realized Beau wasn't next to us, but I could hardly focus on that. All I could think about was how much Linda meant to me, and how I didn't know if I could ever forgive myself for bolting out of her home the day before and not chasing after her that morning.

Finally I had cried myself out and I sat up a little, wiping my eyes and sniffling loudly. A tissue box was put in front of me, and I looked up to see Beau holding it. "I talked to Matt," he said.

"What happened?" I asked, taking the tissue box and blowing my nose loudly.

Beau sat down and leaned his elbows on his knees. "She was found on the lawn of an elderly couple who claim that when they opened their front door to get the

paper, she was just lying there. At first they thought she might be drunk, but then they noticed all the blood."

"Thank God they were home to help her," I said, so grateful to that couple.

"Yep," Beau agreed. "Anyway, they said that when they went out to see if she was all right, they could see that she was really hurt, and they coaxed her to lie down and the husband went in to call nine-one-one while the wife stayed with Linda. During the time it took the ambulance to arrive, Linda was talking but she wasn't makin' much sense. The one thing the wife said she managed to understand was that Linda was anxious about someone named Mary Jane, and that she really wanted to have someone warn her about something."

"What?"

"Linda never said. The elderly woman tried to get Linda to give her more information, because she was worried that maybe Linda wasn't the only one who'd been attacked and hit over the head. She was thinking maybe this Mary Jane might be off in the woods somewhere, hurt too."

"Why off in the woods?" I asked. That was a curious thing to say.

"Well, the old lady said Linda kept pointing to the woods behind her house."

My brow furrowed. A small hint of recognition sprang to my mind. "Beau, where exactly does this couple live?"

"Oh, this all happened on Loamloch. You know how there's that stretch of road that butts up right next to those woods?"

I sat forward. "Did you say Loamloch?"

"Yeah. Why, you recognize it?"

"My grandparents used to live on Loamloch," I said. That couldn't have been a coincidence. "What was Linda doing over by my grandparents' house? They haven't been alive for years."

"I don't know, Mary Jane," Breslow said. "I guess we'll just have to wait for Linda to get out of surgery and tell us."

We waited hours for news of Linda's condition and at last, right around three o'clock a doctor showed up to give us a report. "Mrs. Chadwick came through the surgery very well," he said. "She had a severe skull fracture and we've put a temporary stent in to relieve the pressure, but she is doing very nicely, given her condition."

"Can she talk?" Breslow asked.

The doctor shook his head. "No, I'm afraid not. We've induced a medical coma at this point to give her brain a chance to heal. We'll be concerned with swelling and any sign of infection for the next several days, but I'm quite optimistic about her chances."

I sagged against Heath, so relieved I started crying again. And then I launched myself at the doctor who'd saved her and hugged him fiercely. "Thank you, thank you, thank you," I told him.

He chuckled good-naturedly and patted me on the back. "It's okay, miss. Just doing my job. By the way, do you know how we can get ahold of Mr. Chadwick? We don't have a record of insurance."

"They're divorced," I told him. "But you can call her

attorney, Montgomery Holliday. He handled her divorce, and I'm positive he made sure Linda's insurance was taken care of."

Linda's husband had left her two years earlier for a younger, much dumber model. Grant Chadwick had been a fairly wealthy man, and through e-mails and phone calls, Linda had given me the blow-by-blow throughout their divorce. Daddy had made sure she had received a very good settlement, which included a provision for her health insurance. In fact, I could remember a chat with Linda about it and she let me know she was so pleased that Daddy had even thought to include that, because she couldn't have afforded it on her own.

Since we weren't allowed to see Linda, Breslow, Heath, and I headed out of the hospital to grab a bite to eat. I wasn't hungry, but Heath insisted that I get something, so I humored him by ordering soup and a veggie sandwich. Over the meal we discussed what'd happened to Linda, and I confessed to Beau that I thought she knew something about the Sandman that she wasn't telling us.

"How would she know anything about the Sandman?" he asked.

"She went to school with Sarah Porter," I said, trying to hide the fact that Linda was Mama's best friend.

"So did your mama, right, Mary Jane?" Beau wasn't stupid. He knew I was hiding something.

Heath had been oddly quiet from the time we'd left the hospital, but he chose then to chime in. "You know what I think?"

"What's that?" I asked, jumping on the chance to change the subject.

"I keep going back to Scoffland's murder. And I can't understand why he was killed."

"Wrong place, wrong time?" I suggested.

But Heath frowned. "Which brings up another question. Why was he there alone in the first place? The coroner said he'd been dead a few hours before the crew arrived, right?"

Beau and I nodded.

"Okay, so why? What was he doing there?"

"Checking out the place before the crew showed up? You know, getting a scope for the work involved," I suggested.

Heath frowned. "Several hours before the crew arrives, though? I've worked construction, and that'd be a weird thing to do."

"So you think he might've been the target?" I asked. That hadn't occurred to me, as I'd just assumed that Scoffland had been in the house at the wrong time, and maybe he'd seen something he shouldn't have.

"Worth checking out, don't you think?"

I pulled out my cell and called Gilley. "Yo! Yo! Yo!" he said. "Whaz up?"

"Can I speak to Gilley, please?" I said.

He laughed. "Sorry. What can I do for you, sugar?"

"You're in a good mood."

"Michel's job ended early and he's flying down here on Saturday for your daddy's wedding. He's going to be my plus one."

I rubbed my temple. My father's wedding was in

three days. How the hell was I supposed to attend the wedding with a crazy spook and a killer on the loose? "Gil, that's great, but I need you to do some more research."

"Okay, and speaking of that, I have stuff to report."

"What?"

"No, no, you first."

"Okay," I said. "I want you to look into Mike Scoffland. See if you can find a connection to him and the Porters."

"The construction dude who was killed by one of his workers?" Gil said.

"Yes."

"What kind of a connection might I find?"

"I don't know." And then a thought occurred to me. "See if there's anything connecting him specifically to Glenn Porter."

Heath's brow shot up. "That's right! He's a real estate developer, right?"

"Yeah," Breslow said. "That could be the connection."

"Glenn . . . Porter," Gil repeated, and I suspected he was taking notes. "Anything else?"

I set the phone on the table and hit the SPEAKER button so that Heath and Beau could hear. "I think that should do it. So tell us, what did you find?"

"Well, for starters I think I've figured out who crafted that Ouija board."

"You did?" I said.

"I did," Gil confirmed. "I got ahold of an art historian in Louisiana who was an awesome source of informa-

tion. He's an expert on the occult history in that region, and especially knowledgeable about Ouija boards. I sent him the picture you took, and he was able to tell me immediately who created it and gave me some history on it."

"Do tell," I said anxiously.

"To begin with, the board is actually an incredibly rare piece and insanely valuable. In fact, he'd like me to put him in touch with the owner so that he can make an offer."

"How much is he offering?"

"Twenty-five grand," Gil said. "And when an art historian is offering you a giant wad of cash like that, you know he can get double or triple that price on his own."

"Whoa!" I said.

"I know. Crazy, right? Anyway, the elaborately painted flowers and filigree indicate a style that was popular in Portugal in the early nineteen hundreds before showing up here. The board from the playroom was designed and created by a much sought-after artisan, named Paco Padesco."

"Where did Padesco settle when he came here?" I asked.

"New Orleans, of course," Gilley said. "Anyway, my source in Louisiana happened upon Padesco's journals, which include sketches and receipts for all the Ouija boards he sold. Padesco was pretty well-known in his day, and his boards were very popular with the wealthy spiritualist set. He sold them on a fairly exclusive basis, demanding crazy money for them. Oh, and he also de-

signed the planchettes, which he said would only work on his boards.

"Now, the planchettes Padesco designed were a sort of interesting device. Most of the traditional planchettes were solid with a small hole where you were supposed to put a pen or a pencil to aid with automatic writing. That morphed into the creation of the Ouija board, which had the letters of the alphabet and a set of numbers printed on it, and the planchettes became solid and ended in a point, which would point to the letter in question. But other sets took the original planchette, with the small hole for a pen, and enlarged the opening so that a letter could be seen through the hole.

Padesco took his boards and planchettes to the next level. He created very elaborate boards with lots of color, which he said would awaken the senses of the living and attract the dead. And then he had his planchettes molded out of sterling silver and he sold a bunch like that, but he saved his most expensive creations for his wealthiest clients. In these planchettes he'd put a gem in the hole rather than just leaving them open. He theorized that by using a pure metal like silver and putting a highly polished gem in the loop instead of leaving it empty, the energy of both the spirit and the medium would be exponentially magnified, throwing open the floodgates to communicate with the other side."

"No doubt he was onto something with that theory," I said. "The Sandman didn't get here from some crappy cardboard-and-plastic Ouija set—that's for sure."

I looked to Heath to see if he agreed, but he was staring at the phone with his brow furrowed. "Can I see

your phone for a sec?" he said. I motioned for him to go ahead, and he picked it up and began to tap at it.

"What's happening?" Gil asked.

"Hang on," Heath told him while we all waited for him to show us what he was doing. And then he simply stared at my phone and said, "Gil, are you looking at the photo M.J. took of the board and the planchette from the playroom?"

"Uh, no, do I need to?"

"Yes," he said, setting my cell down in the middle of the table again, and I saw that he'd pulled up the last image I'd taken of the board and the planchette. To Beau and me he said, "Does anything look out of place to you?"

The deputy and I leaned forward to look closely at the screen. "No," I said, and Beau also shook his head.

"What am I supposed to be looking at?" Gil said from the speaker.

Heath pointed to the planchette. "Em," he said to me. "Look close."

I did and all I saw was the beautiful silver planchette with its amethyst crystal gleaming in the light from my flash. "I am, Heath. I don't see anything odd. What is it that you've noticed?"

Heath leaned in too. "See how the board is covered in dust?" he said. Beau and I nodded. "But the planchette doesn't have a speck of dust on it. And if it's made out of sterling silver, why isn't it tarnished?"

My jaw fell open, and we heard Gilley say, "Holy shit! Heath's right! That thing looks practically showroom ready."

Heath then swiped his finger across the screen. "And look here," he said, moving to another image that I'd taken much earlier of a section of the playroom near the door. "See that?"

"It's a footprint," I said, of the imprint in the dust.

"Yeah," Heath said. "But Beau and I were never over on that side of the playroom. It's to the left of the door and we stuck to the right. Now, I can't say for sure that it's not your footprint, Em, but neither one of us walked over that way."

"Neither did I," I whispered, amazed that I hadn't noticed the footprint in the dust when I'd photographed that section of the playroom. "I walked in to the right too, and I'd kept Everett on my left, circling around the table with the tea set to photograph the room. That's not my footprint, Heath."

"Can someone catch me up to speed, please?" Gil said.

"Someone else entered that playroom before we did and planted that planchette," I told him.

"But who and how?" Beau said. "The room was sealed tight."

"Could there be another entrance to the playroom that we don't know about?" I asked.

Everyone fell silent while we all considered that. "I don't see how," Heath said. "I mean, it's easy to see how the architecture of the playroom was hidden on the outside by the magnolia tree, but there didn't seem to be any other doors or windows in it. And it wouldn't make sense anyway because this footprint is facing into the room from the door. Someone came through that

door and planted the planchette; then they probably walked back out the way we came in, and I think their footprints might've been obscured by ours when we walked in to investigate."

"So, how the heck did they get into a sealed room?" I asked. "And why was that planchette planted there?"

"To wake up the Sandman," Gil said. "Remember, Padesco said the planchette wouldn't work without his board, and probably vice versa."

I shook my head. None of this was making any sense. "So the board and the planchette have been separated for forty-five years, and now someone thought it was a good idea to put them back together? Why? For what purpose?"

"It's got to be Glenn Porter," Heath said. "I mean, you guys saw his office. He must have three hundred planchettes nailed to the wall."

"Wait. What?" Gil asked. I filled him in on our visit to Porter's office and he whistled appreciatively. "That's just playing with fire," he said.

"But how does that work?" I asked them all. "I mean, why would Porter make it so obvious by displaying all of those planchettes in plain sight? He'd have to know we'd think he was responsible for both Scoffland's murder and Everett's."

"He is an arrogant SOB," Beau pointed out.

"Arrogant I'll give you, but he's not stupid, Beau. And again, I gotta ask, why would he use the Sandman to kill Scoffland, and, if we really want to get technical with this, why would he then kill Cisco?"

"He committed suicide," Heath said, referring to the

construction worker who'd thrown himself out the window at the mental hospital.

"Did he?" I said. "Beau, you remember what Matt said? He said that the windows at the hospital were triple-paned. No one should've been able to break through all three—so how did Cisco manage that kind of a physical feat if he wasn't possessed by the Sandman at the time?"

Heath nodded. "She's right. You'd have to have superhuman strength to do that, and only someone possessed or on serious drugs would be able to do something like that." And then Heath seemed to have another thought. "You know what else bothers me?"

"What?" I asked.

"Do you remember when we first got to the Porter house, and that stuff was being thrown off the balcony and we went inside to get away from it and the air was a little thick with dark energy, but then . . ." Heath paused, as if he was searching for the right words.

"Then there was a shift," I said, remembering back to when he and I were in the yard after escaping the house through the window and he'd told me he'd felt it.

"Godzilla," Gilley said.

I rolled my eyes at the phone, but Heath was nodding. "Yeah, Em. The energy shifted right before that big black shadow showed up and tried to attack Gil. I felt it."

"So what are you saying?" Beau asked him, and I knew he had to be confused.

I sighed heavily, because I suddenly realized exactly what we were up against. "He's saying that there isn't

just one evil spirit at work here. It seems we might be dealing with two."

"*Two?*" the deputy gasped.

"Yep," Heath said. "One significantly less powerful than the other, but two separate dark entities were at work in that house."

"But when we went back there to look for the Ouija board, you guys said you didn't feel anything weird."

"That's true, Beau," I said. "Which means both spirits were either dormant or on the move."

"Do you think they were both being controlled by Padesco's board and planchette?" Gil asked.

I shrugged even though I knew Gil couldn't see me. "I don't know, buddy. But I hope so."

"Why do you hope so?" Beau asked me.

Heath answered for me. "Because once we destroy the board and the planchette, we can safely lock those spooks up together forever."

"Still, it would help to know who the other spook is."

"He felt way more powerful than just a grounded spirit," Heath remarked. "I mean, those planters were heavy and that took some serious power."

"Very true," I said. The whisper of an idea was starting to form in my mind, and I so hoped I was wrong.

"Okay, so we have more questions than answers," Beau said. "If we go back and push Porter on all this, I know he's gonna lawyer up. We'll need to come up with a different angle to work."

"We've already got one," I said. "Sarah Porter. I think she knows what happened in that playroom, and

maybe if she can admit that her brother had a hand in Everett's murder, we won't have to look to him for answers."

Heath and Beau nodded and we started to get up to pay our bill when Gil said, "What should I do?"

"Gil, I still need you to connect Mike Scoffland to Glenn Porter. Maybe if we can find some bad blood between them, we'll have a motive that will lead us to more evidence for Scoffland's murder. Oh, and I really want to know more about the Sandman. If Glenn Porter has had that planchette for all of these years, and if he knew where the board was, maybe he used it before now. See if there's been anything to hint that the Sandman has been around in Valdosta. Maybe there's been some freaky occurrences that no one's reported to the police, but maybe they've talked about online."

"That's a lot of work," Gil grumbled.

"Yes, but no one else could do it," I said, stroking his ego a tad.

"Fine," Gil said. "But you'd better bring me back some ice cream tonight."

"Cookies and cream?"

"Yeah, that sounds good. And don't forget the sprinkles."

We headed out, backtracking our way over to Sarah Porter's again. This time we made it all the way up the front steps and Breslow knocked. The door was opened by a woman wearing a maid's uniform, who looked warily at the deputy. "Yes?"

"Afternoon, ma'am. I'm Deputy Breslow. Is Miss Porter available?"

The maid put a hand to her heart and sighed with relief. "Oh, then she's all right?" she asked.

"All right?" Beau repeated. "I'm sorry, but I'd like to speak to Miss Porter. Is she in?"

"Oh, no, sir," the maid said. "She's at the hospital."

"The hospital?" I said. "Is she ill?"

The maid focused her large brown eyes on me. "Well, in a manner of speaking, ma'am. Miss Porter, sometimes, she don't get along so well, you know?" The maid tapped her forehead to give us an indication of Sarah's issues. "Anyhow, she checked herself into the psychiatric clinic the day before yesterday, and wouldn't y'all know it? There was some sorta riot and she got herself hurt. They took her to South Georgia to treat her, and she's supposed to be home later on today, which is why I'm here makin' sure everything's all neat and tidylike."

Heath and I exchanged a look. Sarah had been at the mental hospital when the Sandman had wreaked such havoc?

"What time is she due back here?" Beau asked.

"Oh, sir, I don't rightly know. Maybe in an hour or two? I could have her call you, but she might be tired. Maybe it's best if y'all call on her tomorrow?"

He tipped his hat and said, "Thank you, ma'am. It's nothing pressing, so we'll do just that."

With that, he turned and we followed him back to the car. "We're really going to wait until tomorrow to talk to her?" I asked once we'd loaded ourselves inside and Beau had started the car.

"Nope," he said. "But I didn't want the maid to let Sarah know we were coming back today to interview her. I'd rather show up at the hospital where she has some support if she gets upset about our questions, and doesn't already have a heads-up that we want to speak with her beforehand. She'll be more honest if she's off guard."

"She's pretty fragile, though, huh?" I said.

"Yes. And one of the sweetest, most caring people you'd ever want to meet. It really bothers me that Everett was found in her playroom. Wait till you meet her and you'll see what I mean."

We arrived at the hospital for the second time that day and headed inside. Breslow tipped his hat and inquired about Sarah and we were given a room number. We found it on the second floor next to the stairs, and the deputy knocked lightly before entering. "Miss Porter?" he said, opening the door a fraction.

"Yes?"

"It's Deputy Breslow, ma'am, and two others. May we come in?"

"Oh, Beau, is that you?" she said. I couldn't see Sarah, but I could hear her. She had a wavering, thin voice without much strength. "Come on in here and let me look at you!"

Heath and I followed Beau into the room and found Sarah sitting up in the bed. My first impression was that she was a tiny creature, no taller than five feet by my estimation, and reed thin. She was very pale as if she really didn't get out to enjoy the sun, and her hair was rather wispy, graying at the temples, and pulled

back into a severe-looking bun, but tufts of it had come loose, giving her a disheveled appearance.

She was fully clothed, and I swore she was even wearing shoes, but her legs were mostly covered with an afghan and there was a bandage on her head and a bruise under her right eye. "We heard you had some trouble yesterday," Beau said.

"Well, you heard right," she told him, pulling at the afghan to better cover herself. "I was just starting to feel better too when all that trouble started." Then she seemed to notice Heath and me and she added, "And who are these two, Beau? Did you bring friends to see me?"

I stepped forward and offered her my hand. "Hi, Miss Porter. I'm Mary Jane Holliday, and this is Heath Whitefeather. We're assisting Deputy Breslow on an investigation he's working on."

She took my hand, smiling and nodding, but then she stopped shaking my palm and looked closely at me. "Did you say Holliday?"

"Yes, ma'am."

She put a hand to her lips. "You're DeeDee's daughter."

"Yes, ma'am."

She stared at me and shook her head as if she couldn't believe she was looking at me. "You look so much like her," she finally said. Her hands trembled a bit and she attempted to cover it by pulling on her afghan again, then trying to smooth her hair. "I . . . I wasn't prepared to have guests," she said, the lightest blush touching her cheeks.

"We're so sorry to intrude," I told her.

"I loved your mother," she said suddenly. "Dearly. We were once very, very close, she and I." She looked at me again and I saw her eyes water. "I miss her," she said. "Life just hasn't been the same for me since she left, you know."

I blinked hard myself. Her words moved me and I could only nod. She reached out a tentative hand and put mine in hers. She closed her eyes and sighed, and it was such a sad and strange moment. I'd never met Sarah Porter—of that I was certain—but she had been so close to my mother and her love for her still clearly showed. After a moment she opened her eyes again and attempted a smile. Then she let go of my hand and fiddled with the buttons on her sweater.

Heath moved up next to me and extended his hand. "Nice to meet you, Miss Porter."

She seemed a bit startled by his sudden appearance at her side, but she took his hand and her smile broadened. "What a handsome man you are!" she exclaimed, then with a wink added, "Are you single?"

He laughed and leaned a little against me. "Sorry, ma'am. I'm taken."

She gave him a mock pout. "Just my luck."

We all laughed. And then Breslow came forward a little more and I knew it was time to get serious. "Miss Porter, we need to talk to you for a few minutes about something that could be a little distressing. Is that okay?"

"Of course, Beau," she said, and for emphasis she reached over to the bedside table and lifted a bottle of pills. "They gave me happy pills today."

I covered my mouth to hide a smile. What a sweet woman. "We need to ask you about your cousin Everett Sellers," Beau said.

A cloud came over Sarah's face and her smile vanished. "Oh, that," she said. "I take it you found him."

I was a little stunned by her statement. To me it meant she knew what'd happened to him. "We did," Beau said. "Can you tell us about that day, Sarah? The day he disappeared?"

She stared at her hands for a long time without answering and I wondered if she was going to. At last she lifted her gaze to me, and there were tears in her eyes. "Do you believe in signs?" she asked me.

"I do, Miss Porter," I said, because that was the truth.

She nodded. "I thought you might. Before she died, your mother came to me, Mary Jane, and she said that she would send me a sign someday. Something lovely. Something special. Something I couldn't miss. She told me that on the day that my sign came from her, it would be time to tell the truth. And here you are, in the flesh. Something lovely. Something special, and something I couldn't miss. It's time to tell the truth about Everett, and I'm prepared to do that, but, Mary Jane, I have to ask you . . . are you quite sure you want to hear it?"

I nearly faltered and my heart pounded in my chest. My mother was there that day. I could see it in Sarah's eyes. I swallowed hard, shored up my courage, and said, "Yes."

"Your mother figures into the story," she added, as if that would make me change my answer.

"I know she does," I told her. That was the truth, too.

She nodded and went back to focusing on her hands, which continued to tug nervously at the buttons on her sweater. "Everett was an evil, evil young man," she began in a voice barely above a whisper. "He liked to cause pain in others. Especially me. The first summer he came to visit, I was seven and he was thirteen. He seemed to sense that I was weak and he looked for many ways to taunt me. Torture me. Humiliate me that summer, and as if that weren't bad enough, he began to touch me in places and force me to touch him in places that I knew were bad. Worst of all, he had my brother watch."

I balled my hands into fists. The thought of a seven-year-old as small and frail as Sarah Porter must have been, being sexually abused like that while her brother stood by and watched was so horrible, I could hardly stand it.

Sarah paused for a moment, as if the memory were still so close, it hurt her physically to recall it. And then she continued. "It went on like that for weeks, but at last he was sent home and I hoped it was for good, but the next summer he came back, only this time he brought this terrible thing with him. It was a board game, he said, and with it he could control the universe."

Sarah lifted her chin to look at me. "By that time, Mary Jane, your mother had become my dearest friend. I think she saw how fragile I'd become, and she was such a kind girl, always nurturing sick and injured birds and bunnies back to good health. I think she saw me as an injured little creature too, and certainly I was,

because by that time, my brother had taken to touching me in bad places too."

I sucked in a breath and Heath wrapped an arm around my waist. Sarah must have been so defenseless against the horrors inflicted upon her at such a young age.

"Anyway," she went on, "DeeDee began spending more and more time at my house. I think she sensed that I was in trouble and she did her best to protect me. And for a while, she did. Although I never told her what was going on, she somehow sensed that my brother was doing things to me, and she threatened him by saying that she'd tell my mother if he didn't leave me alone, and you knew your mother. Even at eight years old she was a force to be reckoned with.

"Well, Glenn stopped preying on me, but then Everett came to visit again. He'd begged his parents to come back and stay the summer with us, and as they had more money than even we had, my mother obliged.

"At first I thought that maybe things would be okay between us, because he gave me a present on the first day he was here. It was a beautifully painted board with a silver disk that he said was magic. He said he'd show me how to play with it if I was nice to him, and I was nice to him; I got him cookies and milk, and told him how smart he looked in his new summer clothes.

"I was wary, of course, but I wanted so desperately for things to be normal that all I could think to do was please him so that he wouldn't hurt me again. And for several days and nights things were normal. But then, one afternoon while your mother and I were in my lit-

tle playroom, having tea, the silver planchette that came with the board began to move.

"Your mother and I sat there, scared to death and too frightened to even breathe! The planchette swirled around, and around, and around on the board, always moving in a particular pattern. First to the *S*, then to the *A*, then to the *N*, and on and on. I don't know who said the word out loud first, if it was me or your mother, but one of us eventually spoke its name. The second that happened, the room erupted with an energy so intense, it knocked us both over. We were scrambling to our feet when Everett suddenly burst into the room, laughing, and with him was my brother, but it wasn't my brother. It was something possessed. 'Hello, kiddos,' Glenn said, but it wasn't his voice—it was something else entirely. And then Everett grabbed me, and my brother grabbed your mother, and they raped us both."

I felt the blood drain from my face, and I tasted bile at the back of my throat while my knees buckled. Heath held me up and attempted to move me over to a chair, but I resisted and forced myself to stay put. If my mother could endure that unspeakable violation, then I could damn well endure hearing about it.

If Sarah noticed my reaction, she gave no indication. She merely continued to stare at her hands and recite what happened. "Afterward, your mother and I were left alone to clean ourselves up. There was blood, you see, and tears. Everett took the board and the planchette with him, and as he left the room, he let me know that he could call up that evil spirit anytime he liked.

"DeeDee told him she was going to tell our parents

what he and Glenn had done, but Everett slapped her across the face and said that if either of us ever told anyone, he'd have his evil spirit kill us, and we had no doubt that it would. He also told her that he expected her to come back the next day, because, as he put it, 'Why should Glenn have all the fun?'"

I shuddered and felt sick to my stomach, and beyond that, an anger so intense it was frightening churned in the middle of my chest, but I dared not move or speak and interrupt the story. I had to know all of it. For myself and for Mama, I had to hear the full story.

Sarah took a deep sad breath then, and continued. "DeeDee helped me clean myself up even before she tended to herself, and then she ran home, and I knew by the way that she hugged me at the door that she never planned on coming back. And for several days she did stay away, but then one morning she came to the door, and I took one look at her and I knew something terrible had been happening.

"She said that the evil spirit, the Sandman, that Everett had called forward had been coming to her at night. He'd nearly killed her twice."

Tears streamed down my face. I had never imagined my mother had been through something so horrible, and it destroyed me that she'd endured all of that at such a young age.

"That day we hatched a plan," Sarah said. For the first time since she'd started her story, she looked up at Beau. "We never intended for anyone to get hurt. We simply wanted to get the Ouija board away from Ever-

ett and destroy it. So, during my mother's party, while everyone out in the yard played croquet, DeeDee and I snuck up to Everett's room and gave it a thorough search. We found the board, but not the planchette, so we brought it down to the playroom and were talking about how to destroy it, but DeeDee said she was worried that destroying the board wouldn't be enough. We needed the planchette, she said, because she was convinced that it was the true source of Everett's power over his evil spirit.

"Somehow we needed to trick him into telling us where it was. I told her I knew just how to do it, and I hurried up the stairs to my older brother Jack's room.

"Jack was Mother's favorite, but he was hardly a decent young man. He spent most of his short youth addicted to drugs. They would make him loopy and you could ask him anything when he was high and he'd tell you. I thought feeding some of my brother's drugs to Everett would make him confess where he'd hidden the planchette. I knew that Jack hid his drugs in his room, which we were never allowed to go into, but I risked it on that day because we were desperate, and found a stash of little white pills hidden under his mattress. I brought these down and DeeDee and I then mashed them into a powder and put them in the sugar bowl of my tea set, mixing it with a fair amount of sugar to hide the powder. Then we went to the kitchen and made a batch of very tart lemonade, telling our maid to pass a note to Everett when she saw him. We'd asked Everett to meet us in the playroom, but he had to come alone.

"We then went back to the playroom and hoped that he obeyed the note. DeeDee and I knew we were no match for my brother and Everett—drugs or no drugs, we'd be in real trouble if they both showed up—but to our relief, Everett did arrive alone, wearing a sick smile and toting a croquet mallet.

"We offered him some lemonade and he took a sip. When he made a face, and complained about how sour it was, DeeDee calmly offered him some sugar, which she spooned into his cup. She and I held our breath as Everett drank down the lemonade. It was a hot day outside and he was sweaty from croquet."

Sarah paused to take a sip of water from a glass at her bedside table. The irony of the cup and its little red rose wasn't lost on me. "Anyway," she continued. "I'm sure DeeDee and I expected the drugs to immediately take effect on Everett, but they didn't, well, at least not in the way we expected. Instead of getting sleepy and dopey, he became agitated and angry. To this day I don't know what drugs we gave him, but they worked against us, not for us. I'll never forget the way he turned to the door of the playroom and shut it, locking us in. He then demanded that we take off all our clothes.

"DeeDee refused and told him that she'd scream, and that's when he reached into his back pocket and pulled out the planchette. He waved it at us and laughed when we cried out and scuttled back. He told us that all he had to do was say the Sandman's name, which he did three times, and in front of our eyes Everett turned into a demon."

Sarah shuddered against the memory, and I recalled the face of the demon captured very briefly by Beau's camera. "He came at us," Sarah continued, her voice barely audible. "He attacked me first and bit my arm so cruelly, I thought I'd black out from the pain. And then he was choking me . . . and then . . ."

Sarah stopped speaking and I had to work over and over again to hold back a sob. My poor, poor mother. What horrors had she endured that summer?

"And then?" Beau asked gently.

Sarah closed her eyes, whispered, "I'm so sorry, Dee," and then more clearly she said, "And then DeeDee killed Everett with the croquet mallet."

Chapter 14

Heath took me from the room and held me as I cried and cried. My tears were bitter, and heartbroken, and angry, and so, so sad. To my knowledge, my mother had never mentioned anything to anyone about what'd happened, because if Daddy had ever learned what Glenn Porter had done to her when she was just a child, he would've killed him dead.

Finally Beau came out and told us the rest of the story. "She says that after DeeDee struck Everett with the mallet, she swung the thing again and busted the planchette. The girls then kept their heads enough to pick up some of the evidence, the planchette and the sugar bowl, and DeeDee snuck out of the house with them while Sarah planted the mallet in her brother's room, then joined everyone outside just in time for lunch, which is why no one noticed her missing. Later, Sarah says she purposely spilled some punch on her

dress, and her mother took her to her bedroom to pick out something new to wear, and that's when they both stumbled on the body of Everett, or at least that's what Regina Porter thought.

"Sarah told her mother that she'd seen Everett and Glenn fighting earlier in the day, which just by coincidence they had been, and Regina went up the stairs to look for her son, only to find the bloody mallet in his room and assume that Glenn Porter was responsible for murdering Everett."

"That's some pretty clever thinking on the part of an eight-year-old," I said, still feeling weak in the knees.

"It is," Beau agreed. "But Sarah has always been the brightest of the Porters. She skipped several grades from what I remember and had a full ride to some fancy school up North when she had her first nervous breakdown and became something of an invalid."

"I wonder if Sarah's issues had less to do with a weak mind and more to do with the struggle to hold inside all those terrible secrets and memories," I said.

"What happened to her and DeeDee should never happen to any little girls," Heath said bitterly. He looked mad enough to kill someone himself.

"So Regina Porter thought her son had killed Everett," I said, getting back to the story. "Wouldn't he have just denied it?"

"I'm sure he did, but whatever Regina believed, she never confessed it to Sarah. Instead, she shut closed the door to the playroom, and told Sarah to sit on her bed and not to utter one single word. About twenty minutes later, a worker arrived to board up the door leading to

the playroom and cover it in drywall. He worked for several hours, and Sarah watched him from the bed. He never looked at her and he never spoke to her, and he never asked her why he was covering up a door in her room—he just did the job, painted the wall, and left. The next morning, Regina opened the door of Sarah's room accompanied by Sheriff Maskill—who was sheriff before Kogan—and Regina told the sheriff that her daughter Sarah had the flu and had spent much of the previous day in bed. By this time Sarah was catching on that her mother was telling people Everett had gone missing, not that he'd been killed inside Porter Manor. The sheriff didn't even ask Sarah if she'd seen Everett; he just nodded to her and they left her alone.

"She says that a day or so later, she overheard Regina talking to DeeDee's mother. She told her that DeeDee was not allowed to come back to Porter Manor, and she was to have nothing to do with her daughter or the family ever again.

"Sarah isn't sure if Regina ever knew the real truth. More than likely she didn't want any of Sarah's friends in the house where they might smell something foul coming through the wall. The staff was also dismissed under the pretense that Regina thought one of them might be responsible for Everett's disappearance, and if she couldn't identify which servant it might've been, she was going to fire them all.

"The family existed in that big house for over a year before they hired any new staff. She says that's how long it took for the smell to finally leave her room."

I wiped my eyes and sniffled loudly. "She had no

choice," I insisted. I meant my mother and Breslow seemed to know it.

"Of course she didn't, Mary Jane."

My lip trembled. "This is gonna kill Daddy."

Breslow was twirling the brim of his hat between his fingers. "I don't see any reason it should get back to Mr. Holliday."

I looked at him hopefully. "You won't tell him?"

Breslow eyed me sympathetically. "I think it's like Glenn Porter said: if there's no body, there's no crime." Then he made a point to glance at his phone. "Would you look at that? I forgot to hit the RECORD button, and anyway, I didn't read Sarah her rights, so her confession wouldn't be admissible, and anything you two overheard is just hearsay. No, I think that Everett Sellers is gonna remain a missing-persons case from here on out, unless a body shows up, which hopefully it won't."

I wanted to hug Breslow, but settled for putting my hand on his arm and mouthing, "Thank you."

We waited in the hallway for a bit until I had collected myself, and then we slowly made our way down the corridor.

Just when we got outside, my own cell rang. It was Gilley. "Yo!" Gil said. "I think I hit pay dirt."

I put the phone on speaker and the three of us huddled close. "Go for it," I told him.

"Okay, so, first I looked into Scoffland. Now, according to tax records, he did a little work for Glenn Porter about five years ago, but it was a small job, and he was paid five grand and that was the end of it. I was hoping

for something more current, but there's nothing. There're also no phone calls logged between Porter's phone and Scoffland's."

Breslow cocked an eyebrow. "How were you able to get phone records?" he asked sharply.

I waved at him impatiently. "If he tells you, you won't like it, Deputy, so how about, just for the sake of putting Porter behind bars for Scoffland's murder, we ignore that for now?"

Breslow frowned but gave a reluctant nod. "Okay, go on," he said to Gilley.

"I was ready to stop at the small job Scoffland did for Glenn five years ago, but the man kept the best tax records I've ever seen, so I went back in history looking for anything that might connect him to the Porters, and wouldn't you know it? Up until about fifteen years ago, Scoffland submitted annual invoices to them for the exact amount of twenty thousand dollars a year."

"Fifteen years ago," Breslow said. "That's around the time that Regina Porter died."

"Wanna know when Scoffland began submitting invoices?" Gil sang.

"Let me guess," said Heath. "Nineteen seventy-one."

"Ding, ding, ding!" said Gil. "We have a winner! And by winner I mean that in August of nineteen seventy-one there was an invoice for six hundred dollars, which was promptly paid, and about a week later, there was a second invoice for twenty thousand dollars, and that was also promptly paid."

I gasped. "He was the worker who covered up the door to the playroom!"

"That's what I was thinking," Gil said. "He must've figured out that Everett was behind the door he sealed over at Porter Manor on the day that Everett disappeared, and he blackmailed Mr. and Mrs. Porter for years."

"So what was the purpose of going to the house the night he was murdered?" I asked. "If he was going to try to blackmail Glenn, then why would he uncover the door, open it up, put the planchette there, and cover it back up?"

"That's for you fools to figure out," said Gilley. "But hold off on that until I tell you what else I found."

"What?" we all said in unison.

"Well, I looked into anything spooky that might've been going on in Valdosta which could explain the Sandman's presence—"

"We don't need that anymore, Gil," I interrupted. Heath eyed me curiously and I explained, "The planchette was destroyed back in 'seventy-one. Sarah said Mama destroyed it. . . ." My voice trailed off as I realized what I'd just said.

"Destroyed it?" Gil said. "Then how did it show up in the playroom?"

"Hold on," I said, quickly tapping my screen to get back to my photos. After pulling up the one of the planchette, I said, "This is either the same planchette or a copy good enough to call the Sandman up."

"Oh, it's an original," Gil said. "Remember, I showed it to my historian buddy, and we were able to see the faint outline of Padesco's signature carved into the silver. If it weren't for the dents around the rim of the crystal, the thing would've been in mint condition."

I used my fingers to expand the image and do a close-up of the planchette. Sure enough there were small nicks and a few dents to the silver near where the crystal was. "So, maybe Mama destroyed the crystal, but not the planchette, and that was good enough to lock away the Sandman," I said.

"It would've been," Gil said. "According to Padesco's journal, which I've had a great time reading through, it takes a perfectly unflawed crystal with fairly soft vibrations to be able to create a window big enough for something as powerful as the Sandman. The original crystal would have been amethyst, no less than sixteen or seventeen carats, and it would have had to have been absolutely flawless, which is a seriously rare find."

"So someone duplicated the gem," I said.

"Yeah, but who?" Heath said.

"Don't know," Gilley said. "But I know who it's not."

"Who is it not?" the three of us said in unison.

"Sarah Porter."

I wanted to say "Of course," but I was curious about Gilley's reasoning, so I said, "Why do you say that?"

"About eight months ago a maid who worked for her started posting videos to her Facebook page showing objects being tossed around Sarah's house of their own free will. In one of the videos, you can even see Sarah Porter huddling under her piano, crying hysterically. Shortly after that, the maid quit, saying the house had suddenly become haunted and she wanted no part. A little while after that, Sarah began checking herself into the mental clinic for long weekends. At one

point her house was even listed for sale, but no one wanted it, so it came back off the market. Oh, and I also found a power of attorney for Sarah held by her brother, so if you guys think he's trying to hurt her with the Sandman, I'd make sure she's got some protection until you can shut that thing down."

The three of us looked back toward the hospital. Sarah hadn't mentioned anything about that, at least not with me and Heath in the room. "Did she say anything about the Sandman coming back to you, Beau?"

"No," he said, shaking his head and looking a little shocked.

"That son of a bitch Porter," Heath hissed, a flash of anger returning to his eyes.

But then the most random thought came into my head about an e-mail Linda had sent me a year earlier when she was struggling so much to deal with her husband's affair and the divorce. There was a line in that e-mail that played across my mind's eye, and it changed all of my thinking. "What?" Heath asked me, and I realized I'd been staring down the street as so much began to come together.

"Gil," I said, already heading toward Beau's car.

"Yeah?"

"We'll have to call you back." With that, I hung up and motioned for the boys to get in without any further explanation because I needed to work through the sequence of events on my own. I pointed in the direction I wanted to go and Beau pulled out of the space. It took us only two minutes to get to the destination and I got out of the car, shrugging out of my fishing vest, and

tossing it on the seat. I didn't feel like I needed it for what I was about to do. I then stood for a moment looking up at the giant elm tree that I swore I'd stood under just a few days earlier. "Where are we?" Heath asked as he came up next to me. I noticed he'd taken off his vest too.

"My grandparents' house."

"Looks empty," he told me.

"It's owned by a nice couple. He's an administrator at the hospital and she works there as a nurse." I turned slightly and saw the giant building we'd just come from just over the trees to my right. "I met them the last time I was home and missing Mama. Behind here there's a trail that leads down to the river, and she and I used to take long walks together there."

I didn't explain more than that; I simply headed up the side of the house to where the yard met the woods and the trail. The three of us walked in silence and for the second time since I'd been home, I felt the spirit of my mother come close to me and wrap me in the most comforting, loving quilt of energy.

I spoke to her in my mind as I walked, telling her how sorry I was for all that she'd been through as a little girl. How proud I was of how brave she'd been. How amazed and blessed I felt to have had her as a mother. The whole time I thought she did nothing but listen and love me, and for just a moment, for just a tiny second, I forgot that she had crossed over, and believed that she was there with me, walking to a place we used to often visit.

At last we arrived at a large boulder that butted up

next to a giant elm. I climbed up the boulder just as I'd watched my mother do every time we came here. "What's in here?" she'd say, leaning in toward a hollowed-out section of the tree's trunk. I'd laugh and take wild guesses. "A bunny! A plate of cookies! A magic carpet!"

Mama would lean her head in the large hole and pretend to look around, and then she'd pull it out and say, "Why, no, love dumplin'! It's not any of that!" She'd then put her hand in really far, which told me the hollow was fairly deep, and then she'd pull her fist out, open her palm, and there would be all sorts of individually wrapped candies. "All I found in there were these!"

I loved coming here with her. She always made each moment with her feel magical.

"Hey, now," Heath said with a bit of alarm. "Deputy, you see that? Is that blood?"

I closed my eyes on top of that boulder, the memory of my mother atop it fading as I thought about poor Linda. I knew she'd come here. I knew Mama had told her all about what'd happened that day, how she'd hidden the planchette in this hollowed-out tree, but she'd kept that sugar dish on her vanity to remind her of what she'd done. Of the life she'd taken. Of the penance she'd have to pay one day.

It made me remember something else. Something a bit out of context that now made total sense to me. Not long into Mama's illness I'd overheard Daddy yelling at her. He almost never raised his voice to her, so it was particularly startling to me. He'd yelled, "Goddammit, Madelyn! Why don't you fight? You're just giving up, and I can't lose you! I can't! *So fight*!"

He'd yelled that last part so loud at her, his anger fueled by his desperation to keep her with us. But even from the early days of her diagnosis, she'd seemed resigned to the fact that she was dying. That there was little hope. I'd never acknowledged that because it was too painful to consider, but now I knew that it was true.

My mother had died of cancer, but it was the guilt that'd killed her. Guilt over an act of self-defense that she could never forgive herself for.

For a moment I ignored Heath and Breslow, who were busy examining the drops of blood littering the trail, and instead I poked my head into the hollow and saw something catch a small ray of sunlight that was peeking in behind me. Reaching down, I lifted out several pieces of the smashed crystal and the wooden cigar box my mother had kept the planchette in. Inside the box were a dozen small refrigerator magnets in the shape of fruit. A pineapple, a banana, an apple. I remembered what I'd told little DeeDee about getting some magnets, and I wondered if in some strange and almost magical way our two worlds really had met between two planes of existence where the laws of time and space didn't apply, but words spoken between two souls would have weight and measure and meaning when we went back to our separate realities.

Had DeeDee taken my advice and covered the broken planchette with them, ensuring that the Sandman would remain locked down? There was a part of me that truly hoped it'd gone that way.

I set the cigar box with the magnets back inside the hollow. Then I examined the pieces of the smashed

crystal, which were beautiful, and it was hard to imagine something once so perfect had been part of such a terrible instrument.

"Look at this," Heath said, pointing to a large stick with blood on it.

"Linda was attacked here," Breslow said.

"You think Glenn Porter could've done it?" Heath suggested, not noticing that I was shaking my head.

Breslow too shook his head. "No, couldn't have been him, Heath. We were in his office at the time she was attacked."

"Well, then who?"

I cleared my throat and Heath looked up at me.

"Whoa," he said, seeing the fragmented gem in my hand. "What'cha got there, babe?"

"The original crystal from the planchette. Mama hid it here and told only one person in the whole world what it was and where it was hidden."

"Who?"

I jumped down from the boulder and said, "I'll tell you, but first we need to head over to Glenn Porter's office before it's too late."

Breslow insisted that he call in the scene of Linda's crime to one of his other deputies before we ran back to the car. I knew he didn't like to leave all that evidence out in the open, but I felt a sense of urgency that made me push him to heed me.

He drove quite fast through the streets, which I was grateful for, and still it took us a bit to reach Porter's office, which further cemented my theory that Breslow was right and Glenn couldn't have been the one to at-

tack Linda. She was attacked probably right before or even during the time we were interviewing him, and Wells was alerted to the scene while we were on our way to Sarah's house. Porter couldn't have attacked Linda and gotten back to his office in time for us to interview him, and he certainly couldn't have left his office and attacked her before we reached Sarah's house. When we were nearly to Porter's office, Gilley called. "I hacked into Scoffland's bank records. There's a deposit to his account for ten thousand dollars the day before he was murdered. I don't have the corresponding invoice yet, but I'm working on it."

"Don't sweat it," I told him. "I already know who paid him."

"Are you going to fill me in?" he asked.

"Yes. Tonight, when I bring you that ice-cream cone."

"Don't forget the sprinkles!"

"Okay, Gil, gotta go." I hung up as we had just arrived at Porter's office, and no sooner were we out of the car and dashing up the first set of stairs than the police radio in Beau's car crackled with noise. He hurried back to the car and listened through the open window, then took the mic, yelled into it before throwing it down, and took off running up the steps at a much more urgent speed. He passed Heath and me without even pausing and we chased after him, hampered slightly by the rush to put on our vests. "What's going on?" I yelled at the deputy's back.

"Dispatch just got a nine-one-one call from inside this building!" he yelled back.

I stopped in my tracks. I had an inkling what was

going on inside and realized how unprepared we were. "Breslow, *stop*!" I shouted.

Heath eyed me over his shoulder, saw the look of panic on my face, and moved faster up the stairs to grab the deputy by the shoulder. "Let go!" Breslow yelled.

Heath tightened his grip and said, "Wait!" Then he turned to me expectantly.

"We need spikes!" I called, turning back toward the car. "Heath, don't let him go in there without me!"

While Heath held tight to Beau, I raced to the car and grabbed the duffel from the backseat. It was insanely heavy, but I had no time to open it and grab as many stakes as we might need, so I just threw it over my shoulder, dug deep, and began to power my way back up the many stairs. As I was about midway to Heath and Breslow, who was still trying to tug out of Heath's grasp, there was a terrified scream from inside.

Breslow shoved Heath aside and dashed up the remaining steps, pausing only a moment to kick the door in and dart inside.

Heath came down the stairs to me, grabbed the duffel, and pulled me along up the remaining steps.

Just as we crested the last stair before the ones leading to the front porch, something came whizzing out of the house straight at us. We ducked in the nick of time, but Heath didn't dive quite fast enough. A planchette struck him just above his right eye and he lost his balance and fell to the side, landing hard on the stakes. There was a sickening crunch and he cried out in pain.

Unfortunately, he was still gripping my hand and

effectively pulled me with him, and I landed on him. I scrambled to my feet and put my hands on his side because he was moaning and curling his knees up in pain. "Ohmigod! Ohmigod! Heath! Heath!"

His eyes were squeezed shut and he was hissing through his teeth, but he managed to roll off the duffel, shove it weakly toward me, and gasp, "Help . . . Breslow. . . ."

I shook my head; how could I leave him? But then the front door to the office slammed shut before it opened and slammed, then opened and slammed, and soon it was joined by a dozen other doors.

The Sandman had come for another visit.

Chapter 15

"Go!" Heath said, his shaking hands trying to pull on the zipper to the duffel.

I slid mine under his and unzipped the bag. Grabbing four or five spikes with each hand, I said, "I'll be right back."

Heath wheezed and tried to get to his feet, and I realized he hadn't meant to send me alone inside; he was going to try to come with me, even though he'd clearly broken a few ribs and was having a hard time breathing. "Stay here!" I yelled at him, giving him the fiercest look I could muster.

Still, he shook his head but I simply got up and ran to the remaining stairs. I crouched low near the door, watching it open and slam, open and slam, and counted the beats, trying to time my decision to rush it.

It opened and I was just about to duck through when another planchette came whizzing out with all

the force of a ninja star. I pulled my head back just in time, and then clenched my jaw, determined to get my ass inside.

I counted four more beats, then made my move. Launching myself through the door, I ducked and rolled to the side, nearly crashing right into Breslow's unconscious body.

Over my head planchettes were whizzing past us and striking the walls. Under the desk I saw Chloe, her eyes wide as saucers as she trembled and hugged her knees. She looked at me with such fear, and I motioned to her to stay put.

Turning away from her, I reached for the leg of a chair and pulled it down on the ground. I then pulled it in front of Breslow to give him a shield against the onslaught of planchettes, and then I turned my focus to the office near the end of the hall. There seemed to be a great deal of shouting going on in there and I knew that things were about to reach a point of no return.

Gripping the stakes, I pulled myself on my elbows down the hallway. Planchettes were zipping out of the room, and periodically there was the sound of one making a striking sound and a loud cry right after, along with the thundering noise of the slamming doors and objects striking the walls.

Inside there were horrific screams, some high-pitched, others a little lower, but all of them terrible. I paused midway down the hallway and pulled a metal planchette from the wall where it'd struck. It had an empty loop that was just big enough for the largest piece of the broken amethyst I'd pulled out of the hol-

low. With trembling fingers, I set down my spikes before taking out the broken-off piece of crystal and placed the piece in the middle of the planchette. Next, I held it there with my fingers and extended my arms fully away from my body so that the planchette wouldn't be hovering over the magnets. After taking a deep breath, I closed my eyes and allowed all the fear, anger, and anguish I'd had to deal with over the past few days course through my energy until I practically pulsed with emotion. I then gathered all that emotion and channeled it straight down through my arms all the way to my fingertips and into the planchette. My fingers and the improvised planchette vibrated with energy, while I simply waited for the Sandman to notice.

Abruptly the slamming doors and whizzing planchettes halted.

And then something stepped into the hallway and I trembled anew. A huge shadow appeared from the doorway, and within its darkness I saw two red glowing eyes.

"Miss me?" I asked, fear now overriding all other emotions because I had no idea if my improvised plan would work.

The most horrible laughter filled the hallway and I found myself close to abandoning my plan and making a run for it. But I'd come this far, and if Mama could face down this demon as an eight-year-old, then, dammit, I could, too.

The Sandman considered me for a long moment, his beady eyes greedy with a deadly kind of lust. "What's the matter?" I asked to taunt him, while holding the

amplified energy of the planchette out toward him and willing all that anger and fear and anguish to ratchet it up a notch. I knew the old crystal and all my emotion were too much temptation for him to resist. "Are ya chicken?"

There was a roar and the shadow moved so fast, I was barely able to register anything more than a blur of darkness as he dived straight at me. In the second before he hit me, I clenched my jaw, closed my eyes, slammed the planchette against my chest, and in my mind's eye called up the image of my mother cradling me in her lap, filling me with all of her love and protection. In the next instant, I felt the full force of the Sandman hit me dead center in the chest, exactly where I was holding the planchette.

The weight of the demon was beyond description. It felt as if my very soul were being crushed. I knew I was protected by a layer of magnets and the energy of my mother's love, but his power was immense and I could feel myself fading under the pressure.

Gritting my teeth, I called out to her in my mind's eye. *Mama!* I cried. In an instant I felt her. Like a beacon in the darkness, she was there, her energy joining with mine as we fought the Sandman together.

Still, the most difficult thing I've ever done in my life was to reach down with one hand and grab hold of the spikes I'd set next to me, then lift them and lay them flat against the planchette on my chest. Immediately the pressure lessened and I was able to weakly come fully to my senses and take a deep breath. I'd trapped the Sandman between layers of magnets, and as long

as I could hold him this way, he couldn't get out. But there was another force here in the house, one that I'd have to deal with as well, and I hadn't yet figured out how to do that.

I lay there for a bit, panting, and then I managed to call out to the person responsible for bringing the Sandman back. "Sarah," I gasped. "You're in there, right?"

"So you've figured it all out, have you?" she asked, her voice so sad.

I was still so weak from the blow of the Sandman's full force that I felt I needed a minute to collect myself. At the edge of my energy, Mama hovered protectively, but I could tell that her energy was dissipating too. It'd cost her to come from the other side and help me against the Sandman, and I didn't know how long she could keep herself near me. Weakly I got to my knees, still holding the planchette at my chest, and shuffled down the hallway to the open door of Glenn Porter's office. Thinking I could get a breather by having Sarah tell me her side, I said, "I haven't figured out all of it yet. Why don't you tell me and then we can see what to do about Everett?"

"He's dead," she said, and I wondered whether she meant Everett or Glenn.

"I see," I said. "So, tell me what happened."

"How did you trap the Sandman?" she asked me, avoiding the question.

"I've got him stuck between layers of magnets, but I'm not sure if I can hold him for long."

"You'll need to destroy the crystal," she said, and I knew she meant the one she'd fashioned to fit into the

planchette she'd discovered in the tree and was holding in her hands right that very moment.

"Yep," I told her. "Tell me about what happened to make you go looking for it, Sarah."

I heard her sigh, but then she said, "You have to understand, Mary Jane, growing up in that house, it was the worst kind of existence. My father was impossibly cruel, my mother was distant and cold, my older brother was a drug addict who died recklessly, and my sister was a self-absorbed narcissist. And my brother Glenn, well, he was in a class by himself.

"He was as cruel as Everett ever was, but far more cunning. Whatever Glenn wanted, Glenn got. The only thing standing in his way was me, and the only weapon I had to use against him was that I knew what'd happened to Everett, and I'd told my mother that Glenn had killed him.

"Glenn was locked away for several years because Mother believed him a wicked boy who'd nearly brought the worst kind of scandal to our door. I learned that he had no idea Everett was even sealed up in our house. How could he with his room so far from mine? Still, I managed to let him know that if he ever touched me again, I would lead the sheriff right to Everett's body, and I would point the finger at him as the killer. I asked him whom the sheriff would believe, Glenn or me, and he seemed to understand that I was not someone to be trifled with.

"Still, a few years after Everett died, the doors in our house began to slam shut on their own. It happened a few times a week, but it got more intense over the

years, and our family grew very afraid. The door to my room slammed most often, and I begged my mother to let me move down the hall. She allowed it, but then that door began to slam too. I think Mother and I both knew it was Everett, and eventually Glenn figured it out too.

"Not long after that, I discovered Glenn in the woods behind our house playing with a Ouija board, and after spying on him I realized he was actually communicating with Everett. It wasn't long before our house became a constant source of violent spectral activity.

"Glenn used the planchette to control Everett, who'd become something so monstrous and powerful that for a long time I wondered if it weren't the Sandman come back. I considered going to the police, but Glenn always threatened me by saying that if I ever went to the sheriff and told them that Glenn had killed Everett, he'd really let Everett loose.

"What Glenn did to us on a daily basis with Everett, however, was enough to keep all of us in check, even Mother. If Glenn were punished for something, my mother's favorite china would smash to the floor. The day Molly was given a new car, she was tripped by an unseen force on her way out the door and broke her ankle. And me, well, Glenn and Everett tortured me most of all.

"My toys were routinely broken, my doors slammed incessantly, and my things went missing. One night my father actually attempted to intervene on my behalf— the only act of kindness he'd ever shown me—and he told Glenn that he knew he was controlling the ghost

in our house and that if he didn't stop it, he'd throw Glenn out. We found our father at the base of the stairs the next morning, the back of his skull smashed in and his neck broken.

"Glenn never said as much, but I know he had Everett kill our father.

"Then, after Mother died, Glenn moved out to start up his own company. Which failed miserably of course. And when he was nearly out of money, he came to me, but after all those years of torture, I wouldn't lend him a dime. I'd been very careful with my share of our inheritance, and I still held a fifty percent stake in the family home. All of the taxes were paid out of my share, but I levied liens against the property for his share just to make sure he didn't get off scot-free.

"Glenn, however, found a way to get to me despite my best efforts to keep him at bay. I've always had a bit of difficulty knowing what's real and what's not. Glenn used that against me and ratcheted up Everett's activity. Everett became very violent, his power increasing as my brother funneled his hatred of me into the spirit. At last I moved out of the house, hoping that would give me some peace, but Everett simply followed me to my new home, and one morning I snapped. Glenn had me committed and while I was in the mental clinic he won a judgment for power of attorney over my affairs. He then put our family estate up for sale, something I never wanted to have happen, knowing what evil and what skeletons lay within those walls, but I was powerless to stop it.

"And, perhaps it was out of desperation that I even-

tually concluded that I had to fight fire with fire. If my brother could use Everett against me, perhaps I could use something even more powerful against him. That's when I got the idea to call upon the Sandman. That very day I happened to bump into Linda Chadwick at the grocery store, and I formed a little plan.

"DeeDee and Linda had been so close, I wondered if Dee had told Linda where she'd hidden Everett's planchette. I knew she'd destroyed the crystal, but I wondered if I could repair the planchette. If only I could find it, perhaps I could use it to control the Sandman against my brother so that he never, ever thought of using Everett to harm me again.

"I took Linda out for lunch the next day. She was having a rough time of it with that divorce going on, and I slipped a little pill into her drink. By that time I was well familiar with pills. She told me everything, how DeeDee had confessed to her that she was terrified your daddy would know she wasn't a virgin, and the ordeal we'd been put through at the hands of my wicked family. She'd told Linda where she'd hidden the planchette, and that she'd made sure it could never harm anyone again."

I squeezed the planchette at my chest a little tighter. I'd remembered the e-mail from Linda saying she'd had lunch with a friend named Sarah, but that she'd had too much to drink and she'd had the most terrible hangover the next day. She'd specifically said she barely remembered the lunch at all, and she'd hoped she hadn't embarrassed herself.

"I found the planchette rather easily, hidden in that

tree, and because the old crystal had been broken by DeeDee, I began to experiment with new crystals I had made especially to fit the hole. It took a little while, but finally, I had the perfect flawless gem."

I thought it ironic that Sarah didn't realize the largest piece of the old crystal probably would have worked if she'd tried it. The chunk of crystal was broken, for sure, but it still held no inclusions within its depths, and hadn't it just worked perfectly well for me a few moments earlier? Still, I didn't want to comment and throw Sarah off track with her confession, so I kept quiet and let her continue.

"By this time of course my brother was well into his next scheme," she said. "I discovered he was angling to buy back our family home at a significant discount from Christine Bigelow. He thought that by setting Everett loose upon the construction workers, Christine would be unable to renovate it, and Glenn could then buy it back for less than he'd sold it for, make a tidy profit, then parcel off all the land without having to include me in the deal.

"I, on the other hand, wanted Porter Manor back too, as I had never agreed to sell it. Glenn had done that while he'd had the power to do what he wanted with my affairs. I thought Glenn's plan was actually quite bright, and if I acted quickly, I thought there was a way to get my brother out of my affairs once and for all and get Porter Manor back as well. If workers were scared off by Everett, imagine how terrified they'd be if the Sandman began to haunt the halls. So I called up the man who had originally sealed up the room and asked

him to unseal it, let me into the playroom, then seal it right back up again. I discovered in playing with the planchette, which will work with any board, really, that all you have to do is say the Sandman's name three times and, as long as your will is strong, he appears to do your bidding. At least initially. Like Everett I learned that after a time, you don't even need to hold the planchette to summon or control the demon, but that is the place from where he emerges. Like a genie from a bottle he springs to life from the planchette."

"So, knowing your brother would tear down that wall to get into the room to see what you'd hidden there, you planted the planchette in the playroom," I said. "And had Scoffland reseal the room. Once Glenn entered the playroom, you'd unleash the demon. Was that how you planned it to go?"

"Yes. That's it exactly," she said.

"How'd you get Glenn to agree to go over there?"

"It was so simple," she said with a sigh. "I called my brother and told him a lie, that I'd alerted the police to where Everett's body was located, in a sealed room hidden in my old bedroom. I also told him that I'd planted evidence there to implicate him in the murder, and that if questioned, I'd point the police in his direction. I knew that would lure him to the scene, and then I could unleash the Sandman on him and he'd never, ever want to set foot on that property again. That is, if he survived the night.

"But the plan backfired on me. While I hid in the room across the hall, waiting for my brother to arrive, for some reason, Mike Scoffland came back to the

manor. My brother found him there, about to pull out the drywall he'd tacked up the day before. I think Mike must've thought I'd put something valuable in the hidden room, and perhaps he wanted to take it before his workers showed up. Or maybe he was simply curious about what was hidden behind that door for all these years. Maybe he simply wanted to see Everett's remains to be certain we'd done him in. Whatever the cause, when Glenn discovered him in my old room he became furious, and the two began to argue. Hiding in the room across the hall, I became very afraid that they'd discover me, and I think the Sandman used my emotions to make an entrance. Before I quite knew what was happening, the Sandman possessed Mike, who then attacked my brother. The pair struggled for a bit, and Mike was definitely winning when Glenn got his hands on a nail gun and killed Scoffland with one click of the gun. Mike hit the floor, my brother felt for a pulse, and then he simply panicked and fled the scene.

"Realizing what I'd done, I too fled the scene. It wasn't until the next day that I had worked up enough nerve to go back to the house and retrieve the planchette and the board and get the Sandman back into the planchette. By that time, you had already discovered the hidden room and what lay beyond."

"What about Everett's body?" I asked. "Did you steal it from the scene?"

"Oh, no," Sarah said. "That was Glenn's doing. He didn't want Everett's remains to be connected back to him like I kept threatening, so, sometime after I retrieved the planchette, he snuck into the playroom and

retrieved Everett's body; then he buried him in my backyard, knowing I'm not physically capable of digging him up and moving him again. I guess Glenn figured it was only a matter of time before Beau did a search of our properties. He'd been working steadily to turn the tables against me ever since he killed Mike."

"And what about what happened at the mental hospital?" I asked next.

"Oh, that," Sarah said with a tired sigh. "Once the Sandman learned that you were DeeDee's daughter, it was all I could do to keep control of him. The day after he killed Scoffland, Glenn sent Everett to attack me at my home and I broke down again. My maid checked me into the hospital, and I thought I'd be safe, but I made the mistake of bringing along the planchette. I didn't want Glenn to get his hands on it, but they gave me drugs which weakened my will and let the Sandman loose again. Before I could get my wits about me, one of the patients attacked me and I was knocked unconscious. When I came to, the place was in chaos. At first I tried calling the Sandman back just by saying his name, but he was becoming too powerful. He wasn't listening to my commands and for a time I couldn't find the planchette to force him back, but I finally did. It'd been knocked under one of the beds."

I realized that must have been the moment when all the chaos abruptly stopped. I had one more question for her, but it was a difficult one for me to ask. Still, I managed. "Why did you hurt Linda, Sarah?" I knew it'd been Sarah who'd attacked Linda, because my grandparents' old house was a mere stone's throw

away from the hospital where we'd interviewed her. Hell, I even remembered that when she'd told us what happened the day Everett died, she'd been fully dressed, even wearing her shoes. "Linda came to see you this morning, didn't she?" I pressed, knowing Linda had left Mrs. G.'s and gone straight to the hospital. "She must've realized that she slipped up and mentioned to you that she knew where Mama had hidden the planchette and that you were the only one who knew about the Sandman and how to control it."

She didn't answer me at first and the silence stretched out between us. At last she said, "Yes, she came to see me. She accused me of retrieving the planchette and using it to call up the Sandman. I denied it, but I knew she could tell I was lying. And then, from my window, I saw her get into her car and drive straight over to Loamlach. I knew she'd check the tree to see if the planchette was still there. It was easy to slip out of my room down the stairs and over to the river. I was back in an hour, and none of the nurses even knew I'd been gone." I shook my head in disgust but didn't voice my feelings. A moment later Sarah said, "Is she dead?"

"No."

"Good," Sarah said, and there was no trace of malice in her voice.

"But why?" I pressed. "Why would you hurt her? She did nothing to you and you already had the planchette."

"She did nothing to me?" she repeated. "Mary Jane, she hurt me worst of all."

"How?" I couldn't fathom Linda ever hurting a single soul, let alone small, frail Sarah Porter.

"She took away my DeeDee," Sarah said, a waver in her voice. "Linda stole the truest, best friend I ever had."

Now it was my turn to be quiet, but then I was reminded that I didn't have the luxury of waiting too much longer. Mama's energy was quickly fading and the Sandman was pushing hard against the magnetic barrier I'd placed him in. "Sarah?"

"Yes, Mary Jane?"

"It's time," I told her.

She didn't answer me and I waited several long moments to work up the courage to carefully get to my feet, still pressing the planchette against my chest, and step around into the open doorway. Sarah was sitting on the floor, holding the Sandman's real planchette and on the floor next to her was the body of her brother. He was riddled with dozens of planchettes, impaled to death by the very devices he'd so coveted.

Sarah looked at my free hand and the spikes and she said, "May I do the honor?"

I considered not trusting her—she was a murderer after all—but then I considered that I didn't have the mobility to hold on to the planchette on my chest and destroy the other one at the same time. Bending my knees and extending my hand, I offered her one of the spikes. She raised it feebly and brought it down on the crystal. It took her several tries, but at last the thing was broken and then she laid the spike lengthwise on the surface of the planchette.

Tentatively I lifted one of the remaining spikes in my free hand and knocked the gem out of the center of the

planchette at my chest. The metal stopped pulsing with energy immediately. The Sandman had been disarmed. "Everett?" I asked her next.

She pointed to Glenn's desk. Stepping carefully around the planchettes littering the floor, I approached the desk warily. In the center I saw that Glenn had painted the surface to resemble a large Ouija board, and there in the middle was a worn photo of Everett Sellers. One of the only remaining planchettes on the opposite wall began to rattle and I knew it was about to aim straight for my head. I lifted my hand holding all the remaining stakes high, and brought it down as hard as I could in the center of the desk. For a moment, nothing happened, and then the planchette simply fell to the floor.

I surveyed the terrible mess and my gaze finally came to rest on Sarah, who lifted her chin, and looked at me with such tenderness. "You look just like your mother," she said to me. "And she was the most beautiful woman I ever knew."

I swallowed hard, but continued to hold her gaze without tears.

With a sigh Sarah sat back, looked at me, and held up something small hidden in her hand. Belatedly I realized she was holding on to a prescription bottle. "My happy pills," she said, her words slurring.

I gasped. "Ohmigod, Sarah! No!"

She closed her eyes and fell back with that smile still on her lips. And then she was gone.

Chapter 16

The moments after Sarah's suicide were awful. I was torn between trying to help her, Breslow, and Heath, and it was a tough call as to whom to help first. I had to recruit Chloe to help Breslow, and Heath had somehow managed to crawl up the steps and make it to the front porch, but that's as far as he could go. I called dispatch, looking for backup, which finally arrived.

The reason it was so late getting to us was that there was a four-alarm fire at Porter Manor, and nearly the entire mansion and some of the surrounding woods went up in smoke.

The cause was determined to be arson, and I had no doubt that Sarah had set the fire. She'd known when she'd made her first confession to us in the hospital that her dream of ever owning or living in Porter Manor again was gone.

Christine was totally heartbroken, but Daddy prom-

ised her that they'd rebuild such a grand manor that no one would even remember the Porter place, and in the meantime they had a perfectly lovely home to live in, which I could now attest they did.

Heath and Breslow were taken to the hospital and X-rays confirmed that my sweetheart had suffered three fractured ribs. How he'd even stayed conscious, given the amount of pain he'd been in, was something of a miracle.

Beau had suffered several blows to the face and head by flying planchettes, but Chloe had ridden with him in the ambulance, and last I heard, she was sweetly nursing him back to health.

As for Deputy Cook, he came to immediately after the Sandman was banished once again to the lower realms. No surprise, he didn't remember a thing about attacking Sheriff Kogan and Kogan actually surprised me by subtly altering the official report to read that Cook had become light-headed and fallen while holding a knife, accidentally stabbing Kogan. No charges were filed, and I heard that Cook went right back on duty, although for a while he'd also been ordered to wear a fishing vest with a few magnets in the pockets—just in case.

All the other victims of the Sandman's possession had also woken up confused and remembering nothing about the incident at the mental hospital. No charges were officially filed there either, although how Kogan had managed that, I still wasn't sure.

Linda woke up just a day later too, not remembering much about her attack, but able to smile and hug me, and there were no signs that she'd have any lasting damage, so I was incredibly relieved. She didn't make it to

Daddy's wedding, but I thought that might've been for the best. Linda had loved Mama, and it was a hard thing to watch the love of Mama's life marrying someone else.

I knew that for a fact.

Even though the ceremony was small, it was still lovely all the same. Michel—Gilley's man—flew in and they made such a handsome couple. Daddy barely batted an eye when he was introduced to Michel, and I had to give him marks for that at least.

And, despite the pain Heath was still in, he managed to slow dance a few songs with me. As the party was winding down, I went inside and walked from room to room, taking it in and thinking about Mama and how much I missed her. She would have loved the wedding. I knew she was there in spirit of course—she was never one to miss a good party—but it still hurt to think that I'd never come through these doors again and feel her presence as intensely as I had before Daddy and Christine took up with each other.

That said nothing about how I felt about Christine, however. The more I got to know her, the more I adored her, and I was so happy for her and Daddy. . . . It's just that, well . . .

"Hey," I heard Gilley say from behind me as I lingered in the parlor, gazing at a framed photo of me and Mama from when I was about four.

"Hey," I replied.

He came up and put an arm across my shoulders. "How you doin', sugar?"

I laid my head on his shoulder. My best friend always knew when I needed him. "I'm fine," I said.

"Hell of a week, huh?"

"It was."

"Great party, though."

"Awesome."

"You okay?"

I smiled. "You already asked me that."

"Yeah, but now I want you to tell me the truth."

A well of emotion bubbled up from my chest and I hid my face from Gil as I tried to wipe the tears away quickly. "It's just . . ."

"Hurts, don't it?"

I nodded. "But it shouldn't," I said. "I mean, Christine is lovely, and I know she's not replacing Mama, but he's still Daddy, and even though we've had our share of ups and downs—"

"More downs than ups," Gil said.

"That's true, but even still . . . he's so tender with her, Gil. So nice. Like he was with Mama, but with me, he's, well . . . gruff, and aloof, and . . ."

"A pain in the keister?"

I chuckled and wiped my eyes again. "Yes, that. But it's more than that. Why can't he be like he was with me before Mama died? I mean, I had this ray of hope when I first saw him with Christine that he'd turn into that loving, caring man that adored me when I was little, but in the days since the fire, we're as aloof with each other as ever."

Gil nodded like he knew just what I meant. "M.J.?"

"Yeah?"

"Did you ever think the problem might not be with Monty?"

I turned to look at him with furrowed brow. "What's that supposed to mean?" I snapped.

Gil shrugged. "Did you ever think that maybe, just maybe, you're still angry at him for pulling away from you when you needed him most and that all those years of his hard drinking took a toll on you, which you haven't quite forgiven him for?"

"No, Gil," I said defensively. "When he went through the program, he apologized to me for all of that and I told him right then that I forgave him."

Gil's face softened and he looked at me with such sweet understanding. "Sugar," he said. "Forgiveness isn't a decision. It's a process."

My breath caught at the wisdom of his words, and I took that in, thinking back to all those times I'd had my guard up whenever Daddy called, or we met face-to-face. And since I'd been home, I'd spent most of my time investigating a set of murders and busting a demon, and hadn't made any real time to hang out with my own father.

And yet I'd held the memory of my mother as close to me as if she'd died yesterday. I'd put her on a pedestal and adored her from afar and Daddy had always paled in comparison with her, and since learning about the horror that'd happened to her as a young girl, I'd elevated her even more.

How could Daddy ever compete with that? No wonder he was distant from me.

Leaning in, I gave Gilley a giant hug and then stepped back and said, "Would you excuse me?"

"You headed back out?"

I nodded. "I think it's time the groom danced with his daughter, don't you?"

Gilley beamed at me and squeezed my hand. "I do. But after, do you think we can we go for ice cream?"

"It's a deal, honey."

Making my way outside again, I wound my way through the wedding attendees, stopping to kiss Heath on the cheek, while he grimaced in pain but tried to put on a good face as he watched the dancers on the dance floor. "You okay?" he asked me, reaching up to squeeze my hand.

"Yes," I told him. "I am. I know you're hurting, but there's one quick thing I have to do before we go. Is that okay?"

"Take your time, babe," he said, forcing a smile. "I can always nurse one more beer."

I kissed him again, then moved away and over to Daddy, who was dancing with his radiant new bride. Tapping him on the shoulder, I said, "May I have this dance?"

Daddy turned to me and a mixture of emotions played across his face—surprise, delight, and also perhaps a bit of melancholy I supposed was caused from all those years we'd spent at war together.

"Of course I'll dance with you, baby girl," Daddy said, bowing to his bride, who winked at me as her new husband took up my hand. We danced without saying a word for a bit, and then Daddy leaned back and stared at me intently and I was shocked to see tears fill his eyes.

"Daddy? Are you okay?"

He shook his head. "It's nothing, honey," he said, pulling me close again. But after a minute he said into my ear, "It's just . . . you look so much like your mother tonight. And I always thought she was the most beautiful woman in the world. I guess I never realized how much like her you are. Your beauty and your spirit, you get all that from Madelyn. And, baby girl, you just . . . take my breath away."

I swallowed hard and wiped a tear from my own eye. Nothing he could've ever said could've been more wonderful than that.